Widow's Walk

Part 1: The Precipice

Kenneth Spillias

abbott press®
A DIVISION OF WRITER'S DIGEST

Widow's Walk
Part 1: The Precipice

Abbott Press books may be ordered through booksellers or by contacting:

Abbott Press
1663 Liberty Drive
Bloomington, IN 47403
www.abbottpress.com
Phone: 1-866-697-5310

ISBN: 978-1-4582-0726-5 (e)
ISBN: 978-1-4582-0727-2 (hc)
ISBN: 978-1-4582-0728-9 (s)

Library of Congress Control Number: 2012923294

Printed in the United States of America

Abbott Press rev. date: 2/18/2013

FOREWORD

The journey of Jim Donovan was initially conceived and began as a short story. Somewhere in the recesses of my mind, and for no apparent reason, I had conjured an ending to a story that seemed, to me at least, entertaining and thought provoking. Since a story's ending needs a story, I set out to create that as well, and so was born Jim Donovan and the Widow's Walk.

Putting the story aside for a while and re-reading it some time later, it became immediately apparent that it contained a major flaw. I had provided no explanation of who Jim Donovan was; where he came from; what his life experiences were; what he thought and felt; or how he had gotten to where he was. In short, there was no connection to what made him tick and why the reader should care about what happened to him. To bring Jim Donovan to life, I would need to transform the short story into a full length novel.

It was in the course of writing this, my first novel, that I experienced the phenomenon I had heard successful novelists describe, but that I found difficult to comprehend. At some point—exactly when I cannot say—the characters I created, to whom I had given histories, personalities, thoughts, feelings and emotions, and character traits, both good and bad, came to life. While I continued to map out in my mind what was going to happen next, I found that as I wrote, the characters often took control and directed the action, based on what they would have done or said next, even creating story sub-plots that I had neither planned nor contemplated. In a very real sense, the book began to write itself—as enjoyable an experience as I ever could have imagined.

The result, to date, is this book and the one to follow. The places described are, for the most part, real. The characters, however, are fictional and any resemblance to persons, living or dead is purely coincidental.

I have received significant support, both moral and editorial, from numerous friends and family members throughout this process. I am truly grateful to every one of you. I would like to particularly acknowledge my wife, Monica, who generously tolerated my spending so much of our leisure and vacation time writing rather than romping in the surf with her; my good friend, Chuck Elderd, whose constructive suggestions sharpened and improved several key passages in the book; my publishing attorney, Alan Kaufman, who not only vetted the book to keep me out of legal trouble, but also provided editorial suggestions born of many years of experience in the publishing world; and my sister-in-law, Robin Spillias, who has served as editor, critic, counselor, agent and overall guide through the process of publishing and publicizing this work. Without her encouragement and support, *Widow's Walk* would still be an unfinished manuscript.

To Geoffrey, Alicia and Stephanie

'Tis the fool whose quest consists
Of seeking love's attentions.
Life's treasures flow to those whose love
Pours forth with no intentions.
To Give Love

Chapter 1

EATH. IT WAS COMING. FUNNY, during his life he had died and been reborn so many times, in so many ways. But the real thing, *real* death was coming now, right here on this widow's walk. He was left to wonder what control he ever had over the outcome, over his final fate.

Yes, it was time to die. He was certain of it. The wind and rain and hail and lightning were so intense, the thunder so deafeningly loud, that it could be only a matter of seconds before his eardrums shattered and his veins burst. It would be the explosion of the carotid artery, he imagined, that the coroner would ascribe as the cause of death.

He was aware of the storm-battered lady on the porch below, beseechingly gazing up at him—pleading, for her life and his. But he could do nothing, say nothing, not even look at her—though he desperately wanted to. He was frozen, but not with fear. He *was* afraid, but his paralysis came from far beyond the power mere fear had over him. He was a pawn in a titanic struggle, tearing at him from opposite directions and about to rip him apart no less gruesomely than the ancient rack. But even then, he knew that that would not be the end of it. There would be no end.

Frozen, until one side or the other got the upper hand. A pawn, yet the central figure in this battle. Wondering whether he could any longer have any impact on the ultimate outcome.

He heard her pleading wails again. How he wanted to put her mind at ease. How he wanted to hold her and comfort her. But he couldn't. And he knew he never would again. Yet in the midst of his own struggle, he was determined to fight for her as well.

Could it really have been less than three days ago, the Reverend Jim Donovan wondered, that he last stood so confidently before his congregation and told *them* how to run *their* lives. He chuckled—a pitiable chuckle the lady below could neither hear nor see.

Wait till they hear about this, he thought.

Three days. An instant that now seemed an eternity. *Eternity,* he thought. *That's what's going on. That's what the voice and the visions are about. That's* . . . There it was. The voice again. Loud laughter. Words. Heard, and hearable, only by him.

Suddenly a piercing pressure enveloped his neck as if it had been placed in a vice with the screws tightening. His head lurched up involuntarily forcing his eyes to stare into the cloudy morass of a turbulent, starless sky. He tried to close them, not wanting to see anymore, hoping that by doing so he could find peace—either in sleep, or in death. But they wouldn't close. Like it or not, he would see what it wanted him to see.

His eyes remained fixated. He didn't know for how long. But he knew it didn't matter—that time, as he had always understood it, no longer had any real meaning. A day ago, a year ago, a decade ago—it was all the same now. For the Reverend Jim Donovan, the *when* no longer mattered. He had only to concern himself now with the *what.*

The clouds swirled before his motionless eyes. They seemed to be taking a shape, something familiar to him. No, not something. Someone. A face. A face he knew. Actually, a face he once knew. It was blurry. He knew he knew her, but he couldn't make her out.

Then, sharply, her face came into focus. There was instant recognition followed immediately by the sensation of a mule's kick to the stomach.

It was Rachel—seventeen-year-old Rachel Feinberg. He tried to avert his eyes. They would not move. He had no choice. He would have to watch.

Chapter 2

H E HAD NEVER NOTICED JUST how rich the color in her eyes was. They were a deep, dark brown that set him to fantasizing about swimming around with her in a large vat of dark chocolate.

What are you staring at?" she asked in a voice soft and fetching.

He knew it was a softball question, meant to elicit a compliment and move the action forward. It could be something simple—like "You really have pretty eyes." But when it came to girls, Jimmy Donovan found that for him, nothing was simple.

His tongue tied, his stomach churning, he struggled to overcome his fear of looking or saying something foolish. He knew, of course, that sitting there, against the thick trunk of a majestic oak with Rachel Feinberg, saying nothing as he fought his own silly emotional battle within himself, is what made him look foolish. Knowing that didn't help.

"Well?" she lightly insisted, flicking the bangs off her forehead with a slight cock of her head.

"Well what?" he spit out reflexively. He wished he could take the words back the second they jumped from his tongue.

"What are you staring at?" she repeated, again offering him the opportunity to see where flattery could get him.

Jimmy had always felt that Rachel was a pretty girl, with those large expressive eyes that were now holding him in a trance, dark brown, almost black, hair that flowed over her shoulders to the middle of her back, and thick, luscious lips that seemed to be permanently poised for some wet and sloppy kissing. She *was* pretty, and he knew that was exactly what she wanted to hear.

His heart was racing now. A bead of sweat had formed on his forehead and began working its way between his eyes. *This is silly,* he thought. *Say something, stupid. Anything.*

"Nothing," he finally answered, averting his eyes from hers and none-too-deftly wiping the sweat from his brow.

"Nothing? You look into my eyes like forever, and you say you're staring at nothing?" She turned her head away from him. "Boy, you sure know how to make a girl feel good, Jimmy Donovan."

He was horrified. He felt like a complete idiot (*Nothing new there*, he thought). But before he could begin apologizing for his social klutziness, she put her hand to his cheek and stroked it gently.

"Relax Jimmy." She smiled a broad toothy smile. "You need to learn to just go with the flow."

Her words were soothing and comforting. She moved her hand from his cheek to the back of his head and pulled him towards her. Her full and fleshy lips met his. It wasn't a wet and sloppy kiss. It was brief, but tender—and enough to arouse him. He drew his legs up towards his chest hoping she wouldn't see the bulge in his pants. Try as he might to consider his erection a point of pride, five years of Father McTighe's brand of sex "education" was not easy to overcome, even with the help of Rachel Feinberg.

"You're embarrassed," she said. He saw her looking down at his crotch. She sounded amused, yet her smile was disarming. Jimmy's embarrassment melted away and he slowly lowered his left leg giving her an unobstructed view.

Take that Father McTighe, he thought to himself, proudly and defiantly. He smiled. Her smile broadened. She placed her left hand on his left thigh and kissed him again—this time wet, and sloppy, and long.

Jimmy was amazed that he had managed to find himself alone with Rachel Feinberg in the woods at twilight. He knew that if he had dared to plan such a thing, he could never have made it happen. As they embraced and locked lips, he kept opening his eyes, looking at her face as they kissed, then looking up at the brilliant orange and yellow leaves above them. He kept thanking God for these days of Indian Summer—that last gasp of teasing, summer-like weather in the middle of fall. He looked back at her face. Suddenly her eyes popped open, startling him.

"Aha! Caught you!" she said, pointing her finger accusingly at him. "What are you looking for, an audience?" Her finger stopped pointing and began to caress his lips. Before he could say anything, she started to giggle.

"Well, Mr. Exhibitionist, it's too late for that. Everyone's gone. It's just you and me."

Everyone *was* gone. And Jimmy wasn't exactly sure how or when it had happened. One minute, he and his best friend, Tony Scarlotti, were taking turns flying over the creek on an old tire swing. The next, they were chatting it up with Rachel and her two friends—Rebecca Walters and Debbie Minton. They all lived in the same neighborhood on the hill overlooking one of the last wooded areas left in their corner of Pittsburgh's suburbia. And while he and Tony spent a great deal of time in the woods, he had never seen any of these girls there—so their appearance had been quite unexpected.

The girls were seniors—a year ahead of Jimmy and Tony—and ran with a crowd that Jimmy knew would never include him. After all, Debbie and Rachel were cheerleaders. Rebecca was on the swim team and had placed third in state in the one hundred meter freestyle. They were as "in" in the in-crowd as you could be.

And Jimmy? What a joke, he thought. Jimmy Donovan in the in-crowd—with the cheerleaders, the jocks and their anointed hangers-on. Jimmy Donovan—well above average intelligence, below average athletic ability, unassuming and unnoticeable in appearance—all five feet ten inches of him—totally lacking in social skills and so invisible to anyone who really mattered at school, other than Tony, that these girls, these neighbors of his, pretended like they had to ask him his name when they happened upon each other at the creek.

Yet, there they had been, like old pals. And in another moment, while Rachel and Jimmy talked—a conversation she started and was carrying because he never could have—everyone else disappeared.

Jimmy decided to stop analyzing the situation and just count his blessings. He was *alone with Rachel Feinberg. And she wanted him.* Her words echoed in his ears. "It's just you and me." And as they did, fear overtook him.

She's sure to have done it before, he thought. *How can I make sure she doesn't realize that I haven't?*

"Jimmy. Don't you think now is a good time to stop and go home?" the ever-present strictures of Father McTighe whispered in his brain.

"Go away Father," Jimmy mumbled.

"What?" Rachel asked, looking and sounding bewildered.

"Huh?"

"I thought you said something, Jimmy. Were you trying to tell me how much you want me?" she said, as she ran her slender fingers through his hair.

She didn't wait for an answer. She kissed Jimmy again. Her fleshy, lipstick-less lips seemed to engulf his. When she stopped she smiled at him and pecked him softly on the nose. Then she slowly slid down the trunk of the tree until she was lying on her side next to him. Gently, she tugged on his arm bringing him down to her.

Jimmy's primal instincts kicked in, and kicked Father McTighe out. He embraced Rachel and kissed her passionately. This was new territory for him. But, after all, he was almost sixteen and he figured it was about time.

Rachel's knee slid between his legs. Their bodies became intertwined like vines on a tree. His unleashed passion was driving him to want every bit of her. But how to get there? What should he do next?

It was a question he didn't have to answer. He felt Rachel pulling his right arm away from its embrace of her. She took his hand in hers and placed it on her breast. There may have been a bra and a sweatshirt between them, but *by God,* he thought, *I've got Rachel Feinberg's breast in my hand!*

There would be no stopping him now, he decided. Within thirty seconds his hand was inside her sweatshirt grabbing a handful of breast-filled bra. Her knee was now planted firmly against his crotch. They were both groaning expressively and loudly, but Jimmy knew there was no one to hear them but the creatures of the wood.

Rachel pulled her lips away from his and whispered in his ear.

"Undo it."

"Undo what?" he whispered back.

"My bra. Undo my bra."

As she placed her lips back on his, he slipped his hand around to her back and felt for the clasps. He had never really examined a bra closely so he didn't have an intimate knowledge of its mechanical workings, but he knew they hooked up somehow in the back. He found the clasps soon enough and tried to figure out through touch exactly how they operated. In the midst of passionate arousal, he decided, was not the best time to be trying to figure this out for the first time.

As he fumbled clumsily with the insidious contraption, he cursed his inexperience under his breath. He opened his eyes and saw Rachel looking at him. She stopped kissing him again and backed her head slightly to where they could both see each other's full face.

"You need the key," she said.

"Key? What key?"

"The key to unhook my bra."

Now he really felt stupid. He had never heard that you needed a key to unhook a bra.

"I . . . I don't have the key. Where would I get the key? Don't you have it?" Jimmy was unable to hide his bewilderment.

At that, Rachel sat up and looked down at him.

"You've never done this before, have you?" she said.

Lying there, looking up at Rachel, Jimmy felt small and helpless. With all his heart he wanted to deny it. But it was true. The closest he had come was when he and Tony's younger sister, Maria, went through the tunnel of love that summer at Kennywood Park. Even then, when Maria stuck her tongue in his mouth as they kissed, he didn't know what to do. As dumb as he felt then, this was much worse.

"You haven't, have you?" Rachel repeated.

"No. Not really," Jimmy answered. He figured he had just lost any opportunity of experiencing Rachel Feinberg.

"As it should be," he heard Father McTighe say as the good priest began to work his way back from the deep recesses of Jimmy's mind.

Rachel smiled.

"Well Jimmy Donovan, in that case, you just lie back and let me do all the work."

She untied and slipped off his tennis shoes. Then his sweat socks. She threw them up the hill beyond the trunk of the tree. She took his hand and pulled him up into a sitting position, then pulled his shirt up over his head and off.

Jimmy was stunned. A few seconds earlier he had felt like a complete rube. Now, Rachel Feinberg was undressing him!

She gently pushed him down again and unsnapped his jeans. Then she began to unzip them, slowly, as if relishing the unhinging of each tooth of the zipper, one by one. He was so aroused he felt as if his erection would burst through his pants any second.

When she finally got the zipper all the way down she slipped the jeans off, then his jockeys, and threw them up the hill with the rest of his clothes.

Jimmy lay there before her. He was incredibly excited. At the same time he felt very embarrassed—lying there buck naked while she was still totally clothed. For a moment she just looked at him. Her eyes scanned his body, stopping at his private parts. He didn't think it was possible, but the way she looked at him created even greater arousal.

Still smiling, Rachel softly placed the fingers of her left hand on his testicles. An electrifying sensation coursed through his body. Slowly she moved them up the shaft of his penis. Jimmy knew that it wouldn't take much more to make him come.

"Damn!" she said, removing her hand.

"What's wrong? What's wrong?" Jimmy asked desperately.

"I've got to pee."

"You've got to pee? Now?"

"Yes. Now. When you've got to go, you've got to go," she said. "Stay right here. Don't move. I'll go up the way—in the trees up there." She pointed up the hill behind them. "But you've got to swear you won't turn around and look."

"What am I going to see?" he responded. "It's gotten dark. Besides, *you're* the one getting an eyeful."

"I don't care. You've got to swear. Do you swear?"

"Yes. I swear. Just hurry back. Please."

"I will baby."

She kissed him and playfully tapped his penis. She got up, took a few steps and paused. Then she continued up the hill, the sound of her sneakers rustling fallen leaves and broken twigs, disappearing into the deepening darkness.

The ground felt cool against Jimmy's naked body. The dirt and leaves caused him to itch a bit, but by this time of the year most of the mosquitoes were gone. They never really bothered him much anyway. Despite the warmth of the Indian Summer day, the night was starting to get a little brisk. The coolness felt good to him—titillating his exposed private parts even more.

"What are you doing, Jimmy?" The voice of Father McTighe crashed into his thoughts bursting his moment of solitary sensual pleasure.

"I'm just lying here, Father."

"Don't take that tone with me, young man," the prelate's voice scolded him. "You know what I mean."

"Oh Father, leave me alone," Jimmy pleaded. "Don't mess this up for me."

He strained to get the priest's voice and all thoughts of Father McTighe and the years of admonishments about pre-marital sex out of his mind. He looked up towards the darkened sky and clasped his hands behind his head.

"This is wrong, Jimmy, and you know it. I've told you over and over."

"I know you have, Father. Over and over. But . . . but she's done it before. It's not like I'm taking advantage of her." Jimmy began to build his case. "Besides, she's not Catholic. She's not even Christian. It's probably not even wrong in her religion. So see, I wouldn't really be hurting anyone." He felt his logic was inescapable.

"You'd be hurting yourself in the eyes of God."

Sure. There it is. The eyes of God pitch, Jimmy thought to himself. He knew that he couldn't win this argument, but he was determined to push forward. Too much was at stake to let his Father McTighe-formed conscience get in the way.

"But Father, then why did He make it feel so good? It seems awful cruel for such a good and just God to make me want something so bad, and to tempt me with . . . with Rachel Feinberg! I mean, Jesus!"

"You know the answer to that, Jimmy. God made us as he made us. And blessed us with free will. The temptation—that's not from God. You know where that comes from." The voice in his head paused. "And don't use Jesus' name that way."

Jimmy knew that for him this conversation was a losing proposition. He had already lost his erection. If he couldn't remove this morality play from his mind before Rachel got back . . .

Rachel. It dawned on him that she had been gone for quite some time now. He listened intently into the woods above him—to see if he could hear the sound of tinkling, or of footsteps returning down the hill. Nothing.

He sat up, figuring it would help him hear better. Still, nothing. In fact, what he heard was dead silence—no wind blowing through the trees. No birds. No sounds of the woods. No Rachel. Nothing.

He called out in a normal tone of voice. "Rachel." He didn't want to sound foolish by betraying his growing anxiety. No answer.

He turned his head to face up the hill in her direction. "Rachel." Louder this time, but still as matter-of-fact as he could sound. Still, no answer.

He was getting worried. He wondered if something could have happened to her—if she could have gotten lost, or hurt. He yelled out. "Rachel!"

Silence.

Jimmy decided he better get dressed and find Rachel. He stood up and went around the trunk of the tree to where she had thrown his clothes. He reached down to where he was sure she had tossed them. He felt nothing but leaves, twigs and dirt. He felt around the ground in an ever-widening circle—but no clothes.

He was confused. He was sure this was where Rachel had put his clothes. It was dark now and hard to see. He got down on all fours and crawled all around the area of the tree, reaching out, groping for any article of clothing that could lead him to the rest.

He began to panic. He crawled frenetically around the tree, further and further out from it. But there were no clothes. And no Rachel.

Jimmy's anxiety turned to fear. Rachel, and his clothes, were missing, without a sound or a trace. If this was some kind of foul play then Rachel could be hurt, or worse. And he would be the next target—a pretty vulnerable one at that. If it was some sort of trick or practical joke—but how could it be? They would have seen or heard something. *No,* Jimmy thought. *Something's wrong. Something's terribly wrong.*

He realized that nothing in his life had prepared him for something like this. He was a typical teenage boy in a typical middle class family. His father, a vice-president at Mellon Bank, was not much of an outdoorsman and had never taken him camping, fishing, hunting or anywhere where survival skills would be necessary. Jimmy had never joined the Boy Scouts—never had much interest. Right now he wished he had.

He decided to call out once more. "Rachel! Anyone!" Still, nothing but deafening silence.

It was clear to him now that wherever she was, whatever had happened to her, Rachel was not coming back. He would have to find his own way out of this. He looked up the hill where the path ultimately led to the cul-de-sac that sat at the end of the street on which he, Tony and Rachel lived.

Jimmy couldn't see anything except a faint glow from the house lights and street lights that seemed to hover high above him in the now otherwise pitch black, moonless night sky. He had grown up playing in these woods and knew them well. From where he stood, it was about one hundred yards up the slightly winding footpath to the nearest backyard, which happened to be Rachel's house. His best bet, he decided, was to climb the hill to the edge of the woods and work his way through the trees and underbrush along the cul-de-sac until he got to Tony's house, two doors to the left of Rachel's. He hoped Tony was home by now. He'd still have to figure out how to get Tony's attention, and help, without anyone else noticing. He decided he'd worry about that when he got there.

Jimmy began his trek up the hill. He stayed along the right side of the path to use the trees and the thicker underbrush off the path to guide him along, much as he surmised a blind man might walk part on and part off an unfamiliar road or sidewalk to keep his way.

The woods seemed unusually still to him. The only thing he could hear was the sound of his walking on dried out fallen leaves and the occasional "damn" he muttered when his bare feet encountered a sharp pebble or broken tree limb.

Jimmy's fear subsided. His mind became preoccupied with working his way up the hill and figuring out what he would do once he got there. It was going to be embarrassing enough, he thought, explaining this to Tony. He was downright mortified at the prospect of being seen like this and having to explain to anyone else, especially his parents. Or worse, Father McTighe. And then there was Rachel. What if something bad *had* happened to her? It would be his fault—no question about that. Everyone would blame him. He would too. He would never forgive himself. He . . .

Jimmy thought he heard something—off to his right in the trees. He stopped. He was about one-third of the way up the hill. He listened for a few seconds. Nothing. *Just a squirrel,* he thought.

He started walking again, slowly holding his right arm out towards his right front to feel for the next tree along the path. He squinted hard trying to make out objects ahead of him and looked anxiously for a light at the top of the hill.

He heard it again. He was sure this time. It was the sound of something or someone walking slowly—as slowly as he was. Two legs or four? He couldn't tell. It was off to his right. He guessed about ten or fifteen yards from the sound of it. *Too big to be a squirrel,* he thought.

Jimmy stopped again. It stopped. A deathly still hung in the air. No breeze. No sound. *It's not natural,* he thought. He took a few more steps. As he did, so did his shadowy companion. He stopped. It stopped.

This is not good, he thought.

He was getting scared again. He had never seen a really dangerous animal in these woods. He had heard his father say that encroaching development was driving most of the animals away and that it wouldn't be long before these woods made way for more houses. But something was out there now. And it seemed to be stalking him.

Maybe it *was* a person. Maybe it was Rachel, trying to find her way up the hill and just as scared of his noises as he was of hers. He turned and looked in the direction of the footsteps.

"Hello?" he said quietly, his voice quivering, afraid to shatter the unearthly stillness. "Hello, Rachel? Is anyone there?"

There was no response.

"Hello?" he said a little louder. Still, no response.

He squinted hard, trying to see something, anything--trying to at least make out the form of who or what was tracking him. He could see nothing.

Suddenly, Jimmy began to tremble. It began with his hands, quickly worked its way up his arms to his upper torso, and down into his legs. His teeth began to chatter uncontrollably. Instinctively, he folded his arms to warm himself. Strangely, he didn't feel cold, but his entire body was acting as if he was freezing.

Jimmy stood there, shaking all over, trying without success to will it to stop. The trembling was becoming violent. His shoulders and neck were aching from being wrenched back and forth and in all directions. His vibrating legs were becoming rubbery. He felt they wouldn't hold him up much longer.

He tried to turn to start walking or running back up the hill. It seemed as if he had lost all control over his voluntary muscles. His fear was turning to terror. What if he was having some kind of seizure? Maybe the sounds he heard were an hallucination, part of the seizure. Maybe he was going to die, right then, right there. He thought of the shame he would bring to his parents—their fifteen-year-old son, found dead and naked in the middle of the woods.

He couldn't let that happen. He tried to scream out. His lungs and vocal chords would not obey his mind.

The trembling wouldn't stop. Jimmy's eyes stared out into the dark void of the woods. He thought he saw something—like two points of light jumping all around trying to follow his shaking, bobbing head. He worked hard to focus his vision on the points of light. Somehow he felt they could help him, if he could only see what they were.

For several seconds they kept hopping around as the trembling continued to rattle his head. It was hard to focus. He started having double vision. It made it seem as if there were four or more points of light—moving all around and through each other.

Without warning, the trembling stopped. The sudden relaxation of his body almost caused Jimmy to collapse to the ground. He reached out and leaned his left hand against the nearest tree to steady himself. He was exhausted and breathing heavily. He took a long, deep breath.

He covered his eyes with his right hand as he wondered what had just happened to him. He felt relieved, but was still scared. This was definitely the most frightening thing he had ever experienced. He was ready to get the hell out of there. He lowered his hand from his eyes and looked into the woods where the points of light had danced before him. And there they were. There were only two of them now—clear and stationary—side by side. They disappeared for an instant, then reappeared. A few seconds later, it happened again. And again. And again.

Jimmy knew he was looking at a pair of blinking eyes. And he knew they were looking at him. They were lower to the ground than his, so he assumed it was an animal of some sort. But from where he stood there was no way of telling what kind. He wondered why he could even see its eyes, since there was no light around to reflect off of them. But they were there, and they seemed unmistakably interested in him.

Jimmy felt a momentary chill. He noticed that the wind had picked up just a bit. As he continued to look at the deliberately blinking eyes, he began to feel light-headed. He feared he was about to experience another attack of the shakes. He closed his eyes. *Please God,* he thought. *Not again.* He opened them. The light-headedness was gone. So were the eyes in the woods.

There was only one thought in his mind now—to get out of those woods as fast as possible. His nakedness was no longer an issue. And his concern for Rachel's welfare had now taken a back seat to his concern for his own.

He turned and immediately began running up the hill. He still couldn't see but his body and mind were on automatic pilot now, calling upon the memories of all of the times he had gone up and down this hill to guide him like some sort of implanted road map. He didn't look back. There was nothing behind him, real or imagined, that could mean anything good for him. Soon, he saw a light flickering through the unseen branches of the trees before him. He would soon be at the end of the wood. *But then what?* he thought.

As Jimmy approached the top of the hill, Rachel's house quickly came into view. From the front it was a two-story, yellow brick home. From the back, where he was approaching it, the basement and garage made it look like an imposing three-story house. The garage doors were to his right. Above them he could see the windows to the kitchen and dining room. He guessed that the windows above them on the top floor were probably the master bedroom.

There were no lights on in the dining room or the bedroom, but the kitchen lights were on and the curtain was open allowing the light to flood out onto the driveway and the lawn. On the left side of the house he saw a bathroom window and another bedroom window on the top floor. Below them were sliding glass doors—probably the family room he figured—leading out onto a square wooden porch. He could make out a dim light peeking through the closed curtains of that room.

Under the porch was a patio which also had sliding glass doors leading from the house. He could see two metal garbage cans against the back wall to the right of the doors, and a picnic bench at the far left of the patio running perpendicular to the house. There were curtains on these doors too, which were also closed, leading him to believe that this was probably a finished basement. There was no light at all that he could see coming from these doors.

It was funny, he thought, how he had never been in Rachel's house even though they had lived on the same street for five years, and how he had never really *looked* at her house before even though he had cut through her yard dozens, maybe hundreds of times, going to and from the creek.

He wished he could go right around to the front of the house, knock on the door and make sure Rachel was okay. But even though he was still afraid that something bad might have happened to her—maybe from whatever it was he had seen down the hill—he knew he couldn't just stroll up to her house naked and say, "Hello Mr. And Mrs. Feinberg. You see, Rachel and I were going to do it, and she had to pee, and she and my clothes disappeared, and I had a seizure, and I saw something weird in the woods and I ran up here and now I need to know if she got home all right. And, oh, by the way, do you know if she has my clothes?"

He had to make his way to Tony's first, get some clothes and then he would go check on Rachel.

He had reached the end of the path and prepared to edge along the backyards of the cul-de-sac to get to Tony's house. The kitchen light continued to flow out onto the backyard. *At least they don't have that floodlight over the garage on,* he thought, thankfully.

He worked his way, crouching, through the brush and between the trees behind Rachel's house. As he moved along he kept his eye on the windows and glass doors, ready at the first sign of anyone looking out to hit the dirt and slide back into the woods. He saw no one. But he did see *something.* In the middle of the yard, half way between him and the patio—about fifteen feet away. It seemed to be a clump or pile of something. He crawled to the very edge of the tree line to get a better look. Tennis shoes, white socks, jeans, a shirt—*his* shirt. Jimmy realized he had found his clothes. But what were they doing here? he wondered. How did they get there?

He gave it no more thought. He was really frightened for Rachel now and decided he had to let her parents know what had happened as soon as possible. He had the foreboding sense that every minute was critical and any delay on his part could be disaster for her. He took one last look up at the windows of her house and at the yards and windows of the adjoining houses. No one was there.

He got up out of his crouch and darted towards his clothes. Just before he reached them the floodlight above the garage went on bathing the entire backyard in its brilliant white glow. Jimmy looked up at the lights and froze for a second. When he snapped out of it and went to reach for his clothes, a bright flash of light blinded him. Dazed and confused, he stood there waiting for his eyes to clear. When they did, what he saw horrified him. The curtains to the basement were open. Standing there was Rachel, flanked on either side by Debbie and Rebecca. Rachel was holding a Polaroid camera and the three girls were laughing hysterically.

Jimmy's thoughts swirled incomprehensively. He started to turn and run back into the woods—then remembered his clothes. When he turned back to get them, another flash from the camera blinded him again.

The sliding doors were closed, but he could hear the girls' evil laughter. *What if Rachel's parents hear and look out?* he thought. When his eyes cleared he could see the girls again, reveling in their adolescent cruelty. He reached down and gathered up his clothes. As he turned to run back into the woods, the camera flashed again. And another burst of ridiculing laughter followed after him through the still dark of the night.

Chapter 3

"JIMMY. WAKE UP JIMMY." His mother's voice, though distant and calm, intruded on his silent sleep as harshly as the raucous herald of an early morning rooster.

"Jimmy! Get up! It's seven o'clock! You're going to be late for school!" The voice was clear and present now. And it was losing its calmness. Lower than one would expect from a woman, but not so low as to be mistaken for a man's, Mrs. Donovan's voice immediately commanded respect. And when conveying her displeasure, it became an effective weapon for instilling fear, especially in her son.

"I still don't feel good, Mom," he mumbled from under the covers.

It was Wednesday. Jimmy had managed to avoid the humiliation he was certain to experience at school by feigning illness on Monday and Tuesday. He knew his mother had suspected he was faking it. He also knew she wasn't going to put up with it any longer.

"Well, whether you feel good or not, you're going to school today." She pulled the covers down from over his head. "Now get up and get ready!"

He had no choice. While the thought of what he faced at school actually did make him physically ill, he would have to deal with it sooner or later. He had thought about telling his parents what had happened and asking them to let him transfer to another school. But he knew that wouldn't work. His dad would just tell him some totally irrelevant story from his own childhood that was supposed to show that he went through the same thing and survived it. And his mother would just tell him to tough it out. By now, the whole student body knew, and he was already a laughing stock—but he couldn't tell his parents. He would just have to get out of bed for the worst day of his entire life.

"Okay Mom," he grumbled, not bothering to open his eyes. "I'm up. Leave me alone."

"Hurry up, or you'll miss breakfast," she said, her voice sweeter now, more motherly. He kept his eyes closed until he heard the door close behind her as she left his room.

Jimmy dragged himself out of bed. As he dressed, his mind worked feverishly, still trying to find some way to avoid the painful ridicule his classmates were sure to heap upon him that day. It was no use. Short of running away or killing himself—both of which options received serious, if momentary consideration—there was no way out.

After quickly brushing his teeth, he threw his jacket on, grabbed his school books and darted down the stairs which led directly from the house's top floor, where all three bedrooms were located, to the living room. At the bottom of the stairs a doorway on his right led to the kitchen. He quickly glanced in. His parents were seated at the kitchen table. They were eating breakfast, but he didn't bother to notice what his mother had prepared.

She looked up just as he had reached the doorway.

"Jimmy. Come and eat," she said. "You need to eat breakfast."

He ignored her. He gave his dad a perfunctory wave goodbye, turned to his left and bounded down the small flight of stairs to the lower level hallway, which led to the front door. He stepped out into the brisk, autumn morning air for the four-block walk to school.

"Jimmy! Wait up!" It was Tony, jogging up from behind. Jimmy didn't stop to wait for him. It only took Tony a few seconds to catch up.

"What's up guy?" Tony said, patting him on the back. "Your mom said you were sick. Too sick to return phone calls?"

Tony had called several times since Sunday. Jimmy hadn't wanted to talk to him. Even though Tony had been his best friend for three years, the way things had happened Saturday night made him wonder whether Tony had been involved in setting him up. The possibility made him angry, but he also felt guilty for thinking it. Either way, he had been in no frame of mind to talk to his friend.

"Yeah," Jimmy answered. "I wasn't feeling good. Just wasn't up to talking."

"Not feeling good because you were sick? Or because of what happened Saturday night?" Tony reassuringly placed his left hand on Jimmy's right shoulder as they walked along.

"You know?"

"Yeah. It's all over school."

He turned and looked at his friend. "Are there, um . . .pictures?"

"Yeah. There's pictures."

Tears welled up in Jimmy's eyes. "So now everybody in school's laughing at me and knows what an idiot I am." He turned his head and looked straight ahead as they continued walking. They were two blocks from school—two blocks from Hell. "I should have known. How could I have thought that Rachel Feinberg would really be interested in *me*? How could I have been so *stupid*?"

Tony gently squeezed his shoulder. "You're not stupid, man. Could've happened to any guy. You know how it is. When they get in our pants we lose all sense of . . . of perspective. Just turns out these fucking bitches are the type to use their T and A to play games with guys."

Tony always sounded like he knew what he was talking about when it came to girls and sex and all that kind of stuff. He and Jimmy were about the same age—Tony was two months older. But before moving to Pittsburgh three years earlier, he had spent the first thirteen years of his life in Brooklyn, where—he liked to say—young men (he never referred to himself as a boy, no matter what age he was talking about) learned much more about life much earlier. *If that's so,* Jimmy thought, *why hadn't he seen what was happening?*

Jimmy turned and looked into Tony's eyes. "So, where were you?"

"When?"

"Saturday night? When I was getting castrated by those fucking bitches?" There was a hint of anger, which he didn't try to hide.

Tony removed his hand from Jimmy's shoulder. He placed both hands on his face and rubbed his eyes. He appeared exasperated.

"I know man," he answered. "I feel like such a fool. They sucked me in and played me real good. They told me Rachel really got off on showing guys their first . . . you know, *really* good time, and she wanted to . . . you know, make you always remember her fondly." Tony ran his hand through his thick, black hair. "Man, I just thought it was great you were going to get your first piece of ass. I should've seen what they were doing. I'm sorry, man. I *really* screwed up."

They had used Tony too. Jimmy felt guilty for ever doubting his best friend—his only true friend.

"That's okay," he said. "Wasn't your fault. I'm not in Rachel's league. I should've known."

They were approaching the concrete walkway that led from the sidewalk to the main entrance of the high school. Up to then, he hadn't noticed the other students walking to school along the same route he and Tony took. He couldn't miss them now. Those in twos or groups were whispering and giggling. It was obviously directed at him. Even those who walked alone looked at him through mocking eyes.

As they turned up the walkway towards the steps to the front doors, Jimmy's stomach twisted into knots. His jaw became so tense he doubted he'd be able to put an entire sentence together if he had to. His legs were rubbery and for a brief second he grasped Tony's arm to keep from falling.

Tony stopped and looked at his demoralized friend. In a voice just above a whisper, he said, "Look, Jimmy. Don't let them get to you. Don't let them know you're hurting. Turn it around on them. Laugh it off. Act like . . . like you don't mind being part of the joke. That'll drive them nuts."

It was good advice. He knew that's exactly how Tony would handle it if he was in Jimmy's shoes. But Tony was outgoing, personable, and supremely self-confident—all of the things he wasn't. Tony could pull it off. Jimmy would just have to suffer through being humiliated.

"Hey there, Pee Wee!" The words came from his left. He turned and saw Brent Stockbridge—the first-string quarterback of the football team. Brent was flanked by three other players whose names Jimmy didn't know—and by Rachel, Rebecca and Debbie. The bruiser was holding up what appeared to be two Polaroid pictures.

"I hear Playgirl Magazine is doing a spread on The Smallest Dicks in the East," Brent yelled out. "And it's considering you for the centerfold!" The group broke out in laughter at their leader's cruel joke. "Only problem is, you might not qualify because you at least got to have one and, well . . ."—he held the pictures above his head and squinted hard looking at them—" . . . even with a magnifying glass, they're having trouble seeing it!" More uproarious laughter. They were a pack of hyenas tearing at the flesh of Jimmy's pride.

"Follow my lead," Tony whispered in his ear.

Tony stepped forward placing himself between Jimmy and Brent. "That's enough, Brent," he said in a firm and even voice.

Brent's face went from a smile to a scowl. "Or what?" he growled back.

Tony dropped his books and crouched into a martial arts fighting stance, left foot ahead of his right, his arms bent at the elbows, extended in front of him, the palms of his hands facing the ground. "Or *we'll* just have to put an end to it," he said with that supreme confidence of his. "Right, Jimmy?"

Jimmy began to feel light-headed. He never handled confrontation very well. At home, all it took was a stern look or slightly raised voice from his mother to keep him in line. He had always assumed that he got his "peacemaking" nature—which even he considered a euphemism for "wussiness"—from his father. In business, his father was successful and well respected. At home, he was no match for his wife, who never let sympathy, compassion, sensitivity or other "weak" emotions get in the way of arranging life just the way she thought it should be—structured, organized, rational and efficient. Somehow, in his family, the stereotypical male-female roles as far as sensitivity and emotions were concerned had been reversed. As he had always known, he was his father's son.

He knew Tony was expecting him to back up the boast with a resounding "Right!" He tried, but nothing came out of his mouth. His friend had a brown belt in karate and could take care of himself. But Tony wasn't very big—no more than five feet seven inches and maybe one hundred fifty pounds—and he would need help against four football behemoths, all of whom stood at least six feet tall and three of whom easily went well over two hundred pounds.

Tony glanced quickly at Jimmy. Jimmy knew Tony was expecting him to help bluff their way out of this—or at least make it something a little closer to a fair fight. He tried again. Still, nothing came out.

"You mean you and Pee Wee?" Brent sneered.

The girls backed away as Brent and his pals dropped their books. The four of them spread apart and into a four-point pattern, surrounding Jimmy and Tony.

"This is going to be fun," Brent said, an expectant smile on his face, his fists clenched and raised in front of his chest. Tony had turned his back to Jimmy's to face, as best he could, Brent and two of the hulks. Jimmy was left facing the third massive body realizing that if this guy just *fell* on him it would force all of the air, and probably most of the bodily fluids, out of his body.

"Fight! Fight!" someone cried out. In no time a crowd of students surrounded the would-be combatants. Jimmy could sense their bloodlust. As he looked around, he could also see them laughing—no doubt, at him. More than anything he wanted to be able to beat the hell out of Brent and his goons. Right there, in front of the school and all of these kids. That would show them. That would make them stop laughing at him. But he knew that wasn't going to happen. Instead, he and Tony were going to get the crap beat out of them—and he was just as afraid of the added ignominy that would cause him as he was of the pain and bloodletting he was about to endure.

Damn you, Tony, he thought. *Why do you have to be so fucking cocky?*

Their predicament was desperate. Somehow, that seemed to make Tony only cockier.

"Come on, motherfucker!" he yelled at Brent. "It's going to take more than four pansies from a losing football team to take us out!"

He had hit Brent right where it hurt the most—in his athlete's pride. Jimmy figured that Tony must have realized that the bluff wasn't working, so he had gone to Plan B, whatever that was. Jimmy turned to see Brent's reaction. The reaction was one of rage and anger. He threw a punch at Tony. Tony deftly ducked it, lowered his torso closer to the ground and shot out his right leg, digging the heel of his foot into Brent's solar plexus with enough force to knock him on his ass. He then immediately swung around into a position where he could see the other three as they moved in to attack.

Jimmy was stunned. He remained motionless. He admired his friend's handiwork as if he was one of the spectators, rather than supposedly one of the participants.

Brent's friends were stunned, too. Before they could move, Tony looked at him and nodded his head to the left. "You keep that guy busy for thirty seconds," Tony said, "and that'll give me enough time to take care of the other two."

Jimmy turned to face the towering lineman to his right. Tony had asked for thirty seconds. A lot of damage could be done in thirty seconds. But he knew he had to do it. To help his friend who had put himself on the line to defend him. More important, to help himself. To everyone in the school, he had become a fool and a wimp. This was his chance to show them—to show them all that Jimmy Donovan had guts, and character. Even if it cost him a few teeth.

He raised his fists, as much to protect himself against a thirty-second onslaught than with any expectation of landing any damaging blows. His knees were shaking. His heart was racing. But he *would* fight. In fact, he *wanted* to fight. He could hear the crowd cheering louder now. Tony's blow had whetted their appetite for more action—and blood.

The hulk in front of him, teeth clenched and fists raised, stepped towards him. Jimmy braced himself to receive the first punch. It didn't come.

"All right! All right! Break it up! RIGHT NOW!"

The voice of vice-principal Craig Pickering bellowed as he made his way through the crowd of students. He placed himself squarely in the middle of the fighters and glared at each of them, one by one. Jimmy had never been so glad to see a school administrator.

"What's going on here?" Pickering demanded. No one said a word.

Craig Pickering had been a teacher and school administrator for over twenty years. He was a short man—no more than five feet five inches. But he demanded the respect of the entire student body. This was due in no small measure to the fact that he was a power lifter who could bench press more than any student in the school. Jimmy knew that a quick survey of the participants and the scene would tell Pickering all he needed to know about who was with whom.

"You, you, you and you," Pickering said, pointing to each of the football players. "Go to the principal's office. Tell Miss Link that you're to stay there until I get there."

The four large boys picked up their books and walked into the school.

Pickering turned and looked at the assembled crowd, which had already begun to thin out. "Show's over everyone," he said. "Get to your homerooms." Jimmy watched as the students dutifully obeyed their vice-principal and filed through the propped-open front doors of the school.

Pickering turned his attention back to Tony and Jimmy.

"You two. Come with me."

The boys picked up their books and followed him into the school and to his office. He closed the door and motioned them to sit in the two chairs in front of his nicked and scratched wooden desk. He took his seat behind it. Jimmy noted that the desk had many folders and papers on it—all arranged in neat piles, reflecting the organized character of its occupant. There was a mug bearing the seal of West Virginia University, Pickering's alma mater, and a photograph of a woman and young girl, who Jimmy assumed were the vice-principal's wife and daughter.

Pickering looked at him, all but ignoring Tony.

"Does this have anything to do with the pictures of you that are supposedly making their way around the school?"

Jesus, Jimmy thought. *Even Pickering knows about it.*

"I don't know what you're talking about, sir," he lied, lowering his eyes to avoid Pickering's all-knowing gaze.

"No sir," Tony jumped in. "Jimmy had nothing to do with it. Was just a girl thing between me and Brent."

Pickering ignored Tony's attempt to continue protecting his friend. He folded his hands on the desk before him and leaned toward Jimmy.

"Jimmy, I heard about what happened. Not too much gets by me."

Jimmy knew that was true. Pickering always seemed to know what was going on—so much so that it led to students trying to figure out who his spies were.

Barely moving his head, he raised his eyes to meet Pickering's. The vice-principal leaned back in his chair, his right thumb under his chin and right forefinger resting on his cheek.

"If I can find the pictures, I'll have them destroyed," Pickering told him. "But what happened, happened. And you're going to have to find a way to deal with it. Getting into fights with jerks like Brent Stockbridge isn't the way to do it."

"Yes sir. I know that," Jimmy replied as he nervously picked at the cuticle of his left ring finger.

Pickering leaned forward again. "Look, son. I know that this is going to be very difficult for you. Based on what I heard"—Jimmy had no doubt that he had heard everything—"I imagine it's going to be pretty embarrassing for you."

"Yes sir."

"Unfortunately, there's not much I can do for you to remove the embarrassment. This isn't something that happened on school grounds or during school hours. You're just going to have to tough it out."

"Yes sir. I understand." Jimmy lowered his eyes. *You're a lot of help,* he thought. *Tough it out—just what my mother would say if she knew.*

Pickering turned to Tony. "I know you were sticking up for your friend. Did a pretty good job, apparently."

"Yes sir," Tony said proudly.

Pickering laid his hands palms down on his desk. "Okay. I'm not going to take any formal action—this time. Any more fighting, though, and you'll be suspended."

"Yes sir," the boys answered in unison.

"I'm going to go read the riot act to Brent and his buddies. Hopefully, word will get around to lay off of you a bit," he said, nodding towards Jimmy. "But there are no guarantees."

Jimmy saw sincere concern in Pickering's eyes. It was a look he would not have previously associated with the school's designated disciplinarian.

"I understand, sir. Thank you."

Pickering stood up. "Now get back to your homerooms."

The boys got up and walked out of the vice-principal's office. They stopped at the reception desk to pick up their hall passes from the ever-present, bespectacled administrative assistant, Miss Link. The bell had already rung signaling the beginning of homeroom and they would need the hall passes to authorize their not being in a classroom after the bell. With their passes they stepped out into the deserted hallway.

"Thanks Tony," Jimmy said.

"For what?"

"You know what. For sticking up for me."

Tony placed his free hand on Jimmy's shoulder. "It was nothing, good buddy. You'd have done the same for me."

He wanted to believe that. He would certainly come to Tony's defense if he could do it by using his brains. He wasn't so sure about his fists. Still, Tony was his best friend, and he knew Tony would do anything for him.

"You know it, Tony. I'd do anything for you," he said with false bravado.

Tony smiled and playfully punched him lightly in the fleshy part of his upper arm. "I know you would, good buddy. I know you would."

They turned and headed in opposite directions towards their respective homerooms. Jimmy was secure in the knowledge that Tony might ask him to do many things, but he'd never ask him to fight for him. All the same, it made him feel like less than the total friend he felt he should be, and unworthy of Tony's unconditional friendship.

Chapter 4

ROOM 201 WAS AT THE end of the hall and up a flight of stairs. The homeroom period was only fifteen minutes long—just long enough for the morning announcements over the public address system and any important announcements the homeroom teacher may have.

As he rushed down the hall and up the stairs, Jimmy's mind was still debating with itself over what kind of friend he really was. This distraction caused him to momentarily forget that this was the worst day of his life. He remembered soon enough. When he reached Room 201 he opened the door and closed it behind him. Mr. White, his homeroom teacher, sat behind his desk in the far corner of the front of the room. He appeared to be correcting papers.

Without looking at the class, Jimmy walked towards Mr. White's desk to give the teacher his hall pass. Halfway across the room he heard a muted voice coming from the back of the classroom. "Pee Wee. Pee Wee."

He stopped and turned his head to his left, in the direction of the voice. Loud laughter broke out. He felt as if he was standing naked before the entire class.

"That's enough!" Mr. White said loudly and firmly.

The laughter stopped, but Jimmy could see many of the kids laughing silently to themselves, exchanging snickering glances with each other. He walked the rest of the way to Mr. White's desk and turned in his hall pass.

He took his seat in the front row, second desk from the window, keeping his eyes cast down at the floor and his desk. When he sat down, he could still feel his classmates' cruel, mocking eyes piercing the back of his head. He had already had more than he thought he could bear, and the school day was only ten minutes old.

"Ignore them Jimmy," a voice whispered to him from his right. "They're just a bunch of creeps."

He turned his head to the right and saw Meghan Jeffries leaning towards him, a look of disgust on her face. Meghan Jeffries, the undisputed prettiest girl in the school—golden hair flowing to the middle of her back, a precisely complimentary cream-like complexion and a perfectly proportioned body, no part too big or too small, all parts fitting together as if designed and assembled with the precision of a master watchmaker. Meghan Jeffries, who had sat next to him in homeroom since the beginning of tenth grade. Meghan Jeffries, who he was secretly and madly in love with and who he went to sleep thinking of every night. Meghan Jeffries, who was going steady with Stosh Kowalski, the state heavyweight wrestling champion who would chew up and spit out anyone he even *suspected* of making a play for his girl.

"Thanks Meghan," he whispered back. His eyes were glistening as he fought to hold back tears. One thing he couldn't do is let them see him cry.

"Don't worry. They'll get their jollies for a day and it'll pass," she reassured him.

The public address announcements had started a few seconds earlier. He looked up at Mr. White to see if he had seen them whispering, which wasn't permitted during the announcements. The teacher appeared not to have noticed.

Jimmy slouched down into his chair, his right arm draped over the writing portion of his standard classroom chair/desk combination. He turned his head back to Meghan.

"Not for me," he whispered. "It'll never pass for me."

While he had no hope of ever having Meghan Jeffries as a girlfriend, they had become friends. As he saw it, that in itself wasn't too shabby. For over a year now she had treated him as something of a confidant, telling him about her ups and downs with Stosh and her previous boyfriend, Taylor Cunningham, the point guard on the basketball team, asking him for advice, and sharing with him on many occasions Mr. White's exile to the "time-out" chairs in the back of the classroom for those who violated the no talking policies. Aside from Tony, Meghan was the one person in the school he could count on to empathize with him.

Meghan looked up at Mr. White, then turned her attention back to Jimmy.

"Sure it will," she whispered. "I know you don't believe it now, but some day you'll look back on this and laugh."

It was such an adult thing to say. From anyone else it would have seemed trite. From Meghan, though, it seemed wise, if not particularly helpful in removing the immediacy of his present pain and humiliation. Strange, he thought, how she could seem so wise when counseling him, yet so foolish in making decisions in her own life—like dating guys like Stosh and Taylor.

Jimmy raised his arm, tilted his head towards Meghan and rested his cheek on his hand.

"I'll *never* laugh about this, Meghan. *Never.* But some day, I'll show them. I'll show them all. I'll . . . "

The announcements ended just as the school phone on the wall next to the door started to ring. Mr. White walked over and answered it in a voice loud enough for all to hear clearly and to keep the class quiet.

"Mr. White. Room 201."

He listened for a moment and looked directly at Jimmy.

"Yes sir. Will do." He hung up the phone, walked back towards his desk and stopped in front of Jimmy's desk.

"Jimmy," he said, rubbing his brow with his thumb and two fingers. "Vice-principal Pickering wants to see you in his office."

"Right now?" Jimmy asked.

"Right now."

What now? Jimmy wondered. Had Pickering changed his mind about suspending him and Tony? Maybe he confiscated the pictures? Whatever it was, given the way the day had gone so far, he held little hope that it was a good thing that he was being called back to the office so soon.

As he stood up, Meghan reached out and gently squeezed his hand. It was a gesture he treasured, even if it could subject him to the wrath of Stosh. As he left the classroom, the renewed snickering of the rest of the students followed him out.

Jimmy was only half way to the office when the bell rang signaling the end of homeroom and the movement of students to their first period class. The hallway filled quickly. He avoided all eye contact as he worked his way through the crowd. But he couldn't avoid hearing the diminutive nickname that had been pinned on him.

"Hey Pee Wee."

"How's it going, Pee Wee?"

He pushed his way through the sea of students. When he reached the office, Pickering was waiting for him just inside the door in front of the reception desk. Jimmy saw a look of concern and urgency on the Vice-principal's face.

"Jimmy," Pickering said solemnly, "you need to get home. Right away."

"Mr. Pickering, I thought you weren't going to suspend . . . "

"Jimmy, it's your father. He's had a heart attack."

The words hit him harder than any punch he might have taken that morning. He stared at Pickering for a minute, expecting the words to somehow be taken back—to be told that it was a mistake, some sort of misunderstanding or miscommunication.

"Jimmy? Did you hear me? Your father had a heart attack. You need to get right home." Pickering's voice was urgent, and compassionate.

Jimmy rapidly blinked his eyes several times, as if he was coming out of a trance.

"Yes sir. Uh, uh . . . do you know . . ."

"I don't know anything else, son. Just hurry."

"Yes sir."

He turned to leave, then turned back to Pickering. Without a word, he handed the Vice-principal his books. He would be running the four blocks home and didn't want to be weighted down.

He turned and went back into the hallway. The changing of classes was still going on. He ran through the crowd, almost knocking down a couple of students. They yelled at him, using his new pejorative nickname. He didn't hear any of it. He stormed out the front door, down the steps and across the empty outdoor campus. He ran the four blocks home darting across the intersections with no thought or concern regarding oncoming traffic or the color of the traffic signals.

As he turned the corner of his street, he saw an ambulance pulling out of his driveway. It drove up the street and past him. He noted that it didn't have its emergency lights on.

He rushed to his house and just about crashed through the front door. He bounded up the stairs to the living room. There was no one there.

"Mom! Mom!" he called out.

"In here, Jimmy," his mother's voice wafted out from the kitchen. He ran to it. She was sitting at the kitchen table, still in her morning robe, smoking a cigarette.

"He's dead." She said it with all the feeling and compassion she might have exhibited in announcing that the Dow Jones had fallen thirty points that day. But her inability to show emotion was the last thing Jimmy cared about now.

"Huh ... huh ... how? When? I mean . . . "

"Right after you left for school. Your father finished his breakfast, stood up to go to work, and keeled over—right onto the table."

The reality of his father's death hadn't set in. He had seen no body. There was no evidence to support what he was being told.

"He can't be! He was too young to have a heart attack!" He was marshalling his arguments to disprove the fact of his father's death. His mother just ignored them.

"Paramedics said he didn't suffer." She flicked a long ash into what had been her husband's breakfast dish. "Death was instantaneous, they said."

"No! Nooo!" Jimmy yelled as he pounded his right leg with his fist.

Mrs. Donovan made no effort to hug or comfort her son. He knew she wanted to, but for some reason, she just didn't know how. She hid her inability to nurture and comfort behind a façade of steel and strength, which allowed little room for useless emotion.

"Jimmy, he's gone," she said. "There's nothing we can do about it. We just have to go on without him."

He wanted to cry. He needed to cry. He wouldn't do it in front of her. That would just create a scene—a scene he was in no condition to deal with. He turned and ran upstairs to his room. He closed and locked his door. He threw himself on his bed and sobbed for the death of his father. He knew that as far as his mother was concerned, as long as she didn't see him cry, it didn't happen. As far as he was concerned, she was a cold bitch.

Chapter 5

JIMMY HATED WEARING A TIE. So had his father. He tried to convince his mother to bury his dad without a tie. It wouldn't be proper, Mrs. Donovan had told him. So there he stood, in the Underwood & Sons Funeral Home, looking at his father's lifeless body in the open casket, cloth choke chains wrapped around each of their necks. *At least you can't feel it anymore, Dad,* he silently said as one silver tear rolled down his cheek.

He felt a large hand rest upon his shoulder.

"What do you think, young man? How does he look?"

Jimmy looked over his right shoulder to see a tall, thin, distinguished looking man in his late fifties, wearing a black suit, a white shirt with overly starched collars and a black tie. On his right lapel was a small gold nameplate which read "C. Underwood."

"He looks fine, Mr. Underwood," Jimmy lied. "Almost like he was still alive."

Clyde Underwood was the funeral director who had buried all of Jimmy's grandparents, each of whom had died by the time he was fourteen. He was eight when his father's mother died. Hers was the first corpse he had ever seen and when he did, he cried out, "That's not grandma! That's some kind of dummy!" It was then that his mother had told him that proper funeral home etiquette was to compliment the funeral director on how life-like the deceased looked—even thought it wasn't true.

"I just wish he didn't have to wear that tie," he continued, looking down at his father lying in the ornate casket. "Dad hated ties. Said it was because he had to wear one every day to work." He looked back at Mr. Underwood. "I just don't think he'd of wanted to wear one through all eternity."

"Perhaps," replied Mr. Underwood as he shifted his hand from Jimmy's right shoulder to his left. "But he does look very distinguished. Wouldn't you agree?"

"Yes sir. Yes sir, he does."

And it was true. Mr. Donovan looked as distinguished in death as he had always looked, at least to the outside world, in life.

"You've done a fine job, Mr. Underwood. A real fine job."

"Well thank you, Jimmy. That's very kind of you." He tapped Jimmy a couple of times on the shoulder, then turned and walked up the center aisle between the finely made wooden pews towards the entry salon to the viewing chapel. Mr. Underwood stopped halfway up the aisle where Jimmy's mother was standing looking intently at the floral arrangements framing the coffin of her late husband.

"Is there anything else we can do for you, Mrs. Donovan—before the visitors arrive?" Jimmy heard the undertaker ask his mother.

"No, Mr. Underwood," she answered, never taking her eyes off of the flowers. He thought his mother sounded more like a hostess planning a party than a widow arranging a viewing. "Father McTighe should be here around eight."

"That will be fine," said Underwood. "We will prepare accordingly. If you'll excuse me." Jimmy turned his head and saw Underwood bow slightly and walk out of the chapel. His mother looked at him and walked up to him.

"Jimmy, it's almost seven o'clock," she said. "People will be here any minute." She brushed the fabric of his suit jacket's arms and straightened the knot on his tie. "Now you should be at the door to the chapel to greet everyone as they enter. I'll be here in the front pew." She licked her fingers and ran them over a lock of his hair that had fallen out of place. "When Father McTighe arrives, you come and sit next to me. Do you understand?"

"Yes ma'am."

"And remember, no tears. No matter how much anyone else cries— and Lord knows the faucets will be wide open for your Aunt Liz and your Aunt Mary—you and I must remain dignified. Understand?" She brushed more invisible lint from the front of his suit jacket.

"I understand, Mother," he said with a hint of obvious annoyance. "I understand."

"Good. Good. Now go get in position." Mrs. Donovan placed her hand on Jimmy's back and gently nudged him towards the door to the salon. She then took her position in the front pew of the still empty chapel.

It was at this moment—as he strolled up the aisle of the viewing chapel—that he realized for the first time just how much he would miss his father. He loved his mother, and he knew that she loved him. But they could never be close—not like he was with his dad. William Donovan was a good and kind man—easy-going, with a good sense of humor and utterly devoted to his family and, within proper bounds, to the pursuit of happiness. Mrs. Donovan, on the other hand, was a rigid moralist and perfectionist. She viewed the rules of society (as defined by etiquette and her staid concept of dignity) and of the Catholic Church as absolute and unbending. She attended Mass every morning and chastised her husband for setting a bad example for their child by only attending on Sunday mornings.

Jimmy thought about how he almost always sided with his father in such matters. He knew that this angered his mother, but she rarely showed it. Mary Donovan believed that almost any show of emotion was a sign of weakness—and if it was up to her, weakness would be added to the cardinal sins.

Jimmy took his place in the salon at the entryway to the chapel. He looked at his mother, sitting alone in the front pew facing the open casket of her dead husband. He wondered why it was so difficult for her to open up, to show warmth and caring, even to her only child. He suspected it had something to do with her father who, until he died when Jimmy was thirteen, she seemed to barely tolerate. But this was a family that didn't talk much about feelings, much less family secrets—and Mary Donovan spoke the least of all.

"Oh, Jimmy. He was *sooo* young!"

He turned to see his Aunt Mary—his father's sister—dressed in an ankle-length black dress with a black hat and veil, walking into the funeral parlor and towards him. Her arms were outstretched and she was already sobbing hysterically.

"Oh, Jimmy. You *poor* child," Aunt Mary said as she placed him in a painful bear hug of far greater force than one would expect of a woman who barely reached five feet one inch with heels. "To lose your father when you're so young." She continued to sob.

Holding back his own urge to cry, he returned the hug and sought to console his aunt.

"It's okay, Aunt Mary. He's in a better place."

Yuck, he thought to himself. *That sounded so trite when others said it to me when they heard that Dad died. It must sound just as trite coming from me.*

"Yes he is, Jimmy. Yes he is." She kissed him on the cheek, turned and walked down the chapel aisle to her brother's casket. Jimmy turned his attention back to the salon, not wanting to see the emotional scene that was sure to take place.

It was after seven o'clock and people started to file in—what little family there was, Bill Donovan's colleagues from work and friends of Jimmy's parents. He properly, and with dignity, greeted every one of them.

Tony came, of course, with his parents. They had become good friends with the Donovans when they moved to Pittsburgh from New York. As he was greeting the Scarlottis, he got the most pleasant surprise of all.

"Hi, Jimmy. I'm so sorry about your dad." He turned to see Meghan. She was dressed in a simple navy blue dress, appropriate for a funeral. But no matter how plainly she dressed, she couldn't hide her radiant beauty. She put her hands out, took his and kissed him on the cheek.

"Tha . . .thanks, Meghan," he stuttered. "It's so nice of you to come."

"Since you didn't come to school yesterday or today, I didn't get a chance to give you my condolences. And I didn't want to just call you."

"Thanks Meghan. You're . . . you're really special." He had wanted to say that so many times and couldn't. Of course, he knew she wouldn't take it quite how he would have meant it if he had had the courage to say it under different circumstances. But it didn't matter.

She hugged him. "No I'm not. I'm just a friend, if you ever need me." His legs wobbled and he hugged her back, as much to hold himself up as anything.

She turned and walked down the aisle towards the casket and the first pew where Mrs. Donovan was receiving condolences—*holding court,* Jimmy thought sarcastically. His eyes followed Meghan the entire way, watched her kneel at the casket, bow her head in prayer, then get up and walk over to his mother. *Everything she does spells c-l-a-s-s,* he thought. *Why can't she . . .*

"Hey Jimmy." His attention was jerked away from Meghan by the all-too-recognizable voice of Rachel Feinberg. "Sorry about your dad." He turned to see Rachel, flanked, as always, by Debbie and Rebecca.

"What are you doing here?" he said. It was a tone that he knew his mother would have considered undignified and unacceptable, whatever the cause.

"Came to pay our respects, like everyone else," Rachel answered. Jimmy wondered if Debbie and Rebecca ever spoke when they were with Rachel. "We're neighbors, remember?" she continued as she brushed some non-existent lint from his lapel. Her mimicking of his mother's mannerism—unknowingly done as it may have been—both intimidated and angered him. "Besides,"—Rachel curled the left side of her upper lip derisively—"our parents are here, and they made us come."

Having thus diminished the death of his father, Rachel gave a slight nod of her head, turned and headed down the aisle towards the casket, followed dutifully by Tweedle Dee and Tweedle Dum. He watched them, his anger rising at the thought that their next act of callous disrespect would be feigning concern, and even prayer, while viewing his father's body. And he knew that, at least for now, there was nothing he could do about it.

"Nasty bitches, aren't they?"

"Wha . . .what?" Jimmy said as he turned to find the source of the startling comment. Standing next to him was an unassuming man, slight in build, perhaps early middle-aged, with absolutely no distinguishing characteristics which would, as far as Jimmy could tell, make him stick out in a crowd of two. He wore the same black suit, starched white shirt and black tie as Mr. Underwood. His small gold nameplate read "P. Lachaise." Jimmy realized the man was obviously one of Mr. Underwood's assistants.

"Those young ladies," the man said as he nodded towards Rachel and her pals, "ah, ladies is certainly not accurate—those young girls you were talking with. Very nasty little whores, aren't they?"

Jimmy was floored by the man's bluntness. Yet his direct expression of exactly what Jimmy was feeling created an instantaneous sense of kinship, and respect.

"Yes. They are . . ." he answered, as he looked again at the man's nameplate, ". . . Mr., uh, Lachaise. But how would you know? Do you know them?"

"In a manner of speaking. I know their type." He was standing right next to Jimmy, but his voice had a distant quality to it. Jimmy found himself straining to hear, even though he could hear every word clearly.

Lachaise continued.

"They use their good looks—or sometimes their parents' money or power—to gain popularity, to join the in-crowd. Or they even create their own exclusive little clique, of those they would christen 'the beautiful people.'" He leaned closer, hands clasped behind his back, and whispered in Jimmy's ear in an almost conspiratorial way. "And to keep their status, their position at the top of the adolescent food chain, their *power,* they exclude, they tease, they demean, they humiliate those not deemed worthy of their grace—those like *you.*"

Yes! Jimmy thought. *Yes!* That's exactly what it was like. No matter how much his parents, educators, guidance counselors, school psychologists— all of them—no matter how much they called it a matter of typical high school adolescent behavior, it was much more sinister than that to those like him who were targets of that cruelty. *Yes, bitches and whores are exactly what those girls are. And Mr. Lachaise understands that.*

"But—but how do you know about Rachel and her friends?" he asked, curious as to how this stranger to him and them could be so perceptive.

Lachaise folded his left arm across his chest, rested his right elbow on it and took his chin between his thumb and right forefinger. "I'm . . . a people watcher. I work with people every day."

"You work with *dead* people."

"Yes, yes I do." Lachaise moved closer and whispered in his ear again. "And you'd be surprised how many of the dead people I work with every day are still breathing, walking around, *acting* as if they're alive, when they're not—they're actually dead. They just don't know it yet."

What did he mean by that? Jimmy wondered. There was only one way to find out, he decided—ask.

"How could people be dead if they're still alive, Mr. Lachaise? And what do you mean they don't know it yet?"

Lachaise stepped slightly to his left so he was facing Jimmy head on. He looked straight and deep into Jimmy's eyes.

"Do you know?" he asked.

"Do I know what?"

"Do you know that *you* are dead?"

Jimmy shivered. He felt as if his inner soul was being probed by some sort of unseen instrument.

"Wha . . . what do you mean . . . I'm dead? I'm not—I'm not dead."

"Aren't you?"

Jimmy lost all sense of anyone else being around. He saw and felt only Mr. Lachaise's presence—and the presence of . . . he couldn't quite tell. Fear, yes. But more, much more.

"No. N . . . n . . . no," he sputtered. "I'm not dead. I'm right here. Alive."

"All that anger bottled up inside you—for what Rachel did; for the kids at school making fun of you; for your mother not giving you the love you need; for all of that and so much more."

He couldn't distinguish Lachaise's voice anymore, but he was hearing all of the words—as if he was hearing the man's thoughts. "All that anger. And what do you do with it? Nothing. You keep it inside. You swallow it. You let it eat at your insides. You're letting it kill you."

Jimmy was confused. How did Lachaise know? How did he know about what Rachel did? About his mother? But he *did* know. And he knew about the anger, and what it was doing to Jimmy. If he knew this, he must know more.

"But—but what can I do?" he asked. "What can I do about it?" This man had seen right into his demons like no one before and he needed Lachaise to tell him how to exorcise them.

"You must release your anger, free yourself of it." There was a hissing sound accompanying Lachaise's words now. "Those who hurt you must pay, so that those who would hurt you in the future . . ."

"Good evening, Jimmy."

The sound of Father McTighe's always forceful voice startled him and stopped Lachaise in mid-sentence. Jimmy looked towards the entrance door to the funeral home and saw his parish priest walking towards him.

"Sorry I'm a wee bit late," the cherubic-looking Irishman of the cloth said to Jimmy. "So what do you say you stop standing here by your lonesome and we go see how your mother's doing and get on with the service?"

At the suggestion that he was alone, Jimmy turned to look back at Mr. Lachaise, but there was no one there. The priest took him by the arm and turned to go into the chapel. Jimmy stopped and placed his hand on Father McTighe's.

"I'll be right there, Father," he said. "I've got to go to the restroom."

"Okay then, boy. But hurry it up."

Father McTighe let go of his arm and headed into the chapel. Jimmy looked around the salon for Mr. Lachaise, to finish their conversation. But the assistant to the funeral director wasn't there. He looked in the men's room, the other viewing chapel and the office. Not there either. He went outside and checked the parking lot. Nothing. As he came back to the front entrance another man in the Underwood & Sons Funeral Home "uniform" was at the door. His nameplate read "L. Chamberlain."

"The Donovan viewing is in chapel number one," Mr. Chamberlain said as he held the front door open. He pointed. "That's the one there, on the left."

"Yes, yes. I know," Jimmy answered impatiently. "I'm looking for Mr. Lachaise. Have you seen him?"

"Is he a member of the family, or a visitor, sir? Either way, you may want to check the guest register to see . . ."

"No. No. Mr. *Lachaise*. The guy who works here—with you."

"I'm sorry. You must be mistaken young man. There is no Mr. Lachaise who works here."

"Of course there is!" Jimmy was almost shouting. "He's wearing the same clothes as you, and has the same kind of nameplate, and was talking to me in there and . . ."

"Son," Mr. Chamberlain said as he placed his hand on Jimmy's shoulder in an unsuccessful effort to calm him down. "I don't know who you saw, or who you were talking to, but I can *assure* you, there is no Mr. Lachaise working here."

Jimmy rushed back into the funeral parlor and looked around one more time. When he convinced himself that Lachaise wasn't there, he returned to the chapel. Father McTighe had not waited for him to return and had begun to lead the assembled group in prayer. As he listened to the priest pray to the Lord for the repose of his father's soul, he knew that whoever Lachaise was, everything he had told Jimmy to do flew in the face of what the church, his parents and Father McTighe had taught him.

He was a good kid. He knew he would do what was right. But he also knew it would be harder now. *Jesus,* he thought. *Who is this guy who seems to know me inside out? And where did he disappear to?* Just the thought of Lachaise was spooky, even scary. But the thought of what Lachaise had told him— "those who hurt you must pay"—felt so temptingly, deliciously good.

Chapter 6

"**T**ELL ME ABOUT KATIE O'TOOLE."

The words were soothing, caring, and paternalistic.

Jimmy kept his head buried in his folded arms resting on the table. He didn't want to look up. He didn't want to talk about Katie O'Toole.

"Jimmy? Jimmy. Look at me." The voice was still caring, but insistent now. Jimmy raised his head, slid both hands through his hair, and looked at the man sitting across the rectangular table from him.

"Tell me about Katie," the man insisted.

Jimmy's eyes moved around the bare room with the drab green walls and no furniture but the table and two wooden chairs he shared with his inquisitor. They slowly worked their way back to the man seated across from him.

"What do you want to know?" he asked. His tongue felt heavy, causing him to slur his speech—probably from the damn medication they were giving him, he figured.

"Well, why don't we start with how you met her?"

He wasn't sure he trusted Dr. Pierre Pe're. He had dark, slicked back hair and a black goatee. He was dressed all in black from head to toe, just as he had been every day that Jimmy had known him. He looked more like an evil scientist in a B-grade horror movie than a psychiatrist. Or, he thought, with a black beret the good doctor could have passed for a starving artist hawking his mediocre paintings on the Champs Elysee, as if Jimmy knew anything about how Paris looked. The stark surroundings of the bare room gave him the impression of being in a police or military interrogation room rather than a psychiatric hospital. It was all so incongruent. But he had been talking to Dr. Pe're for almost a week now, and it did seem to be helping.

"I—I met Katie about, um, about a year after my dad died—my senior year in high school." His speech was slow and halting, quite unlike his thrashing and screaming when he was first admitted the week before. The medication calmed him down, but it also made it more difficult to translate his thoughts into words.

Jimmy stood up and walked over to the only window in the room. It had bars and didn't appear to have any way of being opened, lending that much more to the prison-like atmosphere. He looked down from his second story perch onto not-so-well manicured grounds. Stone benches surrounded three sides of a central, non-operating fountain, and white uniformed aides walked and wheeled robed patients aimlessly around as if they were extras on a movie lot whose roles were to provide the appropriate backdrop for his very own unfolding drama.

"Do we have to talk about this?" he asked Dr. Pe're, not shifting his gaze from the scene below.

"Jimmy, you had a nervous breakdown. A pretty severe one. We're here to help you, but you've got to be willing to help yourself—by working with us." Dr. Pe're tapped the table with his hand. "Now, why don't you sit down and tell me about Katie."

Jimmy turned and looked at the doctor. Pe're had taken his pipe out and had placed it into a pouch of tobacco. He pulled it out and packed the tobacco in the pipe bowl, then lit it with a gold-plated lighter.

In each session he had had with Dr. Pe're so far, he had started with a deep seated unease which, somehow, by the end of the session, had turned into a sense of wholeness and unity with the doctor. He would feel much better but, for some reason, he felt guilty about feeling good. It seemed so typically Catholic to him. As he returned to his chair he made a mental note to ask the good doctor at some point how to cope with his Father McTighe syndrome.

"There was this . . . really neat girl . . . Meghan," he began. "Meghan Jeffries. She sat next to me in homeroom for three years. She was just about, well . . . just about the most gorgeous girl you'd ever see. But she wasn't stuck-up about it like most of them. She was . . . she was really nice."

He paused to collect his still sluggish thoughts.

"Did you like her?" Dr. Pe're asked, briefly interrupting the regular hissing sound the mouthpiece of his pipe made every time he drew on it.

Jimmy folded his hands and rested them on the table before him.

"Yes, Dr. Pe're. I did. I really did. Problem was I wasn't the kind of guy she'd go out with. She liked me all right. We became pretty good friends. Buddies. You know what I mean? I could tell her just about anything. And she could, too. But see, she was so pretty I guess she kind of felt like she needed to date popular guys. You know guys from the in-crowd, jocks.

"So our senior year she was dating this guy Stosh—Stosh Kowalski. He was on the wrestling team—a big guy—the state heavyweight champion. And she would always be talking to me about her and Stosh, about their dates, their fights, their making up—you know, confiding in me. Almost like I was her girlfriend instead of a guy."

"How did that make you feel?"

"Well, in one way it made me feel pretty good that she trusted me like that, to tell me her secrets and all. But it also made me mad. Stosh treated her like dirt—like she was his property or something. She was too good for that, and I told her so. But she didn't listen. She was just so caught up in being the girlfriend of big shots."

"Did you ever tell her how you felt?" Dr. Pe're asked, pointing his pipe towards Jimmy.

"Are you kidding? First off, Meghan would've just laughed. She'd of thought I was joking or something." Jimmy leaned back in his chair, slouched and extended his right leg. "Besides, that would've been a sure way of getting the crap beat out of me by Stosh."

He lowered his head and closed his eyes. "I might as well have told her how I felt, because Stosh beat the shit out of me anyway."

Dr. Pe're laid his pipe down on the table and leaned forward towards Jimmy.

"Do you want to talk about that, or do you want to get back to where we were supposed to be going—Katie?"

Jimmy rubbed his eyes and opened them. "You asked how I met Katie. That's what I'm telling you," he snapped back, irritated at what he considered the doctor's obvious lack of insight.

Dr. Pe're leaned back in his chair with an almost satisfied look on his face. "Okay, continue."

For a moment Jimmy thought of ending the session altogether. But he knew that having started down this road, stopping would be more painful for him than continuing.

"So, one day Meghan tells me that Stosh saw her talking with Brad Martin—he was our class president—and got all pissed off because he thinks Brad is putting the moves on Meghan. Meghan swears it's not true, but Stosh doesn't believe it and says he's going to bust Brad up. For days, Brad—now you got to understand, Brad's a pretty big guy, but he's no jock and no fighter—he wants to be an actor for Christ's sake—anyway, Brad tries to avoid Stosh. But Stosh keeps calling him out and threatening to get him alone in the woods one day and really do a number on him.

"So I guess Brad decides that if he's going to get beat up by Stosh, it's better to do it at school where there are lots of witnesses and maybe it can get broken up by a teacher before he gets too broken up.

"Meghan says that Stosh and Brad have agreed to meet in the school parking lot after school. She says she's tried to talk Stosh out of it, but she can't. I ask her why she doesn't threaten to leave Stosh if he hurts Brad, but she says she can't do that either—because she *loves* him too much."

Jimmy takes a deep breath, thinking how ludicrous it was for a girl like Meghan to go with a guy like Stosh.

"Anyway," he continued, "she says she can't bear to watch, but wants to know what happens right away. She asks me if I would go out to the parking lot, watch the fight and as soon as it's over, run down to the gym lobby where she'll be waiting so I can tell her what happened. Like the idiot I am, I say okay.

"So after school, I go to the parking lot. There's a bunch of kids there. Brad and Stosh take off their jackets. Since Stosh is a wrestler, I guess Brad decides to try to box him and"—Jimmy clenches his fist and throws a phantom punch in Dr. Pe're's direction—"he throws the first punch."

Jimmy sits up and bends his head and shoulders down.

"Stosh ducks, grabs Brad by the legs, lifts him up and throws him down on his back on the hard asphalt." The heaviness had left his tongue and he was now telling the story in rapid-fire fashion.

"The crowd pushes in closer and I have trouble seeing over everybody's heads, so I look down and between people's legs. All I see is Brad's head lying on the ground, two fists pummeling him and blood squirting all over the place. When Stosh finally stops, I can barely see Brad's face through the blood—but I *can* see that his nose is broken pretty good.

"So now I run down the sidewalk from the parking lot to the doors to the gym lobby. And Meghan's there waiting. Her face looks all worried and she asks me what happened. When I tell her, she starts crying and saying 'I didn't want that to happen,' and 'Why did Stosh have to do that?'

"*Then,*" he continued, his voice rising in pitch and excitability, "she throws her arms around me and starts crying on my shoulder. Now I'm thinking, man, Stosh Kowalski just beat the crap out of Brad Martin for *talking* to Meghan the wrong way. What the hell will he do to *me* if he sees her *hugging* me? So I try to push Meghan away. I tell her everything will be okay. She just holds me tighter and keeps wailing, 'It's all my fault! It's all my fault!'

"I turn my head and look out the glass doors to the sidewalk and I see Stosh marching toward the doors followed by all his hangers-on—I don't know where Brad's gone—but I try to push Meghan away again. I tell her Stosh is coming. It's no use. She's bawling and holding me tight and when he comes in and sees that . . . the look on his face—it's like . . . it's like he's not even human. The rage. The hate. He morphs into some kind of . . . some kind of beast—flames coming out of his eyes, smoke from his ears. If he hadn't hit me first I'd have probably had a heart attack I was so scared.

"Well, I figure the only reasons my face didn't look like Brad's was that I did a better job of holding my arms over my head as Stosh kept punching me, and Stosh must have felt it was a little unfair, me being so much smaller than him—either that or his hands just hurt so much from the beating he put on Brad."

Jimmy paused again and stared up at the ceiling. The pain of the memory of the precise moment he met Katie seemed, in some ways, almost indistinguishable from the memory of the pain inflicted upon him by Stosh Kowalski—in other ways, a defining moment in his life.

"As I lay there, writhing in pain on the floor, no one thought to see how I was or anything. Everyone seemed to have scattered. Since we were in the school I guess they figured some teacher must have heard the commotion. My luck, Tony—I told you about Tony yesterday—my best friend and, kind of, I guess you could say my protector—Tony's home sick. So I was there alone; my ribs were really killing me; I don't remember the punches, just the pain. So I'm really hurting.

"And then I feel this hand stroking the side of my face, and my forehead, and I hear a voice saying 'Are you okay? Is there anything I can do?'

"I look up and I see this . . . this almost angelic face. She's got short, strawberry blonde hair, freckles and these great green eyes—and she's looking at me, all worried. I had never seen her before. Turns out she was new in school—had just moved from Canton, Ohio."

Jimmy blinked hard several times to hold back the tears. He realized he had been unconsciously wringing his hands so hard they had started to turn white from the lack of blood circulation.

"She started to help me get up," he went on. "Just then, Mr. Pickering shows up. Asks if I'm okay. Then tells me to come to his office. As I start to follow him, she takes my hand in hers, touches my cheek with her other hand, and says, 'My name's Katie—Katie O'Toole. I'm in Mrs. Higgenbottom's homeroom—Room 207.' I say okay. I don't even tell her my name. But the next week, after serving my three-day suspension—Stosh got ten days because they found out about Brad—but I don't know why I got *any* days, but my mother wouldn't appeal the principal's decision—anyway, the next week I went to Katie's homeroom before the bell rang and I found her and . . . Well, that's how we met."

"And you started dating?" Dr. Pe're's voice startled him. As he had been telling his story, it was as if he had been alone and reliving it. For a moment, he said nothing as he watched his therapist stroke his black goatee, which appeared almost devilish on the man's angular face and pointed chin.

"Yeah. We hit it off right away. She was . . . she was really special. She . . ." He couldn't hold the tears back any longer. He put his head down into his arms on the table and wept.

"Would you like to stop for today?" Dr. Pe're asked.

Jimmy nodded his head, not bothering to lift it from the pillow of his folded arms.

⊢•→·◦·←•⊣

He stared straight up at what would have been the ceiling if he could have seen it in the pitch blackness of his room. It was a room without windows. In fact, except for his therapy room, he had seen no windows in any part of the hospital. As he would be led through the hallways by the attendants, he had the distinct impression of being deep in the bowels of some sort of catacombs, each doorway seeming more like the entrance to a vault for the dead than a room for living patients. While Jimmy had never been in a "house of death," he felt the scent of death all around him, although there were, to his knowledge, no dead people anywhere in the building. This was, after all, a mental hospital, not a medical hospital. It was unlikely that many people died here. *Just another effect of my breakdown,* he figured.

The door to his room had an observation portal with a sliding metal panel on the outside. When it was closed, like now, no light shone in from the hallway. The room was sparsely furnished—two beds, two vinyl-covered chairs and a bed pan for each bed's occupant in case nature called before an attendant was available to accompany him to a bathroom.

The bed pan was of no use to Jimmy's roommate, a seventeen-year-old paranoid schizophrenic named Aubrey something or other who spent most of his time strapped in so he wouldn't thrash around when the voices started talking to him. *I thought they had medication to stop that from happening,* he would think to himself each time Aubrey started screaming. He found Aubrey's outbursts eerie and unsettling. Much of what the young psychotic said was confusing and undecipherable. But one thing he kept yelling—it sounded like "Why, red eyes? Why my mother?"—was especially unnerving, particularly once Jimmy learned that Aubrey had carved up his own mother with a butcher knife.

Aubrey was asleep and quiet now. The only sound Jimmy could hear was his own breathing and the occasional footsteps of the floor's night attendant as he paced up and down the hallway tending to whatever duties needed tending to when all of the patients had been medicinally sent to dreamland for the night. Jimmy had cheated the hospital's dream merchant this evening by keeping his sleeping pills under his tongue while pretending to wash them down with the water the nurse provided him in a little paper cup. This night he was in no hurry to get to sleep.

How does he do it? Jimmy wondered. *How does Dr. Pe're get me to open up with him? I don't like him. I don't particularly trust him. Yet, in just a week, I've told him personal and intimate things about my family, myself, all about my inner feelings and fears, my most painful experiences and memories—just about anything and everything.*

He continued to stare into the darkness, allowing his mind to momentarily go blank. When thoughts returned, a feeling of unease overtook him.

The worst thing, he thought, was that Pe're seemed to already *know* what he was going to tell him. It wasn't anything Pe're *said* that indicated he already knew what there was to know about Jimmy. It was just . . . just the way the doctor *looked* at him—with a clear sense of recognition when he talked, especially when he was sharing his pain. At those times he almost thought he saw the corners of Pe're's lips turn up a bit—as if he was stifling a smile.

It's just my imagination, Jimmy thought. *After all, I had a nervous breakdown. My mind can't be operating too effectively.*

What he did have to admit to himself was that he *was* feeling much better since he had been admitted. And despite his misgivings—even his mistrust—of Dr. Pe're, the more he talked to him, the easier it became. Now he wanted Jimmy to talk about Katie. And then, he knew, it would be Veronica.

Every girl or woman he had ever been involved with had been a disaster for him. And that had become his cross, his curse, his obsession—to the point that it had overwhelmed him, caused him to lose control, shamed him. Dr. Pe're held out the promise of gaining control, learning to cope. He would listen to Dr. Pe're, he decided. Tell him what he wanted to know. Follow his advice and directions. He wouldn't resist anymore. The pain was too great, and he didn't know how to make it go away by himself. Father McTighe's words and teachings sure hadn't helped. They couldn't help him overcome his cold, unfeeling mother. They didn't protect him when Rachel Feinberg made him the laughingstock of the entire school. They didn't keep him from getting screwed by Katie and Veronica. They couldn't even comfort him when he lost his father.

Jimmy closed his eyes, moving seamlessly from the blackness of his dark room to the blackness of his inner mind. *I've got the opportunity,* he thought, *and I'm going to take it. It's time to turn to a real professional. God, I hope you can help me, Dr. Pe're. I don't want to hurt anymore.*

He rolled onto his left side. It was time to go to sleep, he decided. For the first time, he looked forward to the next day's session with Dr. Pierre Pe're.

Chapter 7

"**S**O, I THINK WE LEFT off with you and Katie starting to date," Dr. Pe're said, drawing on his pipe which had already been lit by the time Jimmy entered the room. He was, as always, dressed all in black. "Are you ready to move forward?"

Jimmy looked at his diminutive doctor sitting across the table from him, chair pushed back a bit with his left leg crossed and dangling down from his right knee. *How can he look so comfortable sitting in one of these hard, wooden chairs?* he wondered. *And doesn't he have any other colors in his wardrobe? Oh, well. Let's go.*

"Yeah, Doc, I'm ready."

"Good. Let's get started. Why don't you begin by telling me what kind of relationship you had with Katie."

This time there was no hesitation. Jimmy launched right into a description of why and how he fell in love with Katie O'Toole.

"It was instant love, Doc. Something clicked between us from the very start. I don't know what it was, but after two dates we both knew it was the real thing—so we started going steady. Went steady the rest of high school."

"Did you have sex?" Dr. Pe're asked.

Strange question, Jimmy thought. Stranger yet was the way he said the word "sex"—almost as if just saying the word titillated him. Not very professional. But what did he know. Maybe this was just another way for Pe're to bond with him and get him to open up more. Didn't matter, he decided. He continued on.

"No. No sex. You see, we knew we were going to be married some day. And we decided—both of us being *good* Irish Catholics and all—that the first time we'd go all the way was on our wedding night."

He shifted uncomfortably in his chair.

"Took a lot of ridicule for that, too," he said.

"From whom?"

"You know—the other kids in school."

"How did they know what you and Katie did or didn't do?"

"You know how kids are always asking—'Hey, how'd it go last night? Get any?' Girls ask all that stuff, too. And Katie and I were honest. We said how we felt and that we were saving ourselves."

"And the other kids made fun of you for that," the doctor said knowingly.

"Yeah. Teased us. Called us the Odd Couple. Called me Father Donovan and called her Sister Katie. Damn hypocrites. Half of them weren't doing anything either— just bragging that they were, to show off."

Dr. Pe're re-lit his pipe, taking several short puffs to get it going again.

"What about your best friend, Tony? How did he treat you?"

"Tony? Tony was great. He was always defending us. Saying, you know, 'Let them do what they want to do. It's none of your business.' And everybody knew Tony was cool—had done it several times, you know."

"Done what?" Pe're asked, leaning forward with a look of keen interest.

He's a doctor. Could he really be that naïve? Jimmy thought. Then he realized. It was about sex again. His psychotherapist apparently had a bit of the dirty old man in him.

"You know. Sex," he answered.

Pe're's eyes seemed to brighten. "And that made him cool?"

"Well, um, yeah. We were teenagers, you know."

The doctor leaned back in his chair again. "Continue," he said, drawing slow and long on his pipe.

"Anyway," Jimmy continued, "Tony sticks up for us. Stays good friends with us. Double dates with us and all. Tells us maybe we should just keep our mouths shut about it. But we didn't care. See, we knew we *were* different than everyone else. And our love was, too. And I knew— just like Father McTighe had told me it would happen—God was sitting up there in Heaven and he made me and Katie meet and fall in love. And she was the only one for me—forever."

"Is that what happened?" Pe're asked. Smugly, Jimmy thought. He turned his head and gazed out the barred window. A lump formed in his throat.

"No. No, it's not."

"Well . . ."

"Can we take a break?" Jimmy shot back before Pe're could ask another question. He suddenly didn't feel much like talking, although he knew that he would continue. There was no turning back now.

"Sure, Jimmy. Why don't you go get a drink, splash some water on your face."

Jimmy did just that. He went out into the hall to a water fountain right next to the door. He took a drink. The water was refreshingly cold and tasted almost as good as the spring water he and his father would drive three miles to a public park to collect when he was a little kid. He splashed his face. It didn't matter that half the water spilled onto his shirt. It felt good, and made him feel better—and ready to go.

When he returned to his seat in the therapy room, Pe're was packing his pipe again. Jimmy found the aroma of the pipe smoke pleasant. But he found Pe're's constant fiddling with the pipe distracting and irritating.

"Are we ready?" Pe're asked.

"Yeah. Sure."

"Good. Let's leave Katie for a bit. Tell me about Tony."

Jimmy lifted and bent his right leg, rested the heel of his right foot on the edge of his chair, wrapped his arms around his leg and rested his chin on his knee.

"No."

"Why not?"

"Tony's dead."

"How did he die?"

"Being stupid."

"Tell me about it."

There was a minute of silence. Finally, Jimmy decided Pe're would wait him out, so he might as well talk about it.

"One night—it was my first semester in college. I was home for the weekend. Tony was going into the Army but hadn't left yet. So this one night, Tony's parents were out and Tony had a party—a kegger. He got pretty drunk. He could get pretty crazy when he was drunk."

"Were you drunk?" Pe're asked.

"No. I didn't really like beer then. I only had one, and that made me feel woozy enough."

"So what happened?"

"Tony says he heard of a place, a bar, on the Hill where we could get served."

"The hill? What hill?"

"No. Not a hill. The Hill. The Hill District in Pittsburgh. It's an area of the city. Mostly blacks live there. Sort of a poor area."

Pe're nodded.

Jimmy continued. "So he says he's going there and who was going with him. I tried to talk him out of it, but he was determined. He was something of a show-off. Well, another guy, fellow named Jason, agrees to go with him. I never saw Tony again—except at his funeral."

"What happened?"

"Seems he got into a fight with some guy at the bar. I guess they figured he didn't belong there. They never found out who it was, but whoever it was had a knife. Put it right into Tony's heart."

Jimmy put his legs down, slouched down and put his hands in his pockets. Talking about Tony's death was harder than talking about all of the girls who had ever shit on him.

"How did that make you feel?" the doctor asked.

"How do you think?" he shot back, staring angrily at Pe're for asking such a stupid question.

"Well, were you angry at God?"

"No. Just the opposite. I had never hurt so much. I had never felt so much pain . . . and loneliness. I had lost Tony twice. First when I went away to school and he decided to join the Army. And then he died, being stupid. So I prayed and prayed. For Tony *and* me."

"And did God take the pain and loneliness away?"

"I felt He did."

"How?"

"Through Katie. Katie was there for me." Jimmy sat upright in his chair and folded his hands on the table in front of him. "She had come to Penn State, so we could be together. She could've gone to an Ivy League school, you know. But that's how much she loved me. She prayed with me. Kept telling me everything would be all right."

"Did it become all right?"

"Tony's death? No. It's never become all right. But I coped."

"How?"

"Katie. Katie became everything to me. I couldn't have believed it was possible, but we became even closer, more committed to each other and our future. More in love."

It hadn't taken long for the subject to return to Katie.

Chapter 8

"**H**E'S THE DEVIL, YOU KNOW."

Jimmy's midnight daydreaming was interrupted by Aubrey's conspiratorial whisper.

"What?" Jimmy asked, having heard Aubrey speak but not having heard what he said.

"He's the devil," Aubrey repeated. His voice conveyed both conviction and fear.

Jimmy wondered how Aubrey had managed to stay awake with everything they had pumped into him to keep him still and quiet. He continued to stare straight up at the ceiling he could not see.

"Who's the devil?" he answered, just to humor his schizophrenic roommate.

"Pe're. Pe're is the devil. Yes he is. Yes sir. Dr. Pe're is the devil."

Jimmy turned his head towards the direction of Aubrey's voice. The room was pitch black and he couldn't see anything. Nothing, that is, except for Aubrey's face. For no reason he could explain, he could actually make out Aubrey's face in the total darkness. But absolutely nothing else. Just Aubrey's face.

He stared at it for a moment. He could see fear in it—the fear of a crazy man who was in the midst of fighting his inner demons. He knew he should ignore Aubrey—that there was nothing to be gained from trying to have a conversation with a hallucinating psychotic. But it was too late. He had been drawn in and Aubrey's pronouncement, and where it came from in that twisted mind of his, had peaked Jimmy's curiosity.

"How do you know Dr. Pe're is the devil, Aubrey?" he asked in a normal tone of voice.

Aubrey winced. "Shhh. They'll hear you. Can't let them hear you," he scolded Jimmy in an urgent whisper.

"Okay. Okay," Jimmy said, whispering now. "Tell me how you know Dr. Pe're's the devil."

"The electricity."

"What electricity, Aubrey? What about the electricity?"

"Can't you see it? Can't you see?"

"See what, Aubrey? The electricity?" He was always frustrated by Aubrey's disconnected thoughts.

"No! His face. Can't you see him? His face. He's the devil."

Jimmy turned on his side and propped himself up on his elbow. Aubrey's last comment struck him as humorous because the thought had actually crossed his mind from his first session with the psychiatrist that if the devil did exist, he'd look an awful lot like Dr. Pe're.

"What makes you think that Aubrey? Dr. Pe're is just trying to help us."

'No. No. The devil. The electricity—the electricity told me."

"The electricity *told* you?"

"The electricity. God told me." Aubrey's eyes opened wide. "God's in the electricity. That's why they turn the lights out. God talks through the electricity. I know. I hear him all day . . . in the electricity. Don't you, Jimmy?"

"No, Aubrey. I . . ."

"He's after us. Drive us crazy. That's what he does . . . what he's doing. You. Me. Everyone. Gives us poison. Don't eat anything. Don't drink. It's poison. All poison." Aubrey's voice was rising as the words spilled out in rapid-fire fashion. "Don't talk, Jimmy. Don't talk to him. Don't . . . don't listen! Close your ears! Close them up! Like this . . . like this"—Jimmy could see Aubrey put his fingers in his ears—"Poison, Jimmy. His words too . . . everything!" he was shouting now. "God told me! God told me! The electricity! They want to turn it off! Don't let them, Jimmy! Don't let them!"

Suddenly, Aubrey sprang up in his bed, snapping the restraints which had held him down. He looked over at Jimmy and began screaming as he frantically tried to remove the leg restraints.

"We've got to get out of here! Do you hear me? We've got to go! We've got to get out of here! Jimmy, help me! They shut the electricity off! They shut it off!"

Jimmy was about to get out of bed to go get help when he was frozen in place by Aubrey's blood-curdling scream.

"HE'LL STEAL OUR SOULS! THE ELECTRICITY KNOWS!" Aubrey lifted his head towards the ceiling. "HE'S STEALING OUR SOULS!"

The room filled with light. Three large, white-coated attendants rushed in. Two held Aubrey down while the third administered a shot. Within a few seconds Aubrey was still. The three men wheeled his bed out and turned off the lights. The whole process took no more than a minute. And not a word was spoken.

Chapter 9

AUBREY'S OUTBURST THE NIGHT BEFORE, and how quickly and efficiently he had been spirited away, disturbed Jimmy greatly. It was still on his mind when Dr. Pe're entered the therapy room for that morning's session.

"Good morning, Jimmy. How are you feeling today?" Pe're said as he pulled his chair out from the table and sat across from him. Pe're's demeanor was irritatingly cheerful, he thought. More cheerful than he had ever seen him.

"Shitty," he answered sullenly.

"Really? Why don't you tell me about it," Pe're said, shifting immediately to the soothing voice of the concerned analyst.

Jimmy would have none of it.

"What did you do with Aubrey?" he demanded, leaning forward onto the table as far as he could.

"That's none of your concern, Jimmy. We're here to focus on *you*."

Jimmy slammed his hand on the table and stood up suddenly, causing his chair to tip over backward.

"It *is* my concern!" he shouted. "Three goons came in and dragged him away and nobody will tell me where he's gone. Is that what'll happen to me if I make you unhappy?"

Dr. Pe're hesitated briefly and looked him straight in the eye before answering calmly. "No, Jimmy. Nothing will happen to you if you make me unhappy. And nothing has happened to Aubrey."

"Where is he then?"

Pe're looked down as he lit his ever-present pipe.

"Now Jimmy, how would you feel if I started telling all the other residents about your treatment—like, what we talk about in here?"

"I'm not asking you about his treatment. I just want to know where you took him. He was scared. I just want to know he's okay."

The doctor nodded his head ever so slightly towards Jimmy's fallen chair.

"Jimmy, sit down."

Jimmy picked up his chair and sat down.

"Aubrey's fine," the doctor continued. "We just moved him to another part of the hospital—where he could have his own room and we could keep a closer eye on him."

"Can I see him?" he asked.

"Not now. When he's a little more stable, maybe."

"He was . . . he was just so scared."

"Scared of what, Jimmy?"

He wasn't sure he wanted to tell Dr. Pe're much of what Aubrey had said. Despite the doctor's assurances, he felt that Aubrey's outburst had led to punishment of some sort—even though he was psychotic and not really responsible for what he said or did. He still didn't totally trust Dr. Pe're even though every day he felt himself being drawn closer and closer to him.

"Scared of you, Dr. Pe're," he admitted.

"Of me? Why?"

Jimmy squirmed in his chair.

"I don't know, Doc. Why don't *you* tell *me*?"

The doctor leaned back, crossed his legs and smiled.

"Because he's paranoid, son. He's afraid of everything. And everyone."

The easy answer. One Jimmy could not dispute.

"Are you afraid of me, Jimmy?" the doctor asked, looking intently at him.

Jimmy averted his eyes. He looked down at his hands resting on his lap. He began to pick at his cuticles. "A little, I guess."

"A little is okay," the doctor responded. "Do you think I'm out to get you, or to hurt you?"

Jimmy didn't look up. "No, I don't think that," he mumbled.

"Aha!" Pe're barked, startling him. "Then paranoia is *not* one of *your* problems. With that astute diagnosis, if I don't mind saying so myself, I suggest we move on."

Jimmy laughed. It was the first time he had laughed since he'd been there.

"Sure. Okay Doc. I'm ready," he said. And he was. Aubrey and the night before were forgotten—totally and absolutely.

"So, you were about to tell me how Katie betrayed you." The way he made the statement conveyed such warmth and compassion it would have broken down any resistance Jimmy might have had in talking about it. But by this point, there was no resistance. He swallowed hard before beginning.

"It was our sophomore year at Penn State. Katie and I each had our own off-campus apartments. I had moved into an apartment complex with my roommate from the dorm, Billy Taylor—a really good guy; a large, friendly fellow from Tennessee—and Cory Pennington, who had lived in the dorm room next to ours. Katie found a neat attic efficiency in an old house. She shared it with two other girls who had the downstairs bedrooms.

"It was a Tuesday night, early in November. On Tuesdays she had a chem lab from seven to nine. When I could borrow Billy's car I'd meet her at the class at nine and drive her home. Sometimes we'd stop for a pizza or hoagie. That afternoon she told me I didn't need to pick her up after class that night. I asked why not. She said she had a major chem test the next week and that she had made plans with this other girl—I think her name was Cindy—to study together after lab. She said she'd ride her bike to class and ride home when she was done. Then she'd call me."

"Did she call you?" Dr. Pe're interjected.

Jimmy had decided that psychiatrists must feel that they need to interrupt patients to ask questions like these to make it seem like they are doing something other than just listening—to justify the fees they charged and all.

"No." He put his hand up to stop Dr. Pe're from asking "what happened?" The doctor smiled knowingly.

"It was about eight o'clock," Jimmy continued. "I had just settled in to do some studying of my own when I noticed Katie's lab workbook sitting on my coffee table. I realized she must have left it there that afternoon. I figured she needed it for class and for the studying she was going to be doing afterwards with Cindy, so I borrowed Billy's car to run it over to her at class.

"By the time I got to the lab it was almost eight-thirty. Class should have been in session, but the lab lights were off and the hallway was deserted. There was a sign posted on the door saying that lab was cancelled for that night. This wouldn't have concerned me much except for the fact that Katie's bike was sitting outside the building still locked to the bike rack. I couldn't imagine her just leaving it there if she had gone somewhere else to study."

Jimmy paused and swallowed hard. Talking about it was like re-living it. His stomach tightened. His palms had begun to sweat. He didn't want to continue. He looked at Dr. Pe're, who gave him a knowing nod of the head. He sat up erect. It seemed to give him a greater sense of control over his emotions and the situation. He went on.

"I . . . I began walking through the halls to see if Katie and her friend had found an open classroom somewhere in the building to study. But all of the classrooms were empty. As I passed a closed door I heard these muffled voices from the other side. The name plate on the door read "Dr. Carl Roderick." I knew that was her chemistry professor. I figured he might know where Katie had gone, so I knocked on the door. I heard like . . . like feverish whispering, then a cough. Then a male voice said, 'Just a minute.'

"I waited another minute or so. Then, slowly, the door opened about half way. There was a guy standing there looking at me. I figured it must be Dr. Roderick. I'd never met him. He was younger than I expected him to be.

" 'Can I help you?' he says to me. I say, 'I'm looking for my girlfriend . . .' Before I can say anything else, over Roderick's shoulder I see this purse sitting on his desk. I knew the purse. It was Katie's. So now I push the office door completely open and force my way past this guy. On my left there's this couch—and Katie's sitting on it. She looks like a deer caught in the headlights.

" 'Jimmy, what . . . what are you doing here?' she says, acting all innocent and surprised.

" I say, 'What do you mean what am *I* doing here? What are *you* doing here?' She tells me lab was cancelled and she couldn't find her girlfriend to study and she just *happened* to run into Dr. Roderick and asked him to tutor her for the test."

Jimmy could feel the pace of his story picking up. He could also feel his blood pressure rising.

Pe're jumped in.

"Well, that sounds like a plausible explanation. I take it you didn't believe her."

"Doc, she was fully dressed, but both her blouse and slacks were wrinkled. Katie was a neat freak. She never went out that way. She had never given me reason to doubt her before. But . . . but this was too fishy. Know what I mean? I just wasn't buying it.

"So, I turn to confront Roderick. He had sat down behind his desk and was lighting a pipe as if me and Katie were just two students having a meeting with their faculty advisor."

Jimmy glanced at Dr. Pe're who was re-lighting his pipe.

"Then I see this wedding band on Roderick's left ring finger," he continued. "I say, 'Does your wife know that you consider part of your teaching duties fooling around with your female students?'

" 'Aren't you overreacting a bit son?' this asshole says, acting so condescending. 'Katie told you what we were doing. You need to rein in your jealous little imagination.' I wanted to shove his pipe up his smug little ass. Instead, I turn and look at Katie. Her face told me all I needed to know. I stormed out of the office. I hopped into Billy's car and drove around for hours. I couldn't think straight. All I could think about was Katie and Roderick naked, making love on the couch in that office. I could see her hand touching his penis and guiding it into her. Just thinking about it nauseated me."

He put his elbows on the table, stared down and grabbed his hair with both hands.

"It still hurts," he said.

"Keep going," the doctor said.

Jimmy lifted his head and looked at Pe're.

"I prayed that there was an explanation; one that was reasonable and believable; one that would make the thought of Katie touching someone and someone touching her go away and not be true. The more I thought about it, the sicker I felt. It was as if I had been sucker-punched in the gut. I started hyperventilating. I was driving like a drunken fool. Somehow—I don't know how . . . It was a miracle I didn't hit anyone. I wanted to go home to talk to Katie, to have her put my mind at ease. At the same time,

I didn't want to go home. I didn't—I didn't know how I could possibly live with the knowledge that the girl I loved, the girl I had never touched, had been with another man. A *married* man!" Jimmy yelled, slamming his fist on the table. He gazed at the table top a few seconds, biting his lower lip.

"Finally," he went on, "I went home. It was after eleven. Katie was there waiting for me. I knew she would be. I didn't know where Billy and Cory were, but I didn't care. We were alone. 'I need to explain,' she says.

" 'What's to explain?' I say. 'You're screwing your professor.'

" 'No. No, I'm not. I mean, tonight was the first time,' she says. 'I swear.' She says it like that should make it all okay."

His anger was growing rapidly as the image of Roderick's member entering Katie flashed before his eyes over and over like some sort of macabre pornographic slide show intended solely for the purpose of tormenting him. He was reliving an inexplicable pain, and the pain now turned to anger. Pe're remained quiet and let him continue.

" 'Oh, then that makes it okay!' I say. 'You've only done it *once*. And how many times would you have done it if I hadn't caught you?' She pleads with me to listen to her. Says after three years together, I at least owe her that. I say, 'Okay. Explain.' I'm like absolutely determined not to let her talk her way out of this, or back into my heart—like I had somehow already gotten her out of it.

"So she says, 'I don't know what happened, Jimmy.'

" 'You screwed your professor,' I yelled at her.

" 'That's not what I mean,' she says. She tells me that when she got to class there was a sign that lab was cancelled. Cindy's not there and Katie goes to a pay phone to call me. So she doesn't have change, she says, and just then Roderick comes down the hall. She tells him she's trying to call me but doesn't have change, so he offers to let her use the phone in his office. She says sure, that'd be great."

Jimmy closed his eyes, thinking hard to remember the sequence of events as accurately as possible.

"When they get to his office, she says she sees the phone on his desk and goes right to it to call me. She picks up the receiver and puts it to her ear, but before she starts punching my number in, she says she sees Roderick staring at her. He doesn't say anything, but she knows what he's thinking. He wants her."

"How does she know?" Pe're asks.

"Well, she says it's nothing he says or does. It kind of scared her. She said it was like she was in his mind, seeing and thinking what he was seeing and thinking. And what she saw was both of them naked, on the couch, jerking around violently, lots of screaming."

"How did it make you feel to hear her describe that?" Pe're asked.

"Why do you always want to know how things make me feel?" Jimmy shot back, agitated.

"Feelings are the footpath to your soul. And that's where we want to go, isn't it Jimmy?"

He glared at the doctor. "It made me feel like shit! What do you think?"

"Is what I think important to you?"

"No," Jimmy lied.

"Then why don't you just continue your story," Pe're said, seemingly unfazed by Jimmy's mild rebelliousness.

This guy really pisses me off, Jimmy thought to himself. But talking about Katie *was* making him feel better, despite the anger and pain, so he wasn't about to stop now.

"Anyway, she says that, at first, these . . . these images scared her. She wanted to call me and get out of there right away. But as she sensed what he wanted, she said she found herself feeling these . . . these strong urges. She had felt them before, but only for me. And we were always able not to give in to them. But now she said they kept getting stronger and stronger. She didn't know why. Roderick wasn't saying or doing anything—just standing there looking at her. She said they got so strong her clothes actually hurt her skin. All she wanted to do was rip them off and jump on the guy."

"Did she?" the doctor asked.

"She didn't know. She said that from that moment until the instant she heard me knock on the door she couldn't remember what happened. She only remembered bits and pieces of images—like she had been dreaming and woke up and could only remember parts of the dream."

"What *did* she remember?"

"She remembered sex. She remembered feeling pain, but she said she felt joy at the same time. She remembered seeing and feeling Roderick's naked body all over her. She felt lost in it; said it seemed three times larger than real. But she never saw his face. She heard . . . heard a heavy breathing and felt hot breath on her neck, but he never said anything. I could tell by the way she was talking that she had been scared, but that somewhere deep down inside it had really excited her, too. Finally, when she heard the knock on the door, she opened her eyes. She was lying naked on the couch, but Roderick was already dressed. He was sitting behind his desk smoking his pipe. He told her she'd better get dressed. When she heard my voice she just got dressed as fast as she could and . . . well, you know what happened from there."

"So what did you think of her explanation?" Pe're asked.

"I was . . . I was totally conflicted. I loved her so much. I really wanted to believe that somehow this guy had hypnotized her or drugged her or something. That would've made it rape. But she wouldn't say he forced himself on her. Even while she was telling me about it—even the part about the pain—she had this . . . this look of . . . there was the pain and fear, but pleasure, too. I tried to convince her he had done something to her and she should call the cops or something. But she said no—it wasn't Roderick's fault. I should blame her. And then she begged me, over and over, to forgive her."

"So what did you do?" Pe're asked.

Jimmy let out a self-deprecating chuckle. "I told her I needed some time to think. Then the next day I called her and told her I forgave her."

"And was forgiveness divine?" Pe're asked with what almost seemed to Jimmy to be a sneer.

"Hardly."

Pe're drew long on his pipe, tilted his head back and blew the smoke up towards the ceiling. "Take a break," he said. Then he got up and left the room.

Chapter 10

"LET'S FINISH WITH KATIE TODAY, Jimmy." Pe're had taken his customary chair across the table from Jimmy. He had been gone from the room for what seemed to be at least half an hour.

After going to the bathroom and getting a drink from the water fountain in the hall—he had asked for a snack, but the attendant assigned to him enforced Dr. Pe're's orders prohibiting any food or drink other than water—Jimmy had waited alone in the starkly barren room. As he sat there with nothing to do but think, his mind remained stuck in the middle of his experiences with Katie—left dangling by the doctor's prolonged and rude absence.

His anxiety grew with each passing moment. The anxiety quickly turned to anger—anger at Pe're's lack of consideration layered upon the persistent anger at Katie which had been drawn out by that day's session and was being left to fester like the open wound it was. *Interesting,* Jimmy thought, *how the comforting sign on the door to this room reads "Therapeutic Healing Center."* At that moment, it felt much more like an interrogation room to him. *No, make that a torture chamber,* he thought.

"Sure, Doc," he said. "There's nothing more I'd like to do than finish with Katie."

Pe're smiled. "Good. Go on."

Jimmy folded his hands in front of him. "I was determined to save our relationship, even if it meant I had to put Humpty Dumpty back together again. The new thing I had to deal with was how to keep her from giving in to any urges again. We talked about starting to have sex, but we both agreed that would ruin the special character of our love. Katie's answer was that she had experienced "the act" once, but she really didn't remember it and it was like she had never really done it. She assured me she could wait until we were married to do it again. That wasn't good enough for me. I just didn't know how I could trust her again.

"I thought about it a lot. Then the solution came to me. We'd get engaged. As my fiancée, she would officially be mine. I knew that might not keep predators like Carl Roderick away, but it would keep most men honest and, more importantly, I knew it would make cheating unthinkable to Katie. So, I decided to surprise her with a ring. She really liked surprises and there couldn't be a more romantic surprise than being given a diamond ring and getting a marriage proposal." Jimmy unfolded his hands and leaned back in his chair, slouching down a bit.

"I didn't have much money, but I went and bought a ¾ carat ring on installments. I had no doubt that when she slipped that ring on her finger, our love would be sealed forever and I would be able to trust her again. I just knew that that's the way God meant it to be, and that's the way it *would* be."

Pe're leaned forward and pointed his pipe at Jimmy. "So even after what she had done to you, you still saw this relationship as some sort of gift from God?"

"Of course," Jimmy answered. "That's what love is, a gift from God."

Pe're leaned back in his chair and drew on his pipe.

"Interesting. And you still believe this?"

Jimmy stared at the doctor for a moment and decided not to answer the question. He continued his tale.

"Anyway, I picked the ring up from the jeweler. It was a Friday afternoon. My plan was to take her out that night for a really exquisite and expensive dinner, but I wanted to give her the ring in private. I figured that I would go through the whole bended knee bit. I had two classes on Friday afternoons. Katie's last class ended at noon and she usually spent the afternoon studying in her apartment so she could have the weekend free. So I decided to skip class, go to her place, surprise her and propose to the woman I would spend the rest of my life with. Pretty romantic, huh?"

Pe're lifted his eyebrows and said nothing.

"It was about three o'clock when I reached her house. I was really excited. I ran up the two flights of stairs to the door of Katie's room. I was about to knock when I heard a scream from inside her room—a woman's scream. I tried the doorknob but it wouldn't turn. The door was locked. Then I heard another scream. It was Katie."

Jimmy sat up straight in his chair and placed his hands on his legs, grabbing his thighs tightly as he went on.

"I fumbled in my pocket for the key to her room and put it into the lock. As I turned the key I heard a loud grunting. It was a man's voice. Then I heard a loud, long groan. When I opened the door I . . . it was . . . I couldn't believe . . ." He clenched both of his fists and set them on the table. "To my right I saw the naked ass of a man, kneeling on Katie's bed. His back was arched and his hips were thrust forward as far as possible. His legs were placed between two legs of smoother, hairless skin, feet bottoms showing and toes curled down. The man's hands rested on hips which framed the buttocks, which were pressed up against him."

His clinical manner of describing the cruel scene which had unfolded before him was the only way he could maintain his composure in the telling of it. It almost made him seem to be an outside, objective observer. His eyes, which had been fixed on the table top since he began to describe the scene before him, rose to meet Pe're's. Pe're nodded knowingly. Jimmy also nodded, and continued.

"At the head of the bed, I saw Katie's head lying on her pillow, facing to the side, her hands clenching both sides of the pillowcase. I had walked in on my fiancée-to-be right at the moment of Carl Roderick's coming in her. I stood there in shock. They didn't know I was there. Roderick, still inside her, laid his head on her back and grunted, 'God that was great.' Katie turned her head to her right and began to roll onto her back. That's when she saw me standing in the doorway.

"She shrieked, 'Oh my God!' She tried to sit up but the weight of Roderick's body was holding her down. 'Carl, get up!' she yelled as she pushed him away. Roderick still didn't seem to realize I was there. He crawled out of the bed and said, 'Okay. Okay. What's the problem?' Then he turned and saw me staring at him. Then, real smug, all he says is, 'I see,' and starts to nonchalantly get dressed. That's when I knew that Katie wasn't the first person the good professor had cheated on his wife with. It might not have even been the first time the asshole had been caught in the act.

"Katie was in a panic. She didn't know what to do. She jumped out of bed and stood next to her fucking lover and she pleaded with me. 'Oh please, Jimmy! Oh God! I'm so sorry! Oh God! I'm so sorry!' So while she's standing there, naked, pleading with me, all I can think is after three years of loving this girl, my first view of her naked body is while she's standing next to a man who just fucked her!

"I just stood there. I couldn't say anything. My teeth and fists were clenched so tight my jaw and arms ached. Roderick finished dressing and headed toward the door. Just before reaching me, he says—real flippant and arrogant—'Well, I must be going. I'll leave you kids to your jollies.' That was it. Just as he began to brush past me, I started my right fist from below my waist"—Jimmy stood up and re-enacted the scene he was describing— "arced it up and then down into a perfect overhand right landing right on that smug asshole's mouth. He went down hard. I know at least two of his teeth went flying and his face was a bloody mess. Then"—he put his hand in his pocket and took it out—"I took the engagement ring out of my pocket, threw it at Katie and yelled, 'Here, this is for you, you fucking whore!'"

"Then what?" Pe're asked.

"Then I turned and stormed out of the room. As I ran down the stairs I was followed by the image of Katie lying naked in bed with Carl Roderick inside her. It was an image I'll never forget."

"No other images?"

"What do you mean? Like what?"

"Well, what about when you hit Roderick? How did that make you feel?"

There he goes, asking about my feelings again, Jimmy thought. But he realized that Pe're was perceptive to ask, because he had held back on that—on how good it had felt to feel the force of his knuckles on Roderick's teeth, to see the man's blood splatter all over his face, and see his teeth lying on the floor; to feel the sense of power and control it gave him to use violence and to exact revenge. It had felt awesome, and empowering. And that image, too, had stayed with him.

"It felt good," is all he said to Pe're's question.

Pe're smiled.

Chapter 11

JIMMY SLEPT WELL THAT NIGHT. As soon as his head hit the pillow he was out. His sleep was so deep he didn't remember any of his dreams. He awoke refreshed and, for the first time in a long time, looking forward to facing a new day.

He felt so good, in fact, that even the stark bareness of the therapy room had given way to a view of it as a model of utilitarian simplicity. On this morning he bounced in with a smile and a wink for Dr. Pe're who was already there, sitting and waiting for him.

"You seem to be in good spirits," Pe're said as Jimmy took his customary seat across the table.

"I am, Doc. I'm feeling good this morning."

"Any particular reason?"

"Not that I can think of, other than I slept real well last night."

"Getting a good night's rest will certainly make you feel better than not sleeping well. But that wouldn't ordinarily explain by itself the kind of positive mood upswing you're exhibiting this morning." He pointed his pipe at Jimmy. "Think a little harder. What happened between yesterday and today—or what feelings or thoughts you've focused on—that's made you feel so much better."

The psychiatrist's eyes were fixed on Jimmy's. It was as if Dr. Pe're already knew the answer and was trying to telepathically convey it to him. His mind was a blank. They each held their gaze for a moment. Then Jimmy leaned forward, arms crossed on the table, and smiled. The corners of Pe're's lips curled slightly upward.

"I know," Jimmy said in a voice just slightly more than a whisper. "I know why."

"So tell me, boy. Why?"

"Until yesterday, whenever I thought about what happened with Katie, all I could think of was her betrayal; was her and Roderick screwing on his couch and her bed; was her standing there naked with his cum running down her leg."

"And?" Pe're prompted him as he puffed on his pipe.

"And it would drive me nuts. And depress me."

"And since yesterday?"

"Since yesterday, I'm thinking about calling her a fucking whore, and punching Roderick's teeth out."

"And that makes you feel good?"

Of course not! came Father McTighe's booming voice crashing into Jimmy's consciousness. *Cursing and violence are un-Christian! They must not . . .*

"Jimmy?"

"Huh?"

"I asked if that made you feel good," Pe're said.

"I . . . um . . ." *Damn you, Father McTighe,* Jimmy said silently to himself. *Whenever I start feeling good about something, you . . .*

"Jimmy?" Dr. Pe're leaned forward and put his hand softly on Jimmy's forearm. His voice was calm and soothing. "Is something making you feel bad about feeling good?"

"Sort of."

"Your conscience?"

"I guess."

"Let's look at that," Pe're said, leaning back in his chair. "Do you know *why* you felt good about what you said? And what you did to Roderick?"

"I don't know. It . . . it just felt good. And it feels good to think about it. But . . . but it's wrong to feel that way about . . . about . . ."

"It's not wrong, son. It's normal. In fact, it's the first sign that you're on your way back to good mental health."

"But, in church I learned . . ."

"Forget about church!" Dr. Pe're's voice was stern and his countenance had turned harsh. "All church teaches you is to hate yourself for everything you do."

Jimmy was confused. He said nothing. Another long draw on the pipe and Pe're continued his voice again calm and smooth.

"Let's look at why you feel good about walking out on Katie and punching her lover, okay?"

"Okay."

"Katie cheated on you twice. Right?"

"Right."

"And Roderick was an arrogant asshole. Right?"

"Right."

"And you couldn't control that—either Katie's cheating or Roderick's arrogance, could you?"

"No."

"And that depressed you, didn't it? That you seemed to have no control over your life."

"Yeah. I guess so."

"You *know* so." Pe're put his pipe down, put his elbows on the table, folded his hands and rested his goateed chin on them. "And what did you do that afternoon?"

Jimmy looked at the doctor blankly.

"You took control," Pe're said, answering his own question for Jimmy. "You took control of your life. You told a cheating bitch to go to Hell and you punched out an arrogant jerk."

The doctor's crude characterization of Katie and Roderick startled him. But that was exactly how he felt about the cheating lovers. It was clear that Pe're understood him, much better than Father McTighe ever would.

"There's nothing wrong, or bad, about taking control of your life, Jimmy."

"But Doc, what I said and did, I did out of anger—and revenge. How can that be good?"

"Jimmy, listen to me." Now Pe're's voice was barely above a whisper. "Anger and revenge are feelings—just like love, and hate, and pain, and happiness. They're all the same. They all drive us to action in one way or another. If the action is good—is good for *you*—then what's it matter which feeling or emotion drove it?"

Pe're let this thought sink in for a moment. Then he continued.

"Wasn't dumping Katie the right thing for you to do?"

"I think so."

"And didn't Roderick deserve *at least* what you gave him?"

"Yes."

"And didn't it feel good?"

"Yeah."

"And doesn't it feel good to think about it now?"

"Yeah!" Jimmy was beginning to feel as good as he had before Father McTighe's appeal to his better side.

"But, you didn't let it feel good for very long—back then—did you?" As quickly as Pe're had lifted him up, he knocked him back down again.

Jimmy's eyes dropped down. "No. I didn't."

"You let yourself get manipulated and hurt again, didn't you?"

Jimmy could barely mumble his response. "Yes."

"By a woman again."

Pain and embarrassment coursed through his body. He just nodded.

"We have one more boil to lance, son. Are you ready?"

Jimmy looked up at the doctor, tears in his eyes, and nodded again.

"Okay, then. Let's get started," Pe're said, barely disguising his enthusiasm at delving further into Jimmy's psyche, and soul.

Chapter 12

"**I** WAS DEPRESSED THE WHOLE REST of that semester," Jimmy said. He sat slouched in his chair, head down watching his fingers half-heartedly picking at each other. "I had always trusted people. And trusted God. Now I couldn't trust anyone, especially God."

"What did God have to do with it?" Pe're asked.

"If you believed and trusted in Him, God was supposed to lead you to your one true love. You know—your life mate. The *one* person you were supposed to spend the rest of your life with. Part of God's plan."

"And for you, that was Katie."

Jimmy briefly glanced at the doctor, then returned to watching his aimlessly fidgeting hands, now folded on his lap, thumbs circling each other first in one direction, then the other.

"Yeah."

"It was Katie who betrayed you. Why did you blame God?"

"Because He's supposed to be loving, merciful, perfect." Sarcasm dripped from his lips as he described the being which had been at the center of his entire world view—and of his view of himself. "If he's so perfect, how did he screw this one up?"

He expected Pe're at this point to remind him of the concepts of free will and personal responsibility. He was even hoping for it. The doctor just looked at him.

"So then what, Jimmy?"

"Then? Then I spent the rest of the semester feeling sorry for myself. I stopped going to Mass. I wouldn't go out—to parties or things. Billy and Cory and the rest of our friends did their best to cheer me up. You know, drinking and talking with me and stuff. But I just didn't give a shit about anything."

Jimmy sat up in his chair and looked up at the window. He could see the bright blue sky through the bars that right at that moment made the room feel more like a prison cell than a hospital therapy room.

"I just couldn't stop thinking about what I had seen," he said as he turned his head to look directly at his therapist. "I mean, it was so bad I couldn't even sleep. No matter how hard I tried to think of other things— you know, when you're trying to create your own dreams just before you drift off—I just couldn't get Katie and Roderick out of my mind. It was . . . it was like there was this tape running over and over in my mind. Like I was being punished by being made to watch it over and over and over. And when I did get to sleep, every night I would dream about her."

He stopped and looked out the window again.

"What kind of dreams?" Pe're prompted.

"Vivid. Lifelike dreams." He kept staring out the window. "In every one of them, she would betray me. Or make fun of me—laugh at me. Sometimes I'd dream that she actually took a carving knife and cut off my balls and dick. She'd hold them up like a trophy and then I'd hear this applause and cheering. And I'd realize that I was in some sort of stadium or arena—like where the gladiators fought or something."

He turned his face towards Pe're. Tears had begun to flow again.

"Please, Dr. Pe're. Can we stop? I . . . I can't do this anymore. Please."

"No, Jimmy. We can't stop. Not until you've confronted all of the pain that brought you here. Hang in there. I promise you, when we're done, you'll be able to keep from ever being hurt like this again."

Jimmy didn't know how the doctor could make or keep such a promise. But it was precisely what he wanted to believe. So hearing Pe're say it gave him the desire to continue. He slouched back in his chair. He felt tired and defeated. But he was resigned to getting through the ordeal.

"By the end of the semester, I was a wreck. I didn't want to go home for the summer because I knew Katie would be there. I just didn't want to have to face old friends and explain why we weren't together anymore.

Or, worse yet, have to face Rachel or the other kids from high school who had made such a sport out of embarrassing me and bullying me. I never would have made it through the summer. But I didn't have the money to go to school during summer term. And I really didn't want to stay in State College for the summer either."

"What did you do?"

"Billy came to my rescue. Or so I thought at the time."

"How was that?"

"He invited me to spend the summer with him and his family on their farm in Tennessee. He said they had plenty of room and he was sure his dad could get me a job at his company's grain elevator. That's where Billy worked every summer."

"And you accepted."

"Sure. Didn't have anywhere else to go. So why not? At least I'd be away from every place and everything that reminded me of Katie. What did I have to lose?"

"And did it work out as you hoped it would?"

"At first it did. But, like everything else in my life, it got all fucked up too."

"Well, let's see if we can't un-fuck it up then," Pe're said reassuringly. "Tell me about your summer on Billy's Tennessee farm."

"Can I go to the bathroom first?" Jimmy asked. "I really have to go."

"No." Pe're's tone quickly and effortlessly went from reassuring to stern. "We've got important work to do. Part of confronting the weakness that caused you to have your breakdown and brought you to me is developing discipline in your life. When you set a goal, you can't let *anything* stop you from reaching it—not even the need to take a wicked piss. Do you understand, Jimmy?"

His strong desire was to tell Pe're to go to Hell and to get up and walk out the door and go directly to the bathroom. But, something in the doctor's steely expression told him that that would be a big mistake. Instead, he crossed his right leg over his left and pressed his thigh firmly against his crotch in an effort to control the urge to urinate.

"Okay, Doc. I'll try," he said.

"No. You *will*, "Pe're replied. "Now tell me about Tennessee."

Chapter 13

"BILLY'S HOME WAS ON LIKE an eighty acre farm. It was near a town called Clarksville, north of Nashville. Billy told me the eighty acres were what was left of a whole lot larger farm which had been in his family since before the Civil War. They still worked the farm. They raised some corn and soybean. And they had a pretty large vegetable garden for themselves. But it wasn't how they made their main living anymore. Mr. Taylor owned a grain elevator and warehouse in Clarksville. Actually, Mrs. Taylor had inherited it from her father, but Mr. Taylor ran it.

"Billy said it was tough making a living just from farming anymore. He said he heard his parents talk a lot about how much they'd get for the land someday from people who'd want to develop it into houses and stores and stuff. But for now they'd keep farming as much as they could keep up with—or as much as Mrs. Taylor could keep up with because she pretty much ran the farm while Mr. Taylor ran the business.

"While Billy was growing up he worked the farm a little, but mostly his dad had him work at the grain elevator. By the time he was sixteen he was working a full forty hours a week in the summer—and weekends in the winter. Saved up a pretty good amount of money—enough to help him go to Penn State as an out-of-state student. Really pissed his dad off doing that. Mr. Taylor wanted him to go to Tennessee—where he would have gone if he'd of gone to college."

"Jimmy," Pe're interrupted, his voice betraying his impatience. "This is all very interesting, but let's get to the point."

Jimmy's hands fidgeted as he glanced around the bare room in a futile effort to find some object to fix his eyes on in order to avoid fixing them on the doctor. Realizing there was no safe harbor to be found, his eyes returned to the determined glare of his therapist.

"It was really hot," he went on. "It took us about ten hours to make the drive and by the time we got to the farm it was close to dinnertime, but it was still really hot. We drove up this long driveway to the house. When we reached it Billy honked the horn. As we were getting out of the car the front screen door of the house opened. A really beautiful girl came out. She had this medium length, curly black hair. And she was wearing a low cut sundress that came way up above her knees. She had no shoes on and this fantastic smile. She was just drop-dead gorgeous. I figured it was Billy's older sister, Claire, who was supposed to be living in Knoxville.

"She comes running down the steps and calls out 'Billy!' and gives Billy this big hug. Then he says 'Hi Mom.'"

Jimmy rolled his eyes up into his head. "I nearly shit my pants," he said. "I mean, this woman was downright beautiful. Turns out she's only thirty-nine, but she didn't look any older than twenty, twenty-one tops."

"Did you feel attracted to her?" Pe're asked.

"Funny thing. I did as soon as I saw her. Then when Billy said, 'Hi Mom,' for a few seconds—after I got my head back together—I felt kind of embarrassed."

"Then what?"

"Then? Then I got really embarrassed because I realized I had a hard on."

"Did that upset you?"

"Upset me? Why would it upset me?"

"Being sexually attracted to your roommate's mother?"

"No. It didn't upset me. In fact, it was probably the first feeling any woman caused in me since I broke up with Katie. I was just . . . embarrassed. Afraid she might have noticed."

"Did she?"

Once again, as soon as his story involved even the slightest hint of sex or sexuality, Pe're's interest was piqued. The doctor seemed to want to know every detail.

"I don't know," Jimmy continued. "At that point Billy introduced us. Mrs. Taylor came over to me. She took my hand in hers and said, 'Welcome Jimmy. We're so glad to have you staying with us.' She had like these perfect white teeth, and these rich, dark brown eyes. She was really pretty, Doc."

Jimmy's eyes were still looking at Dr. Pe're, but his mind was far away, back in Tennessee, back with a middle-aged woman who looked and dressed half her age, whose minimally enhanced facial features disclosed a natural beauty that time hadn't even begun to betray.

Pe're did nothing to snap him out of his momentary trance, choosing to let him come out of it in his own time. In a moment, he did.

"I was really happy to be there. The change of scenery was really good for me. The Taylors were real nice to me. The farm was a neat place to be. They took me into Clarksville and showed me around and all. Katie, and school, and home—they all seemed so far away and so long ago."

"It sounds like you were very happy," Pe're said.

"I was."

"So, what happened?"

"Just like Billy said he would, Mr. Taylor gave me a job in the warehouse. He said he couldn't guarantee me forty hours a week, but there'd be enough work for at least three days a week. After a few days of relaxing, me and Billy started work. The first week I worked every day. And man was it hard work. I was so out of shape. But I sweated the pounds off. Let me tell you, Doc, there's nothing like working in boxcars full of grain where the temperature gets over a hundred degrees to whip yourself into shape.

"The work was hard, but was actually fun. The guys were cool. When they saw I worked hard they pretty much accepted me. Called me 'College Boy' and would tease me a lot, play practical jokes on me. One time—"

"Jimmy. You're going off on a tangent again. Let's stay focused."

"Sorry, Doc."

There was so much about that summer that Jimmy had found new and interesting. But it was clear that all Dr. Pe're wanted to hear about was the tough stuff. The stuff that had contributed to his being at the institution. The stuff that he was there to fix.

He took a deep breath and ran his hands through his hair.

"Okay," he said, trying to re-focus his thoughts. "I worked on Monday and Tuesday my second week there. At the end of the Tuesday shift, Stubs, the traffic manager, told me that Wednesday would be a light day and that I could take the day off. I was enjoying the work and wanted to make as much money as I could, but I wasn't disappointed. I figured it would let me sleep in. Then I could write to my parents or take Billy's car—he drove to work with Mr. Taylor—and I could drive into Nashville to check it out. Either way, I was looking forward to having some time to myself. In less than two weeks with the Taylors I was feeling like I was beginning to pull myself out of my black hole.

"We ate dinner late that night. Mr. Taylor and Billy had decided to work on the tractor which needed some repairs. It took longer than they expected. Mrs. Taylor cooked a really great meal—pot roast and mashed potatoes. She wasn't too happy about having to keep it warm until Billy and his dad were done. She was afraid the meat would dry out, but once we sat down to eat, no one complained."

"Jimmy!"

"I'm getting there, Doc." Jimmy didn't hide his irritation with Pe're's impatience.

"It was after nine o'clock and already dark when we finished dinner. Mr. Taylor went right to bed. Said it had been a long day and the next day would be, too. Me and Billy went into the family room to watch television while Mrs. Taylor did the dishes. In two minutes Billy had fallen asleep on the couch.

"I wasn't too much interested in what was on TV. And I wasn't tired enough to go to bed, especially knowing I could sleep in the next day. I went into the kitchen and asked Mrs. Taylor if I could help her clean up, but she wouldn't hear of it. There was nothing to do, so I went out onto the front porch. I sat in one of the rockers. There were two of them, one on either side of a two person swing that hung from the porch ceiling. I just settled in for some time alone. There was this beautiful canopy of stars and this great half moon. It was like . . . really serene."

Jimmy knew that going into every detail of that night was drawing the story out, and testing Pe're's patience. *But, damn it,* he thought, *this is important stuff to me. And anyway, it's his job to listen. So he'll just have to listen.*

"After a few minutes," he went on, "I'm sitting there all peaceful and quiet and I hear: 'Oh, here you are. May I join you?' It's Mrs. Taylor stepping out onto the porch. I say, 'Sure.' She sits in the swing and begins to sway back and forth in it. I see she's barefoot again. For some reason I get fixated on her feet. They're kind of small. You know, petite. Her toenails are painted red. Real dainty for a farmer. Anyway, neither one of us says anything for like several minutes. I don't know what to say. She's my roommate's mother. How do you start a conversation with your roommate's mother? I figured if I tried I'd just say something stupid. I felt real awkward. I don't know if she did too. Probably not.

"Finally, she says, 'So, Jimmy, have you enjoyed your time with us so far?'

"'Yes ma'am,' I say. I tell her they've all been real hospitable. And that working in the warehouse was great—that it's actually a relief to do eight hours of work a day without having to exercise my brain too much.

"Anyway, she doesn't say anything. And it, the silence, gets real awkward. She's just swinging on the swing and I'm just sitting there like a bump on a log. So I say, 'It must be really neat living on a farm and having so much land.' Not very stimulating conversation, but what else am I going to say, you know?"

The doctor nodded, and puffed.

"'It's okay,' she says. She tells me it can get kind of lonely, not having neighbors right next door. She starts talking about how being at home all day she didn't get many opportunities to meet new people. And then she started talking about her husband's circle of friends and business acquaintances, how boring and simple they were."

Jimmy chuckled.

"She even said their affairs and—what did she call them?—peccadilloes, yeah, peccadilloes. Even those were stale and unimaginative."

"How did it make you feel when she started talking about these things?" Pe're asked him.

"At first I thought, why is she telling me this kind of stuff? Then she said, 'Jimmy, I'm very glad you're spending the summer with us. It gives me a chance to learn about someone new and interesting.'"

"Did that make you feel more at ease?"

"No. Not really."

"Why not?"

"Well, Doc, I felt like she was trying . . . trying to get me to talk about things I didn't want to talk about."

"Sounds to me like she was just being friendly," Pe're countered.

"Yeah, but I wasn't sure I was ready to be friendly with a female, *any* female, at that point."

"So then what?"

"Well, I don't say anything for a couple of minutes. I keep sitting there. She keeps swinging. Then she says, 'Jimmy, I hope you don't think I'm being overly nosey, but is there something bothering or upsetting you?'

"'No, ma'am,' I say. 'You've all been really great.'

"'No,' she says. 'I don't mean upset about us or being here. It just seems like there's some sort of deep sadness in you, something that's keeping you from feeling real joy, real happiness. You know,' she says, 'mothers have a way of knowing these things.'

"Now I stare straight ahead. I don't look at her because I don't want her to see tears starting in my eyes because now I start thinking about Katie for the first time since I've been there.

"'I'm sorry, Jimmy. I had no right to pry,' she says. I tell her its okay and that I appreciate that she cares, not even knowing me and all. Then she says, 'Sometimes it helps to talk things out, especially with someone who doesn't know you so well and who can be objective.' She says that if I'd ever like to talk about it, she'd be glad to listen."

Jimmy looked up towards the window trying to hide from Dr. Pe're the tears that were forming just at the thought of the conversation on the porch with Mrs. Taylor. Without turning to look at him, Jimmy said, "I couldn't hold it back. I say to her, 'My girlfriend cheated on me, cheated on me real bad. I know I did the right thing breaking up with her. But, I miss her. I miss her so much my stomach just gets all knotted up every time I think of her.' I started to cry. Right there in front of her."

He turned to face Dr. Pe're, tears rolling down his cheeks, reliving in the present the pain and emotions Mrs. Taylor had so easily evoked in him that evening on her front porch. He wiped away the tears with his hands. Then he went on.

"I say, 'How can I get her out of my life, Mrs. Taylor? And how can I get back to where I can ever trust a woman again?' She didn't answer me right away. She just looked into my eyes and I could tell she could almost feel the pain I was feeling. Then she starts telling me that what I've gone through is hard; that it's not easy to get over a hurt like that; but that we all go through heartbreak, and we do survive. 'You will, too,' she says. 'Why don't you tell me what happened. Sometimes it helps just talking about it.'

"Doc, she sounded so loving and . . . and tender. It made me feel that I was in a safe place with a safe person. You know, I never would have been able to talk with my own mother about what happened with Katie. But I opened up completely to Billy's mother and told her the whole story. All she did was listen. She seemed to realize I wasn't looking for advice, just for someone to listen and understand the pain I had felt and that I was still feeling. It was real hard, Doc. I had to stop more than once because of the crying. I really felt embarrassed and childish crying in front of her. But, you know, at the same time there was this . . . this feeling of relief. That was the last place I would have expected to find it—find that kind of, that sense of relief. I told her everything. I went on and on . . . must have talked for the better part of an hour. I described everything—the details of what happened with Katie from the time we met until I caught her cheating the last time; my thoughts, my feelings; the joy and the pain; how Katie's cheating caused me to question everyone and everything I believed in. By the time I was done I felt like I had stripped my soul naked before this woman I had only met a week and a half earlier."

"And?" Pe're interjected.

"And? And I felt an incredible sense of relief. It was like I had been able to transfer my grief to someone who was able to take that grief and make it disappear into herself."

"And what about Mrs. Taylor? Could you tell how she felt right then?"

"You know, Doc, I could. I really could. I could sense that she felt, like, like exhilarated and . . . and like she was experiencing something she hadn't felt in a long time. I was afraid she was going to come over and hug me."

"What did she do?"

"She said, 'Jimmy, you *are* a very special young man. Don't let one bad experience, no matter how bad it was, sour you on love. The right girl is out there, and you *will* find her.'"

"And how did you respond to that?" Pe're asked.

"By changing the subject. I couldn't think of anything else to say right then. So I look up and say, 'Sure is a pretty night sky here, Mrs. Taylor. You can see a lot more stars here than you can back home. Around my house we got too many lights and it blocks out so many of the stars. You've got to go out of town to get a real good view.'

"'Yes, it is pretty,' she says. 'It's even better when you get away from the house, out in the fields where there's no light from the house to compete with the stars.' She says, 'You can see the Milky Way and there are so many stars the sky almost looks like its white with black specks rather than the other way around.'

"So we both looked up at the sky. The half moon was directly ahead of us. Then she gets up from the swing, steps over to me, takes me by the hand and says to me, 'Come on. Let me show you a *really* beautiful night sky.'

"She takes me around the back of the house and we head out into the darkness. The half moon behind us is providing some dim light, but not much. So we walk slow and careful through the backyard into this open field between the yard and a small cornfield they had back beyond. When we reach the cornfield we turn to our left—Mrs. Taylor is still leading me by the hand—and we make our way around the field to its back side. We were now probably about one hundred fifty yards from the house in another open field with grass about three feet high. At this point she stopped. She pointed up at the sky and said, 'Now look.'

"Doc, I've got to tell you, the sight took my breath away. I had never seen such a night sky before. I didn't know that so many stars even existed."

The tears and sadness had left Jimmy now as he thought back on the beauty and wonder of that moment he first gazed at the star-filled sky with Billy's mother. And the more he related to Dr. Pe're what had happened that night, the more both his mind and his body seemed transported back into time. To him, it was as if he was actually reliving the experience all over again.

"'It's something, isn't it,' she says. 'I have all of this right here, and I hardly ever come out to enjoy it,' she says. Then I see a shooting star. But she misses it. Then I see another one. She sees it, too, and giggles—just like a little girl. You know how a little girl giggles. Just like that."

"You found that cute, did you?" Pe're said.

"Can't really say I thought about it," Jimmy responded, "because just about then our eyes shifted from the sky to each other's. And right then I realized that Mrs. Taylor had never let go of my hand. I began to pull my hand from hers, but she wouldn't let go. She was looking in my eyes like she was feeling something—like physical, you know. And I'm thinking, no, that's dumb. I mean, I'm nineteen and she's like thirty-nine, and she's good looking and all. And man, my hormones are starting to rage. It's a pretty romantic spot and all. But I'm thinking it's dumb of me to even think what I'm thinking."

"So was it?" Pe're asked.

"Was it what?"

"Was it dumb of you to be thinking what you were thinking?"

"Turns out, no. Before I realized what was happening, Mrs. Taylor raised herself up on her toes, put her other hand behind my head, pulled me toward her, real gently, and gave me this long, tender kiss. Doc, she had these full, wonderful lips. And it had been so long since I kissed anyone. That only made this kiss that much more exciting and erotic— you know?"

Dr. Pe're put his pipe down. He folded his hands and leaned forward over the table. Up to this point in Jimmy's story about Mrs. Taylor, the doctor had scarcely disguised his boredom. Jimmy could tell that Pe're felt they had gotten to the good part.

"Then what?" the doctor asked, almost eagerly.

"When I opened my eyes I saw Mrs. Taylor looking up at me with a smile. She had this look of like . . . like this mischievous innocence. It made her look half her age, as if she needed anything else to make her look younger. I knew this wasn't right. Man, she was my buddy's mother. So I tried to resist. 'Mrs. Taylor, I can't do this,' I say.

"She kept looking at me. Doesn't say anything. Her one hand was still on the back of my neck, stroking real softly. Then she let go of my hand. She puts that hand around my neck, gives me this full hug and kisses me again. This time it was a long, passionate French kiss. Our bodies were pressed against each other so hard I knew she was feeling my erection.

"I tried to resist. I really did. But I couldn't. I just gave in to it. Before I knew it we were in a full embrace. I was passionately kissing Billy's mother, and I had stopped denying to myself that I was enjoying every second of it."

"And when that kiss ended?"

"I looked at her. She had this impish grin. 'Why, Mrs. Taylor? Why are you doing this?' I asked her. I felt like a kid confused by grown-up conduct I couldn't understand. She placed her left hand on my cheek and caressed it. 'Because you're kind, and gentle,' she says. 'And you have a lot to learn. And I want to be the one who teaches you.' The way she whispered it, it was like, motherly and, at the same time, real seductive.

"So I start to say, 'But Mrs. Taylor . . .' She stops me and says, 'Please, Jimmy. Don't call me Mrs. Taylor. It makes me feel so old. Call me Veronica.'

"'I don't think I can,' I say.

"'Yes you can. Try it,' she says.

"'But I thought your name was Ronnie,' I say. That's what her husband called her.

"'That's what everyone calls me,' she says. 'But I want you to call me Veronica. At least when we're alone. Don't you think Veronica sounds more exotic than Ronnie?' she says.

"So I say, 'Okay, Veronica.' It sounded so strange to hear me say her name.

"She says, 'Now doesn't that sound better than Mrs. Taylor?'

"I say, 'Yeah. But what about Mr. Taylor?'

"Then she puts her index finger on my lips. She says, 'Shhh.' "

"What happened then?" Pe're asked. He seemed to have leaned even further across the table, as if the closer he got to Jimmy, the more he became a part of the story.

"She moved back about three steps. She reached down to the hem of her dress and pulled it up and over her head. She took her bra off. She had these small breasts, not much larger than the nipples themselves. I'm staring at them, you know, and she looks down at them and jokes, 'They were once much bigger. That's what breastfeeding two huge babies will do to a girl.' Then she slips off her panties.

"I could hardly believe my eyes. Veronica Taylor, Billy's mother, stood naked before me. God, she was beautiful, Doc. The way her hair framed her face. And her skin looked so soft and so . . . so perfect. No wrinkles, you know, to show her age or anything. And her eyes. Her eyes were hypnotic. You know, like when they're focused on you you're convinced that you're the only person those eyes had ever seen or ever cared to see. She had these luscious thick lips. I already told you about them."

Jimmy licked his own lips thinking about Veronica's.

"Looking at them," he continued, "I understood why her kiss was so . . . so magical. And she had this petite, perfectly shaped body. Except for the small breasts. But somehow they just made her seem that much more erotic."

He paused, letting himself bask in the memory of that unforgettable moment as if talking about it could make it real again. When his mind returned to the present he saw Dr. Pe're staring at him, breathing heavily, his face flushed and sweating, a boyish smile pasted incongruously onto his chiseled, aged face. *Son of a bitch,* Jimmy thought. *The guy gets off on me talking about my sex life.*

"So what happened then?" Pe're asked in his most nonchalant, clinical manner. It had happened so fast, Jimmy didn't even see the doctor metamorphose from a dog in heat to the consummate, dispassionate professional.

His eyes blinked rapidly, on their own, trying to figure out what they were seeing. *It's no use,* he thought. *This guy's just weird. Better to go back to Veronica than try to figure him out.*

"'Well,' she says, 'are you going to just stare at me all night, or are you going to make me feel like a woman?' That's what she says. I'm just like, I can't believe what's happening. I step over to her and take her naked body in my arms and I give her this big, passionate kiss. She loosens my belt and begins to undo my pants. She looks up at me and, with this gleam in her eyes, she like coos, 'Time for school.'

"And boy did she take me to school. I knew she could tell right away that I wasn't, you know, experienced. And that I was really nervous. I was scared, actually. But she made the fear go away. It was clear that she intended to be pleasured—and she was going to teach me just how to do it."

His eyes looked wistfully up at the ceiling.

"We spent two hours making love in that open field under that incredible night sky. I was amazed. I came four times. The first time was real fast. I felt really inadequate, but she was very patient and reassuring. It was like she knew I was really loaded and that each time I came it would be longer before the next time, and so it was okay. And in that whole two hours I never lost my erection. Not once. What was even better was that she came several times too. I lost count how many."

"During intercourse?" Pe're interjected. He had that little boy grin on his face again. Jimmy didn't care. He was too into experiencing once again his first real sexual encounter to concern himself with the doctor's voyeurism.

"Sometimes from my playing with her. She showed me how to do it the way she liked it. And at least a couple of times from intercourse. One time, we came at the same time, Doc. What an explosion!"

Knowing that Pe're was titillated by his tales of love and sex, Jimmy began to take a perverse pleasure in playing with the mind of the man who was there to fix *his* mind.

"This was sex beyond anything I imagined it could be," he continued. "But it was more than that, Doc. Early on, Veronica told me, 'If you *really* want to enjoy sex, focus on pleasuring the woman, not on your own pleasure. If you do that, you'll experience pleasure beyond your wildest dreams.' Man was she right. Not only did it please me to know that I had made her feel good, outrageously good, but I found out that it inspired her to do amazing things to me—things that created sensations I didn't know existed.

"My fourth time was the time we came together. That one did it. We were both exhausted. We just laid there for a while, looking up at the stars. We realized we needed to get back to the house soon. We agreed that it wouldn't do to fall asleep right there and get discovered in the morning. Before getting dressed, Veronica kissed me on the cheek and sort of dreamily said, 'This is going to be a *great* summer.' Just what I was thinking, Doc. Just what I was thinking."

"This seems like a good time to take a break," Pe're broke in. "Go get some lunch and be back here at 1:30."

That was fine with Jimmy. Reliving his first night with Veronica had brought him great pleasure which was heightened by the knowledge that the telling of that night had turned on the otherwise gruff and hard-assed Dr. Pe're. A break now would allow him to extend those pleasurable feelings a bit longer, before he'd have to tell the rest of the story.

Chapter 14

JIMMY RETURNED TO THE THERAPY room at precisely 1:30. He had skipped lunch. The appetite he had developed wasn't for food. He had gone to his room and spent the lunch hour lying on his bed, eyes closed, replaying over and over in his mind his first night with Veronica Taylor. Why, he wondered, couldn't it have just ended there?

Dr. Pe're entered the room a few minutes later and took his customary seat across from him. He immediately noticed there was something different about the doctor. He was, for the first time, without his ever-present pipe.

"Are you ready to continue?" Pe're asked. His voice seemed somehow different, softer.

"Yeah. I guess so," Jimmy answered. He took a deep breath and returned to the story of Veronica Taylor.

"I read somewhere, Doc, that men reach their sexual peak at eighteen or nineteen, but women don't reach theirs until their mid or late thirties. Is that true?"

"Not in all cases. But as a general proposition, that's true. At least physically."

"Well, it was sure as hell true with me and Veronica. She had this . . . this unquenchable thirst for sex. And she was totally—I mean *totally*—uninhibited. As we were walking back to the house that night . . ."

Suddenly Jimmy's eyes began to burn. He closed them hard several times trying to make it stop. It did, but then his vision became blurred—so much so that he could barely make out Dr. Pe're's silhouette just a couple of feet in front of him.

He began to panic.

"Doc! Doc! Something's wrong! I can't see!" he cried out.

A hand reached forth from the silhouette and rested comfortingly on his.

"It's all right, Jimmy. Everything's going to be fine."

The words came from the direction of Dr. Pe're, but it wasn't Pe're's voice. It couldn't possibly be, but somehow he was sure it was Veronica's voice—as soothing and comforting as it had been that first night he spent with her.

He closed his eyes hard again. When he opened them, the blurred vision was gone. But he couldn't believe what his eyes were telling him. Sitting across from him, leaning across the table and gently holding his hand, was *not* Dr. Pe're. It was Veronica!

Jimmy jerked back so hard his chair fell over backwards, causing his head to hit the floor with a dull thud. The pain was shooting and sharp. His eyes closed instinctively. He kept them closed until the pain in his head subsided a bit. Then, slowly, almost fearfully, he opened them.

Looking down at him, framed by a night sky and thousands of stars, was the beautiful, smiling face of Veronica Taylor. He could feel that he was no longer lying on a cold, hard floor. He was lying naked in the high grass. And Veronica's naked body was lying partially on his as she looked dotingly down at him.

"This is going to be a *great* summer," she said dreamily.

He just stared at her. He knew it wasn't possible. But somehow here he was, in the field with Veronica, reliving—actually *reliving*—that first night. *I must be dreaming,* he thought. He closed his eyes again expecting to wake up either on the therapy room floor or in his bed. But when he opened them, she was still there. And he was still in Tennessee.

"Come on, baby," she said. "We've got to get going before we really do fall asleep out here."

Veronica stood up. Her naked body appeared like a painting against the backdrop of the starlit sky with the half moon appearing to sit on her left shoulder.

He couldn't move. He was confused about what was happening. At the same time, he was enchanted and bewitched, again, by this beautiful, sensuous woman who had introduced him to a whole new world of feelings and pleasure.

Veronica laughed. More of a giggle actually. She leaned over, took his hand and began to pull him up. She couldn't, of course, without his cooperation.

"Come on, silly. We've got to go," she said, still giggling.

Jimmy didn't know what was going on. And he knew how the story with Veronica finally ended. But this part of the relationship with her was so perfect. He decided to put aside his fears, and his confusion, and just go with it to wherever it took him. Besides, he figured, what choice did he have? He was here, and for now he didn't know how to get out.

He allowed himself to be pulled up and fell into an embrace with her. They kissed, and he felt the urge to do it with her again. But she was determined that it was time for them to go.

"I want more, too," she said between kisses. "And we'll have more. Just not tonight."

"Okay," he said, as she slowly and gently pushed him away.

They got dressed silently, the silence itself loudly proclaiming the perfection of this moment and of this night. By now all of his fears and confusion were gone. He was experiencing his first lovemaking experience for the second time. He didn't know how or why, but he wasn't about to let doubt or questioning get in the way of reliving every kiss, every touch, every feeling. It was all as it had been before. And even knowing it would bring him great pain and sorrow, he was as powerless to stop it now as he had been the first time he fell under the spell of this bewitching woman.

⊢•◦•⊣

They walked slowly, hand in hand, back to the house. Veronica was the first to speak.

"Summer will be over before we know it."

"Yes, ma'am. I guess it will." It almost sounded funny calling her "ma'am" considering what they had just done.

"And then you'll be going back to school."

"Yes, ma'am."

"You know what that means don't you?"

"No, ma'am. What does it mean?"

She looked at him and smiled mischievously. "It means we need to take advantage of every opportunity we get."

He smiled back at her. "Yes, ma'am."

"I want it to be fun, Jimmy," she said.

"Me too," he answered. "I know it will be."

"It's not that easy," she said. "Some people confuse sex with love and commitment. To keep it fun, and uncomplicated, we have to have an agreement. No talk of love. No obligations. I have a husband and a family. We're just going to have fun, okay?"

The mention of her husband and family brought Billy to his mind for the first time since before they had entered their field of lovemaking. There was a brief pang of concern which one glance at Veronica made disappear.

"Yes, ma'am. You're the teacher."

Calling her his teacher seemed to bring particular pleasure to Veronica.

⊢⊷⊶⊙⊷⊶⊣

It didn't take long for their second coupling. It was the next day when Veronica came into his bedroom wearing a slinky black negligee, crawled into his bed and woke him up by gently caressing his genitals. Whatever hesitation he may still have felt after the night before completely evaporated in the palm of her hand that day.

As the summer wore on, their sexual escapades grew more brazen and riskier. They had decided that no two encounters would be the same, so each time they were together had to be someplace new. They had sex in every room of the house (Veronica seeming to get a particular rise out of doing it with him in the bed she shared with her husband), in the barn, in each section of the property, on the tractor and in each of the three vehicles the Taylors owned. As the remaining number of new places dwindled, their risk-taking increased. They found themselves doing it on the porch at night while Billy and Mr. Taylor slept upstairs only a few yards away; and in the middle of the day on the roof outside the dormer of the guest bedroom where Jimmy stayed. The greater the risk of getting caught, the more turned on they became.

Nothing was off limits. Veronica relished her role of teacher. And she used it to introduce her neophyte lover to outrageous (at least to him) ideas and techniques. They did every position physically imaginable, utilized a plethora of oils and sexual paraphernalia which they drove all the way to Nashville to purchase (taking advantage of the drive there and back to find two ways of doing it while driving), found bizarre uses for a variety of foods ("Food can be very sexy," Veronica had assured him), and acted out numerous fantasies. Jimmy well knew that he was living every man's *ultimate* fantasy.

By early August he was beginning to have feelings of anxiety and depression over the fact that he and Billy would be leaving in less than two weeks to return to school. He was having a summer to die for and he wanted it never to end. He was addicted to the narcotic-like quality of sex with Veronica Taylor—an addiction which, contrary to their early agreement, he at one point began to mistake for love ("Don't ever say that again. Great sex is *not* the same as love," she had warned him).

He began to scheme in his mind for ways to be with her after the summer; visiting for Christmas, driving down alone and having her visit him in a motel, convincing her to visit him at school. None of the ideas were practical. Deep in his heart he knew that his days with Billy's mother were numbered and that after this summer he would never have her in that way again. So he would make every effort to fully enjoy each intimate moment left.

Many years earlier, when Billy was just a child, Clement Taylor had built his son a tree house in an old oak at the head of the driveway near the road. It was one of the few places left where Jimmy and Veronica had not made love because it was one of the riskiest. The tree house was just a platform with no walls and no roof. The only thing screening its occupants from those traveling the road below were branches and leaves insufficiently thick to prevent anyone looking directly up into the tree from seeing them. If only for that reason, this was one of their steamiest trysts. As they writhed passionately on the blanket they had laid over the splintery deck, Jimmy peered down at passing cars, increasing the volume of his grunts and groans, daring the drivers or their passengers to look up at the pornographic scene playing out above them. By the time they had finished, they were both too sore and exhausted to move.

For a while they laid quietly, Jimmy on his back with his arm around Veronica, her head lying on his chest as she listened to the slowly decreasing rhythmic beat of his heart. He was thinking no particular thoughts, soaking in the full contentment of the moment. Without warning, his contentment was blasted away by the sound of Veronica's voice speaking just two words.

"I'm pregnant."

His torso jolted up into a sitting position, throwing her head off his chest.

"What?!" He was sure he had misunderstood her.

Veronica gathered herself and slowly positioned herself sitting, legs crossed, facing him.

"I'm pregnant," she repeated calmly.

"How . . . how could you be?" he stammered.

"Well, you put the little sperms inside of me and they meet the egg . . ."

"How can you joke about it?" he snapped.

"It is what it is and getting mad about it isn't going to make it go away." She was sounding maddeningly mature and he wanted no part of maturity right then.

"But aren't you too . . . too . . ."

"Too old?" she said, completing his thought. "Did you think thirty-nine year old women are unable to get pregnant?"

"No. I . . . I don't know what I thought. Weren't you on the pill or something? You never asked me to use a condom."

"No, I wasn't," she replied, her voice firm and in control. "And you never asked *me* if I was using anything."

"Why would you take such a chance?" he asked, bewildered.

She uncrossed her legs and laid her head in his lap. She reached up and ran her fingers softly through his hair. "Wasn't risk-taking a big part of our whole relationship? Isn't that what's made it so exciting?"

"Yes, but God, I never thought you'd get pregnant," he answered in a quieter tone, the initial shock having worn off. "How . . . how far along are you?"

"About eight weeks."

"Are you sure?"

"Um hum. Saw the doctor day before yesterday. He confirmed it."

"What are we going to do?" He was finally focusing on how to solve the problem.

"Only one thing *to* do. Get an abortion."

"What?! No! No! You can't get an abortion!" he said heatedly. He lifted Veronica's head off of his lap, forcing her to sit facing him once again. "That's not right! You can't kill the baby!"

"Well, what do you suggest, *Jimmy*?" The way she said his name right then seemed to accentuate their age difference, and made him feel like a child. To hear her call him Jimmy during sex play was endearing. Now, it felt condescending.

"What about putting it up for adoption?" he groped, knowing as he said it the obvious problems with that solution. She readily explained them.

"And what do I tell Clem about my growing belly? That I'm just gaining weight and that all of a sudden, poof, I lost it all?"

"Don't mock me, Veronica."

"I'm sorry, Jimmy. But you *do* see the problem, don't you?"

"Why can't you tell Mr. Taylor that the baby is his? There'd be no reason for him not to believe it." This, he thought, was the ultimate reasonable solution.

"That might have worked," she replied, almost sadly, "except for the fact that Clem and I haven't been together that way since last March. All he'd have to do is do the math."

"You haven't had sex with your husband for five months?" Jimmy asked, incredulous.

"Well, you've kept me pretty busy, and satisfied," she said with a twinkle in her eye and a girlish smile. The smile stroked his ego and had the effect of thawing some of the frost that had developed since she sprang her surprise on him. "And Clem apparently hasn't been too interested," she added.

"What an idiot," Jimmy said, shaking his head. But his attitude about her solution was firm. "Veronica, I can't let you get an abortion. Abortion is murder. And that's my baby inside of you as much as it is yours. I . . . I wouldn't be right with myself and . . . and I know I wouldn't be right with God—neither of us would be—if I let you kill the baby." It was the first time since he caught Katie with Professor Roderick that Jimmy had called upon God for anything.

"But it's *my* body, Jimmy. And I have to decide what's best for me."

"But it's *our* baby!" he insisted.

"So, I'll go back to what I said before. What do you suggest?" Her question held within itself an answer of unassailable logic, but one that he couldn't bring himself to accept.

"I don't know. I don't know, yet." His eyes darted around as if looking for an answer from the trees, the sky, maybe the birds. "Let's . . . let's think about it for a couple of days. We'll think of something. *I'll* think of something. Okay? Can we think about it for a couple of days?"

She softly placed her hands on his cheek and looked lovingly into his frightened eyes. "Okay, Jimmy," she said as she slowly pulled his head towards her and held him close to her chest.

Jimmy was on the work schedule that next morning. He was ready and in the kitchen for breakfast by seven-thirty. He expected to see Veronica making eggs and sausages for the men, as usual. Instead, he saw Clem Taylor at the stove over the sizzling frying pan.

"Mornin' Jimmy," Mr. Taylor bellowed. "Hope you're good and hungry."

"Sure am," Jimmy answered. "Ah, where's Mrs. Taylor?" Keenly interested in her whereabouts, he tried to sound matter-of-fact in his inquiry.

"She went to visit her Aunt Adele in Nashville. Came up all of a sudden last night. Seems Adele's had another bout of bronchitis and Ronnie's gone to sit with her a few days. Should be back by Saturday."

The news struck him like a two ton boulder dropped from a hundred foot cliff. She had sneaked off to get the abortion and he knew there was nothing he could do about it. Anger seethed within him. He struggled mightily to control it so that neither Billy nor Mr. Taylor would notice anything wrong. But the depth of his emotions prevented them from being entirely hidden.

"You all right?" Billy asked him. "You look kind of pale."

"I'm . . . I'm fine," he lied. "I think I might be coming down with one of them summer colds."

"Them's brutal," said Billy.

"If you're not feeling well, why don't you just stay home today," offered Mr. Taylor.

"No. I'm okay. I'll be able to work. I took something for it." Jimmy knew that he had to keep himself busy. If he stayed home alone and stewed about what Veronica was doing, he knew he'd lose it. He would just have to deal with her when she got back.

Veronica returned home as scheduled on Saturday afternoon. She had been gone for four days and when she returned she complained of a little weakness, which she, too, attributed to a summer cold.

"Sounds like what Jimmy might have been coming down with," her husband informed her as he carried her bag towards the stairs leading up to the second floor.

"Oh, really?" she asked, glancing briefly at Jimmy who had fixed a glaring stare on her when she walked in the door and had not let go of it yet.

"Yeah, but he seemed to beat it," Clem Taylor said as he started up the stairs. "Was over it in a day. I'm sure you will be, too."

"Probably," she said as she followed her husband up the stairs.

She spent the rest of Saturday in her room, resting. Billy dragged Jimmy to the stock car races. Jimmy didn't really want to go. He wanted to stay home to look for a chance to talk to Veronica. But he had no choice. When they came home, Veronica didn't come down for dinner that night either. His anger grew.

By Sunday, she seemed to be back to normal. But since Sunday was a church and family day, there was still no opportunity for Jimmy to talk with her alone. At church, he would glance at her and wonder how she could be there worshiping the Lord, knowing what she had just done. The need to address the issue grew more acute within him with each passing moment.

Finally, on Monday, he was alone with her. He had been scheduled to work, but Mr. Taylor received an early morning call telling him that a large order had been canceled, so Jimmy wasn't needed that day. He wasn't disappointed.

When Billy and Mr. Taylor left the house, he immediately confronted Veronica, who was in the kitchen cleaning up after breakfast. He grabbed her arms from behind as she stood before the sink. He swung her around to face him and shouted at her.

"HOW COULD YOU *DO* THAT? HOW COULD YOU *DO* THAT WITHOUT TELLING ME? YOU *PROMISED* TO GIVE US TIME TO THINK ABOUT WHAT TO DO! HOW COULD YOU *DO* THAT TO ME?"

"Do what, Jimmy?" Her voice was firm, and very adult. "Save my marriage? Save your future? Is *that* what you're mad about? Well, I plead guilty."

"You *killed* our baby? You . . . you killed it without even giving me a chance to . . . to decide. Without my permission!"

"Without *your* permission? Look, I made a decision that had to be made. And it was *my* decision to make."

"Not alone, it wasn't."

"Jimmy, we could argue about this forever. But that won't get us anywhere. The truth is—and it's time you learned it—there are consequences to *everything* we do. And we have to live with those consequences. Sometimes we're left with choices, all of which are bad ones. When that happens you pick the lesser of evils and then move on. That's what I did. And that's what *you've* got to do."

"That all sounds *so* easy," he sneered. "So . . . so logical and grown up. So you're the wise grown-up and I'm just the foolish naïve kid. Well, I don't accept that, Ronnie." He used her nickname for the first time, trying to put himself on a more equal footing. Once the word had escaped his mouth, he sensed it made him sound even more immature. "And I don't accept that you had any right to do what you did!"

"Well, Jimmy, whether you accept it or not, it's done. I'm sorry you're hurt. I really am." She shifted from being firm to being soft and caring. "But some day you'll understand that this wasn't only the *right* thing to do—it was the *only* thing to do."

"NO!" he shouted. "I'll *never* accept that. Killing is killing. That'll be on *your* head. But it'll be on mine, too. Because I helped make that baby, and I couldn't protect it from you."

He turned and stormed out of the kitchen.

"Jimmy!" she called after him. But he ignored her. He ran out of the house—out to the field where he and Veronica made love on that first magical night. He sat in the high grass and watched patches of clouds cross the sky. Though he knew he couldn't turn back the clock, his mind continued to search for alternatives to what had happened—as if he *would* be able to change what had happened, if he could only find a solution to the unsolvable problem Veronica's pregnancy had created for them. He sat there for hours. No solutions presented themselves. Nothing changed. The baby—*his* baby—was dead. Murdered. By a woman—a woman he had trusted, maybe even loved. Betrayed. By a woman—again. He didn't return to the house until Billy and Mr. Taylor had returned home from work.

The last week of his stay with the Taylors seemed to drag on longer than the previous ten weeks put together. Jimmy maintained a polite civility towards Veronica, but avoided being alone with her. For her part, she made no effort to speak privately or personally with him. She played the part of woman of the house and perfect hostess as if nothing had ever occurred between them. He marveled at her ability to act so normal in the circumstances, even as he grew angry and bitter about it.

While he was quieter and more preoccupied during that final week, neither Billy nor Mr. Taylor seemed to notice. Finally, the day came for him and Billy to begin their trek north, back to school. After packing the car they said their good-byes. Jimmy politely expressed his appreciation to Mr. and Mrs. Taylor for their hospitality and for making him feel at home. Throughout, he kept his eyes focused mostly on Mr. Taylor. Then, Veronica Taylor walked up to him, put her hands on his arms, kissed him on the cheek, and said to him, "It was our pleasure to have you, Jimmy. Feel free to come back, anytime."

It didn't matter to him whether she was being sincere or not. As far as he was concerned, it was an empty gesture. He knew he would never return. And he knew that she knew it. As he and Billy drove away, he looked back at the house. Mr. Taylor had gone back inside. But, Veronica still stood on the front porch, watching them drive away. She waved, and smiled a smile so wide it seemed to take up her entire face.

When they reached the end of the driveway, he looked up at the tree house in the old oak. Suddenly, he found himself flooded with the memories of that summer—from the first enchanting night under the stars to her explosive revelation among the leaves and branches of that mighty oak. But no matter how hard he tried to think about the wild, stimulating, passionate relationship he had had with Billy's mother, his mind invariably shifted to the fact of the abortion.

Veronica Taylor, the older, experienced woman, had shown Jimmy Donovan the time of his life and in the process had taught him much about loving and pleasuring a woman. Yet, as they drove away, all he could feel was the anger and bitterness—anger and bitterness at her carelessness in failing to use birth control; at her getting the abortion without his consent; at her cavalier attitude about killing their child; at her ability to act as if nothing had happened; at her self-satisfied smile as they drove away. But, most of all, he felt angry and bitter at himself—at the fact that deep down inside, he was glad that she had taken the decision out of his hands; glad that she had made the decision which got him off the hook. In other words, he knew, glad that she had killed their baby. Anger and bitterness, substituting for the enormous guilt that he just couldn't bear.

As he turned his gaze away from the Taylor homestead, he knew he couldn't live with this. He knew he would have to find a way to ease the pain, suppress the guilt and control the anger and bitterness. He had to find a way to protect himself from his own memories. Most importantly, he had to find a way to avoid getting hurt like this ever again.

In addition to teaching him how to pleasure a woman and obtain pleasure from a woman, Veronica Taylor had also taught him there was more than one way a woman could betray you; that if you let a woman too easily into your heart, you were defenseless against her machinations; that despite the conventional wisdom that men used and abused women, it was women who controlled and used men. She taught him that Katie wasn't the exception to the rule. She *was* the rule.

Jimmy Donovan had learned a great deal during his Summer of Love with an older woman. He learned much more than he could ever had hoped to learn from a summer semester at school. He now knew that to survive he had to find a way to harden his heart—to never again allow himself to be so vulnerable.

During the drive home Billy tried to engage him in conversation. But all of Jimmy's talking was in his own mind. Fear, pain, anger and confusion converged in his head until it felt like it was going to burst. Every time he heard Billy's voice it made him think of Veronica; which filled him with anger; which reminded him of Katie; which filled him with more anger; which reminded him that Billy had suggested he spend the summer in Tennessee; which made him angry at Billy for what had happened with Veronica; which made him feel guilty for being angry with his friend, who had done nothing wrong; which confused him, frightened him, made him feel like he was going out of his mind.

By the time they had passed Charleston, West Virginia, he had fallen into a deep depression. The onslaught of negative emotions had overloaded his neurological circuitry. He descended into a dark dungeon from which he saw no escape. The abortion—the murder!—could not be undone. The betrayals would haunt him forever. How could he forget them? The shame, the embarrassment, the guilt would always be with him.

Shame. Embarrassment. Guilt. More memories flooded his mind. Rachel Feinberg. Brent Stockbridge. "Pee Wee." Every put-down, every slight he had ever experienced in his life was back, was real. Then they all stood before him. His classmates, his friends, his family, his tormentors. All together. Looking at him, pointing at him, *laughing* at him.

The pitch-black dungeon got deeper and darker. The laughter got louder and more cruel. Jimmy groped around looking for a door, an opening, some way out. There was none. Now only hopelessness and despair. The only way out, the only release, was death.

"Jimmy? Jimmy? Are you okay?"

He could feel a hand grabbing his arm and shaking him. He recognized Billy's voice. Billy was in the dungeon with him. But Billy was part of the reason he was there—a co-conspirator of those who had brought him to his living Hell. Another false friend.

"Jimmy. Hey, Jimmy. Snap out of it."

The hand shook his arm again. He turned and looked at Billy. Who and what he saw filled him with loathing, contempt, rage. His hands, seemingly on their own volition, reached out and wrapped themselves around Billy's throat and squeezed.

"Hey! What . . . what are you . . .?"

Billy gasped for air while at the same time trying to keep control of the car as it hurtled along Interstate 79 at 70 miles an hour.

"Jimmy, let go," he managed to gurgle. But Jimmy's grip tightened. Billy let go of the steering wheel, instinctively trying to pry Jimmy's hands from their death grip. Without its human guidance, the car swerved to the left, ran off the pavement into the median and began to roll over and over. Jimmy's head slammed into the passenger door window. He felt a sharp pain and a warm liquid—his blood—flowing from the point of impact. Then, quickly, he felt nothing.

⊷•───○───•⊷

"Jimmy? Jimmy? Are you okay?"

The words were the same, but the voice was different. It was the voice of Dr. Pe're. Jimmy opened his eyes. He was lying on his back looking up toward the ceiling, and at Dr. Pe're's face. His head was throbbing.

"You took a pretty nasty spill there, son. Let's go get that cut on your head stitched up."

Pe're helped him to his feet. He put his hand to the back of his head and felt blood trickling out of a cut located on the bump that had formed from his head hitting the . . . the what? The window? The floor? Jimmy was dazed and confused.

"Come on, Jimmy. Walk slowly. You'll be alright." Dr. Pe're was now being assisted by two white-coated attendants.

"But, Doc, I want . . ." He suffered a spell of dizziness. After a few seconds his head cleared. "I want to finish telling you about Veronica."

"I know all I need to know, Jimmy," the doctor said. "Your therapy is almost complete. Go get that nasty bump taken care of and get some rest. We'll have our last session tomorrow."

"Okay, Doc."

Jimmy left the room with the attendants. He was still confused. He realized that he had fallen off his chair and hit his head, but he couldn't remember how, or why. He did remember the instant just prior to his losing consciousness. He also remembered—as if it, too, had just happened—the car rolling over, and hitting his head on the window. And *everything* that had happened in Tennessee. And why didn't Dr. Pe're want to hear the rest of what had happened with Veronica? And how could his therapy be almost done when he still felt so angry, so shamed, so hurt, and *so* depressed? How was this man going to fix all that in just one more session? *Does he think he's God or something?* Jimmy thought to himself contemptuously.

Chapter 15

THE FIRST SOUND JIMMY HEARD the next morning, even before he opened his eyes, was the animated chirping of birds greeting the new day. It was strange, he thought. The entire time he'd been at the hospital, he hadn't heard any sounds from outside except the occasional ranting of patients with ground privileges. Hearing birds for the first time in—how many days or weeks had it been?—made him realize how he took simple pleasures for granted. And how he missed them when they weren't there.

He opened his eyes. Immediately, the birds fell silent. He closed them again. No more birds. Even the simple pleasures are taken from him, he thought.

As he dressed, he searched his mind and his feelings for any sign that he was only one session away from resolving the issues which had caused him to almost kill his friend and himself, and which had landed him in the lap of the strange Dr. Pe're. There was nothing. Not the slightest indication. The gloom, the pain, the rage—they were all still there; still eating at his heart and soul; still keeping him locked in that dark dungeon. He saw no escape, whatever Dr. Pe're said.

Two attendants—the same two who fetched him every morning—arrived punctually, as always, at 9:00 sharp. They escorted him from his room. But instead of turning right to make the customary walk to the therapy room, they turned left.

"Where are we going?" Jimmy asked the smaller of the two, who was guiding him by his right arm. There was no answer. He turned to the big, burly attendant who had him by his left arm. This was a huge man, whose arms and chest betrayed many hours spent in the weight room. On his right biceps bulging out of the short sleeve of his shirt, Jimmy caught a glimpse of a tattoo of a snake baring its fearsome fangs.

"How about you, big guy? Want to let me know where you're taking me today?"

No response from him, either.

They passed the nurses' station on the right and a bank of elevators on the left until they got to the end of the hall. Another right turn led them down another hallway which ended at a single elevator. The smaller attendant pushed the down button.

The doors opened and they entered. This elevator was unlike the others Jimmy had been on in the building. Its floor was carpeted and the walls were wood paneled. There was also an extra floor indicator not found in the other elevators—a "B" located before the first floor.

The smaller attendant pushed the "B" button and the elevator began its descent.

Why are we going to the basement? Jimmy wondered.

The elevator came to a smooth stop. As the doors opened the attendants gently pushed him forward and remained in their positions, apparently for the return ride up. Jimmy stepped out. The elevator doors closed behind him. He looked around at a lush office furnished with black leather upholstery, fine wood cabinetry, plush red carpeting, and an elaborate wet bar to his left.

The walls were covered with a variety of paintings—seascapes, still-lifes—with the back wall having one large painting of a peaceful meadow with waist-high grass and an orange setting sun. Directly beneath the painting was a large desk (black, of course). And seated behind the desk was Dr. Pe're, writing in something that looked like a large journal or ledger.

Jimmy stood silently. In a few seconds Pe're put his pen down and looked up. He pushed his chair back and stood up.

"Good morning, Jimmy," the doctor greeted him.

Pe're looked different to Jimmy than he had ever looked before. Instead of his standard attire of all black, he was wearing beige slacks and a cream colored, button down shirt, open at the collar. And no pipe. *He almost looks . . . angelic,* Jimmy thought to himself.

"Good morning, Doc," he answered.

The doctor walked out from behind his desk and pointed to the leather couch and matching easy chair to Jimmy's right.

"Why don't we sit over here," he said.

"Sure, Doc."

Jimmy sat on the couch and Pe're took his place in the easy chair. The contrast between the cold bareness of the therapy room and the lush opulence of Pe're's office was stark, and somewhat disorienting—as was Dr. Pe're's gentle manner.

"How are you feeling this morning, Jimmy?" the doctor asked. His demeanor was one of caring, and concern.

"Pretty much the same, Doc," Jimmy answered.

Pe're lightly tapped him on the knee. "Well, we're going to see what we can do about that today," he said.

Jimmy wasn't convinced.

"With all due respect, Doc," he said, "we've had a bunch of sessions. And while it has felt good at times to talk about certain things, I don't really feel any better than the day I got here. I don't see how that's all going to change in just one more day of talking to you."

Pe're smiled. "You've got to have faith, Jimmy. Isn't that what your Father McTighe would say?"

Why did you have to bring Father McTighe into this? Jimmy thought. *Bringing up my guilt machine is no way to make me feel better.*

"Faith in who, Doc? God? You?"

"In whoever helps you find the answers you need, Jimmy." Pe're's voice, and the look in his eyes, seemed almost fatherly. "What do you say we get started?"

"Sure. Whatever you say, Doc."

"Okay. Not total commitment, yet. But we'll get there."

Jimmy didn't quite know what to make of the doctor's dramatic change in his look and demeanor. On the one hand, it felt manipulative—in his mind just another therapy technique designed to gain his trust so the doctor could play with his mind. On the other hand, it was working. He was beginning to feel more comfortable, more relaxed. So what if it was just a psychological technique. If it made him feel better, and feel better about himself, isn't that what he was there for? At that moment, Jimmy decided he would have faith—not in Father McTighe, or even God. He would put his faith in the enigmatic Dr. Pe're.

"So," the doctor continued, "when you leave here tomorrow—and I *am* discharging you tomorrow—where do you want to be?"

Jimmy answered, "What do you mean, 'where do I want to be?'"

"Where do you want to be? In your head. In your life."

"I want to be out of this black hole I'm in."

"What's keeping you *in* this black hole?"

Jimmy leaned back, letting himself settle into the soft and comfortable leather couch.

"Pain," he said softly.

"And what's causing the pain?" Jimmy sensed that the doctor was gently leading him back to the subjects of all of their prior sessions.

"Being humiliated," Jimmy went on. "Being betrayed. It's like the story of my life. And it doesn't seem like it's going to ever change."

Pe're draped his right leg over his left and folded his hands on his lap.

"It *can* change, Jimmy. And it will, if you just surrender yourself to this process, and to me, today. Can you do that?"

The words were soft and reassuring. Jimmy wanted to believe that what the doctor was saying was possible, but it seemed like such an overwhelming task, given how worthless and useless he felt. All the same, he knew he had nothing to lose. Father McTighe's "leave it in God's hands" strategy didn't seem to be working. *So, what the hell,* he figured, *let's go with the flow.*

"I guess I can, Doc," he said. "But what can you possibly do to make things different. You can't change what happens to me in my life."

"No, but *you* can. I'm just going to give you the tools."

"What tools?"

"Control. And strength. When you gain control, rather than letting everyone control you, you'll have the strength to avoid being vulnerable, and being humiliated by your vulnerability. And if you *are* betrayed, you'll know just how to handle it so that *you're* not the one feeling the pain."

This was just what he needed to hear. He had always been controlled by others—by his domineering mother, by his protective friends, by girls and women who used, manipulated and betrayed him. By everyone. His life had seemed like a journey on an open, rudderless raft in the middle of the sea—buffeted by constant, overpowering waves that moved him to and fro, at *their* mercy, never letting him control his direction. Never letting him reach solid ground. Now, Dr. Pe're was promising him a better way. He would listen. And he would follow.

"Are you ready?" Pe're asked him.

"Yeah. Yeah, I'm ready," he answered enthusiastically.

"Okay. Good." Pe're uncrossed his legs and leaned forward in his chair. He tapped Jimmy on the knee. "Now, I need you to follow my instructions explicitly."

"What are you going to do?" Jimmy asked. He was putting his trust and faith in the doctor, but he was still nervous.

"I'm going to put you into a mild hypnotic state," Pe're told him. "You'll be able to hear everything I say. And you'll be able to respond to me. You'll just be very relaxed, so we can do the work more easily."

"You mean you're going to put me in some kind of hypnotic trance so you can make me do what you want?"

"No, Jimmy. That's not how it works. Forget about the charlatans you see on television. That's entertainment, not science. I'm not going to turn you into a zombie—just a man."

A man. He's going to turn me into a man, Jimmy thought. *That's just what I want, what I need.* He didn't need to hear anything more.

"Okay, Doc. What do I do?"

"Great." Pe're smiled. It was a friendly smile. At the same time, Jimmy sensed a hint of self-satisfaction, even gloating, in it.

Pe're leaned back and crossed his legs again.

"First, I want you to lean back and place your hands palms down on the tops of your legs."

Jimmy did as the doctor instructed.

"That's fine. Now, keep your feet squarely on the ground at all times, and close your eyes." Jimmy complied. "Good, good. Now, you are to keep your eyes closed at all times. I want you to focus on nothing but my voice. You are to empty your mind of all thoughts and everything else except the sound of my voice. Do you understand?"

"Yes. I understand."

"Fine. We're going to relax now, Jimmy."

"I'm relaxed."

"No, Jimmy. Only respond to me if I ask you a question," Pe're gently chided him.

"Okay. Oops, sorry."

"That's alright." The doctor's formerly sharp and grating voice continued to grow softer, even melodic. "Just do what I say, Jimmy. I want you to start by focusing on your feet. Let your feet completely relax."

Pe're paused for a moment.

"Are they relaxed?"

"Yes," Jimmy answered.

"Good. Now, move up to your shins. I want you to move the relaxation up from your feet through your shins. Just focus on relaxing your shins now." He paused again. "Now your knees and your thighs. Relax your knees and your thighs."

Pe're worked his way up Jimmy's body, part by part, until he had reached his young patient's face. "Now I want you to totally relax your jaw. That's it. Just let your mouth drop open. That's fine. Now I want you to focus on your forehead—the area right between your eyebrows. Now just let the tension there go. Just release it. Good, good. I can see the tension floating away. Can you feel it?"

"Yes," Jimmy answered in a whisper. He had never felt so relaxed in his life.

"Now, Jimmy, I want you to focus only on your breathing. Every time you inhale, you'll actually feel the air come into your body and travel to your lungs. And every time you exhale you'll not only be exhaling air, but every thought in your mind will be pushed out with your breath. Do you understand?"

"Yes."

"Good. Now just breathe. In and out. In and out. Good air in, all thoughts out."

The doctor stopped talking and let him breathe and empty his mind as instructed. Jimmy didn't know how long that went on because having emptied his mind of all thoughts; he didn't know to think of how long it had been. There was some level of consciousness because he could *feel* being in a state of total relaxation. But his mind was completely blank—no thoughts, no images, no . . . nothing.

Pe're's soft voice snuck into the void. "Jimmy? Jimmy, can you hear me?"

"Yes." He heard the sound of his own voice, but was unaware of his lips or tongue moving to make the sound.

"Good. Now I just want you to listen to the sound of my voice, and to what I say. Nothing else. Do you understand?"

"Yes," he heard his voice respond.

"Okay, Jimmy. Listen very carefully, and learn. You've been hurt and humiliated your whole life, because you've been weak. Other people have always been able to push you around, manipulate you, betray you—and you've never been able to fight back. Isn't that true, Jimmy? You've always been weak, haven't you?"

"Yes, I've always been weak."

"And you've looked to others to protect you," Pe're went on. "Your parents. Tony. Father McTighe. God. Haven't you, Jimmy?"

"Yes. Others."

"But no matter how much you look to others for protection, you keep getting hurt. You keep getting bullied, pushed around. People keep deceiving you, using you, taking advantage of you. No matter how good you are to them, they keep hurting you, don't they, Jimmy?"

"Yes."

"You want it to stop, don't you?"

"Yes. Please. Please make it stop," Jimmy's shaking voice pleaded.

"It *can* stop. It *will* stop." Pe're's voice was still soft and gentle, but it was also becoming firm. "You are going to take control of your life. You will need no one's protection. All you will need is what you learn here today."

There was a moment of silence. Pe're had stopped talking, but the last words he had spoken replayed themselves in Jimmy's otherwise blank mind. Then, the doctor continued.

"From now on, you will be strong. You will need no one but yourself for protection. No one will ever get so deep into your heart to be able to cause you the pain and humiliation that Katie and Veronica caused."

The mere mention of their names caused him to tense up ever so briefly. The contrast between that second and the otherwise total state of relaxation he was in was dramatic, and drove home the doctor's message as much as everything he was saying.

"You will stay in control—of yourself, of others, of all situations. You will take care of yourself first, before all others. You have had enough pain in your life, so you will not allow others to hurt you, even if it means they must be hurt. Can you do that, Jimmy?"

"Yes. To stop the pain—yes."

"Good. You've been a small person your whole life, Jimmy. That is going to change. From now on, you will be a big person, a big man. You will walk with confidence. You will speak with confidence. You will allow the powerful forces within you to spill out and let the world know that you are not a man to be trifled with, that you are a man who gets what he wants. Can you be that man, Jimmy?"

"Yes. Yes, I can," his voice responded with growing self-assurance.

"And who will stop you from being that man, Jimmy? Your mother?"

"No."

"A woman?"

"No."

"Father McTighe?"

"No."

Pe're paused. Then, very softly, he asked, "God?"

"No," Jimmy's voice answered firmly.

There was silence. Again, their last exchange played itself out over and over in the otherwise blank void of Jimmy's mind. For how long, he could not know. Eventually, the doctor's voice returned.

"Jimmy, we're just about done. I'm going to slowly bring you out of the hypnotic state. Do just what I tell you, okay?"

"Okay."

"Slowly wiggle your toes. Are you wiggling?"

"Yes."

"Good. Now slowly move your fingers. Fine. Now, I want you to picture the room as you saw it before you closed your eyes—the coffee table in front of the couch, me in my chair, my desk to your right across the room, the painting above the desk. Do you have that picture in your mind?"

"Yes."

"Great. Now I'm going to count to three. When I get to three, slowly open your eyes. Ready?"

"Yes."

"Okay. One. Two. Three."

At three, Jimmy opened his eyes. Everything was exactly as it was when he had first closed them. Pe're was sitting in his chair, looking almost smug, yet still oddly angelic.

"How do you feel?" he asked Jimmy.

"I feel . . . I feel great."

"What do you remember?"

"I remember everything—everything you said. And I remember how wonderful I felt through the whole thing. I want to *always* remember. Can I? Will I?" He could hardly restrain his eagerness.

"What we've done today will always be a part of you," Pe're assured him. "What you choose to remember, and choose to apply to your life, is up to you. I've only given you the tools to make decisions. The decisions are yours to make."

"You've released me from my dungeon, Doc. I don't know how you did it—what magic you used. But I feel great. I feel like . . . like a man."

"Good. Good." Pe're stood up and extended his hand. "Then I think our work is done here."

Jimmy stood up and took his doctor's hand in a firm handshake.

"Thanks, Doc. Thanks for everything. I'll never forget what you've done for me."

"I think you're going to do just fine, Jimmy," Pe're said. Jimmy noted a strange smile on Pe're's face as he said it. His angelic look was gone. His devilish countenance seemed to have returned. It was no matter to Jimmy. All he knew was how good he felt.

"I know I am, Doc. I know I am." He began to walk over to the elevator to leave. He stopped and looked back at Pe're.

"From now on, Doc, call me Jim."

Pe're nodded and smiled, clenching between his teeth his pipe which had suddenly returned, as if out of thin air.

Chapter 16

JIM LOOKED AT THE CROWD all around him. As always, there wasn't an empty seat in Penn State's Beaver Stadium and the crowd was going crazy. The Nittany Lions had just scored to put them ahead 14-10 late in the first half. His date, Nikki Athanasis, threw her arms around his neck and jumped up and down, almost twisting his head off.

"Yea! Yea!" she shrieked over and over. He managed to free himself before she had the opportunity to break his neck. He turned to his right and high-fived Billy Taylor.

"Shit, man!" Billy yelled over the crowd noise. "We're ranked number three. This game wasn't supposed to be so close!"

"Doesn't matter!" Jim yelled back. "Nothing like a seventy-six yard touchdown pass to break their backs! We're going to romp! Give me the flask!"

Billy reached in his back pocket and pulled out a silver flask with the initials "WT" engraved on both sides. He handed it to Jim. Jim was out of Coke, but it didn't matter to him. He unscrewed the cap and took a swig. He let the light, smooth rum roll all around and through his mouth, letting himself fully capture its sweet taste before swallowing hard in one, big gulp.

"Ahh. Great shit, man," he said as he handed the flask back to Billy. Billy took a swig of his own before turning and offering the flask to Cory. Cory didn't seem interested. He was too busy trying to make time—so far, unsuccessfully—with a cute young girl, who hardly looked old enough to be a freshman, sitting in front of him.

Jim turned out to be right about the game. The Nittany Lions did romp, 45-10. But the group of friends didn't stick around until the end. They left at the beginning of the fourth quarter. The game had started at four o'clock to accommodate television and it was running too deeply into their customary Saturday night happy hour (which started any time after noon and lasted until no one was left standing).

As they left the stadium Billy and Cory were a few paces ahead of Jim and Nikki. Billy turned and shouted over his shoulder.

"We'll meet you at the Creamery." Billy and Cory raced off to the small but immensely popular on-campus ice cream shop before Jim could answer.

Jim and Nikki leisurely made their way toward the Creamery, as many other early-departing fans were doing. They walked hand in hand. The sky was clear and the air was brisk. The leaves on the many mature trees that lined the street were at their colorful autumn peak. It was a perfect college football Saturday, Jim thought. The only thing that could make it better would be getting drunk, and then getting laid.

"Enjoy the game?" he asked Nikki.

"Are you kidding? It was great."

He enjoyed her enthusiasm and her ebullient personality. She was a sophomore political science major who he had only just met at a party the week before. He had been immediately drawn to her classical, Greek features—her long dark hair, her dark, expressive eyes, and her proportioned, angular facial features, which, he had decided, would work on an ancient Greek coin as much as the visage of the goddess Athena did. And she seemed to enjoy the fact that she was with a senior. Their ice-breaking date had been the night before, and to Jim there was every indication that she was prepared, even anxious, to take their relationship very quickly to the next level.

After a moment of silence, he decided to dive right in.

"Look, Nikki," he said, "would you like to spend the night with me?"

She looked down at her feet.

"Is it your intention to take advantage of me?" she said, without looking up.

"Well . . . actually, yes," he answered.

She looked up at him. He towered over her by a good ten inches. She smiled.

"In that case, I'd love to."

Now, Jim smiled.

"There's just one thing," he said. "I promised the guys I'd go drinking with them tonight. It's Cory's twenty-first birthday and he's allowed to drink now—legally. So we were going to take him bar hopping. I don't feel it would be right for me to miss that."

"Well," she said as she put her arm through his and brushed her ample breast against his arm, "there are other things I'm sure you wouldn't want to miss, either."

"Now, that is very definitely true," he responded. "So why don't we do this. After we get some ice cream, I'll give you the key to my apartment. I'll go out for just a few drinks with the guys and you can head over to my place whenever. I'll be there no later than . . . let's say, midnight. How's that?"

"Midnight?" she said, a false pout overtaking her face. "You'll probably be pretty drunk by midnight."

He looked down at her, smiled and winked. "I'm even *better* when I'm drunk."

Her pout turned into a sultry smile. "I'll be the judge of that," she said, squeezing his hand. "Okay then," she continued. "No later than midnight. And just to make sure you don't forget what's waiting for you . . ." She stopped, stepped in front of him, reached up on her toes, and gave him a long, deep tongue kiss.

"I won't forget," Jim said, running his tongue over his lips. "You can count on that."

They met up with Billy and Cory at the Creamery. There was already a line almost a block long waiting to get in and out of the efficiently operated ice cream store. They got their cones and the four of them stood around, licking their ice cream and talking. When they were done, Jim handed Nikki his keys, wrote his address down on a napkin, handed it to her and kissed her.

"See you later, Hon," he said.

"You sure will," she replied. Then she whispered in his ear. "*All* of me." With that, Nikki turned and walked toward town.

Once she was out of earshot, Cory turned to Jim and said, "What the hell was that all about?"

"She's spending the night with me."

"But where is she going now?" Billy asked.

"I don't know," Jim replied. "I told her it was Cory's birthday and that I promised to go out drinking with you guys and that I'd be back by twelve. Told her to go to the apartment and wait for me."

"And she bought that?" Cory said, an incredulous look on his face.

"You heard the lady," Jim said with a smile.

"What'll you tell her next week, when I *do* turn twenty-one?"

"I'll deal with that then," Jim answered. "Now, I've got less than five hours to do some serious drinking. So let's go."

"You're something, Jim Donovan. You're really something," Billy said admiringly as the three of them headed to their favorite bar—the one and only bar where Cory's fake identification card would never be questioned, since Cory's older brother was the doorman who checked them.

⊷◦⊶

The bar—called The Cellar—was housed in a basement with its entrance located off an alley. It was crowded as it always was on a football Saturday night. The band was loud and the dance floor was crowded with writhing, jerking, sweating, hormonal bodies constantly rubbing and bumping against each other.

Jim, Billy and Cory managed to get a tall table with three stools and just barely enough room to hold their beer mugs and a basket of shelled peanuts in the middle. The ice cream and the walk from campus to The Cellar had removed their rum and Coke buzz. None of them said anything until their drinks were served and they had each taken one long gulp.

Billy broke the silence, shouting over the loud music and the din of the freewheeling college crowd.

"I don't know how you do it, man," he shouted into Jim's ear. "Ever since you got out of that hospital after the . . . uh . . . the accident summer before last, you've been like . . . you've got this . . . you know, with the babes, man . . . this, this . . . "

"Charisma?" Cory interjected.

"Yeah. Charisma . . . this charisma." Billy took another long gulp of his beer. "And it don't matter how bad you treat them. You screw them, you leave them and they *still* want to be friends with you—hoping someday you'll want to screw them again. I don't know how you do it, man. When I broke up with Amber, she spit in my face, told all her friends what an asshole I am and hasn't talked to me since."

"But you *are* an asshole," Cory said, hoisting his mug inviting a toast to his quick wit. Billy and Jim hoisted their mugs to Cory's wit, touched them together and gulped some more beer.

"So what if I'm an asshole," Billy went on. "So's Jim. At least I made a commitment with Amber. Shit, I went with her for six months. Jim makes no commitment. Goes out with three, four girls at a time." He turned and looked intently at Jim. "Hell, that one time you slept with four different babes in four nights. Now how come that doesn't make you a bigger asshole than me, huh?"

Jim smiled, and said nothing.

"It's the mystery," Cory said. "You know the guy who doesn't let on what he's thinking, or feeling. Makes women want to find out what's inside, what the deep dark secret is. Drives them mad when they don't know, because then they can't wrap you around their little finger. You could see that with Professor Singleton. Man, you could see it drive her nuts. She figured she was so much more intelligent than Jim. More experienced. Older. *Everything*. But man," turning to Jim, "you just mastered her till you were done with her. *Brilliant*. Just *brilliant*."

Cory raised his mug. Jim and Billy responded in kind. Then they all took a drink.

"Are you guys ready for another round?"

All three pairs of eyes turned in the direction of the sound of these words and settled on an attractive blue-eyed blonde. Her eyes settled directly on Jim.

"I'm Amanda. Tina's on break. I'll take care of you until she returns." Her eyes remained fixed on Jim and he understood that her words were meant to indicate she was talking about more than beer.

"Thank you," Jim said politely. "We will have another round."

Amanda smiled and turned to fetch their drinks, never once looking at Billy or Cory.

"See! See there!" Billy said as soon as she had left. "That has nothing to do with mystery, man. We're *all* a mystery to her. But right away she's got the hots for Jim. Just like that . . . that high school girl this summer. What was her name?"

"Amy," Jim answered.

"Yeah. Amy. Amy Van Dyke. Man, she was only seventeen, but you didn't give a shit. And just like this, tonight. You're in a group of people and she picks you right out. Now, Jimmy boy, I'll give you this—you aren't bad looking, but you're not so far above me, or Cory, or Jason, or any of the guys that girls should only be looking at you. And you don't look all that mysterious, either."

Billy was getting drunk and Jim knew that that meant that Billy would never stop talking. He was enjoying listening to his friends talk about his prowess with women, and knew they envied him. And it was almost humorous listening to them trying to figure out what had caused the transformation in his personality and life.

He had never talked to anyone about his sessions with Dr. Pe're; never explained how Pe're had set him loose from all of the fears, inhibitions and restrictive rules of life and behavior which had held him back, caused him to exist at the effect of others and led to such pain and humiliation. He never articulated to anyone how he was no longer operating under any external or internal set of moralistic standards. He just re-made himself and then let himself be. Whatever others thought was no longer of any concern to him. Nor did he feel a need to explain himself.

Women had become his pastime, and his passion. Not in the same way as Katie and Veronica had been. More in the way collecting coins or sports memorabilia was for others. His personal life in the fourteen months since his institutionalization had become almost frantic. Yet, despite that frantic lifestyle and the constant female distractions, his grades also improved markedly. Not only did he feel less stressed, leading to better classroom concentration, but he developed an intensified interest in his field of study—psychology—which he found to be invaluable in steering the course of his numerous interpersonal relationships.

It also provided him some insight into his own behavior—how he was using quantity and withholding to avoid quality and sharing in his relationships. But it didn't matter to him. During his entire junior year he had experienced no pain, no tension, and no pressure to meet others' expectations. Church remained something he had no interest in and he stopped trying to live up to an ideal that didn't exist. And if his own pleasure was the primary focus of his life, he received no complaints about that from the women he saw, for he understood that his pleasure was multiplied tenfold by pleasuring them. That was one lesson he was grateful for having learned from Veronica Taylor.

All in all, life was good. And for that, he had Dr. Pe're to thank.

"Here you go guys." Amanda placed three mugs of beer on the table. She then slipped Jim a small piece of paper before turning and walking over to another table of customers. Jim opened it. It had Amanda's name and a phone number written on it. Billy immediately knew what it was.

"Shit!" Billy said. "Her phone number, right?"

Jim smiled and nodded. He put the slip of paper in his pocket knowing that he would eventually call her.

"Here's to the king," Cory said as he hoisted his mug for a toast. Again, the three friends touched mugs and drank heartily.

"Tell me, Jim," Billy said, now slurring his words with regularity. "What's your secret? How do you do it?"

Billy had asked the question many times before, almost always when drunk. And Jim had answered it many times, each time the same way.

"My secret, Billy?" he said, leaning forward as if ready to divulge the mysteries of the universe. "It's simple, my friend. Live to pleasure— yourself, and them."

"That's it?"

"That's it."

Cory hoisted his mug. Jim and Billy followed suit. As they touched their mugs, they said in unison, "That's it!" Then they chugged their mugs dry.

Chapter 17

DAYLIGHT SEEPING THROUGH HIS TOO thin bedroom curtains rudely interrupted Jim's sleep. His head was throbbing. He looked up at the ceiling as he searched his mind for the memories which would tell him what day it was and what he had done the night before. Then he remembered. He looked to his left at the dark haired girl sleeping next to him. For the first time, he truly appreciated the classical Greek beauty of Nikki's facial features. *Definitely more than a one-night stand,* he thought to himself.

She spent Sunday night with him, too. Sexually, it was an entirely enjoyable night for both of them. It was on Monday, as he watched her get dressed, that Nikki made her mistake.

"It's really neat being able to stay here with you rather than that dank dorm of mine," she said. "Do you think I ought to bring a few clothes over and keep them here?" She walked over to the bed and kissed him. "That way," she said softly, "I won't have to worry about getting back to my place so fast. I'm sure we could find some way to make use of the extra time together."

"That's something to think about," Jim mumbled. He instantly decided that Nikki was looking for more than he was willing to give and that this relationship would have to end quickly.

He was still thinking of how and when to break it off neatly with Nikki when Professor Singh called the Art History 101 class to order later that afternoon. Since this was a general introductory liberal arts course, it was a large class held in one of the larger, auditorium-like classrooms. Jim had no particular interest in art history, but he needed three more general credits, and this was the only one he could fit into his schedule that didn't start at eight in the morning, or end after dinner.

"Please take your seats ladies and gentlemen, so we may begin," Professor Singh announced in an Indian accent which lent an air of international authority to this slightly built, dark skinned man who would seek to instill some measure of rudimentary cultural curiosity into this group of young, football-crazed, Nintendo-raised kids who, for the most part, saw as little relevance and value to their future lives in studying art history as they did in studying algebra. In both cases they were wrong, as Professor Singh kept reminding them, and he declared it his job to correct their misguided views, at least as far as art history was concerned.

"Today we will continue our look at fifteenth and early sixteenth century Flemish art which, as we've previously discussed, was of a style so different from what was evolving in Florence that many sought to distinguish it by giving it a different label from the Italian Early Renaissance. Instead, they called it 'Late Gothic.'"

The professor had already begun to lose Jim. His mind was still busy working on how best, and when, to let Nikki know he no longer had an interest in sleeping with her. He would, of course, like to remain friends, and to keep her on his "emergency" list. Having spent only one weekend with her would make it a bit more of a challenge, but one he was confident he could manage.

Occasionally, he would focus on the screen in the front of the room where Professor Singh was showing slides of Dutch painters like the Master of Flemalle, Jan van Eyck, Rogier van der Weyden and Hugo van der Goes. But his attention would remain focused just long enough to take enough notes to remind him later of what the professor considered important. By now he had learned well the importance of reading your professor in order to excel on the exams. Professor Singh's exams, he knew, were heavily weighted towards the matters actually covered in his lectures, not so much on what was in the large text.

Professor Singh had said more than once that he was close to finishing the *definitive* art history textbook. When he did he would no longer have to rely on the inadequate texts authored by *faux* art experts who believed they could intellectualize a subject that could only properly be taught by bringing the emotional experience of art to life. When pressed, as he was by the occasional precocious undergrad, as to how his book would do this, the good professor's response was: "Wait until the book is published. You will see!" This had been the status of his work in progress for as long as anyone had known—at least as long as he had been at Penn State.

Most of the paintings being shown on the screen had a religious theme. They were of little interest to Jim except for a pair of panels from an Eyckian work called *The Ghent Altarpiece* which depicted a naked Adam and Eve. *Those Renaissance painters really liked their women chunky, he* mused to himself as he examined Eve's plump stomach and substantial hips which were almost enough to draw his attention away from her breasts. He heard little of what the professor was saying about the piece, a problem he seemed to be having with the whole lecture this day. He made a mental note to himself to get a classmate's lecture notes to copy to make sure he didn't miss anything important.

More than halfway through the lecture his wandering mind was captured by a new slide that flashed onto the screen—a slide which he found instantly fascinating. For the first time that day he found himself listening closely to Professor Singh.

"Now this, ladies and gentlemen, is an interesting work called *The Garden of Delights*. It was painted by the Dutch artist Hieronymous Bosch sometime around the end of the fifteenth century or the beginning of the sixteenth century."

As the professor went on to talk about the painter himself, "of whom not much is known," and about his artistic style, "which some describe as weird and consisting of indecipherable and illogical imagery," Jim found himself spellbound by the tri-paneled work staring at him from the screen. The left panel was clearly the Garden of Eden. In the foreground was God introducing Eve, who he had just created, to Adam. In the background above them was a landscape filled with a variety of animals such as a giraffe and an elephant, as well as what appeared to be a variety of sinister looking monsters. Behind the animals and at the top of the panel was a very strange rock formation.

The right panel was equally clear. It consisted of burning ruins and naked people being subjected to odd and outrageous instruments of torture. Without question, this was a frightful, nightmarish vision of Hell.

What was most fascinating was the large, central pane. Its landscape was very similar to that of the Garden of Eden in the smaller left panel. The landscape was populated by a large number of naked men and women doing many strange and peculiar things. In the center of the panel was a circular basin around which many of the naked people rode on the backs of an assortment of beasts and animals. Some appeared to be playing with various fruits and animals, while others romped in pools of water, talked in groups or huddled together. Some were openly and publicly making love.

The picture was a palette of colors, strange juxtapositions and carnal images. It was, indeed, a garden of delights framed by the Garden of Eden on one side and the depths of Hell on the other. The entire triptych caused Jim to look upon a work of art with awe and fascination for the first time.

"So!" Professor Singh's exclamation startled Jim and returned him to the classroom. "We know what the left panel depicts, and we know what the right panel signifies. What can we make of Bosch's center panel—the 'field of dreams' if you will?" It was the first time during this class period that the professor sought to engage his students.

A few hands went up. Jim's certainly wasn't one of them. The professor looked around the classroom and rested his eyes on one particular student.

"Yes, young lady. You in the white pullover. The blonde lady." He was pointing to Jim's right. "Please stand up and give us your name."

A petite blonde seated in the same row as him, about ten seats over, stood up. She was dressed in a white pullover, long sleeved top and jeans.

"My name is Renee Smalley," she said.

"Wonderful," Singh said. "Now, Miss Smalley, would you like to tell us what you think our good friend Mr. Bosch was trying to depict in this piece which, by the way, is without a doubt his most memorable work." The professor expressed this opinion with such unquestionable authority he seemed to be countering a foolishly contrary view held by some unseen, unnamed, obviously mediocre art historian.

"It seems to me to be a very pessimistic view of mankind's fate."

What a brown-noser, Jim thought.

Miss Smalley went on. "There is a straight progression, from left to right, from the Garden of Eden, where our Original Sin occurred, to the actual garden of delight, which is our life here on earth—where we give in to temptation and shamelessly engage in all of the carnal activities shown in the picture. Then, finally, to the depths of Hell, which is the price we pay for giving in to the temptations."

"But Miss Smalley," the professor countered, "what do you make of the beauty of the garden of delight, and of the presence of all of the earth's bounties—food, flowers, animals of all kinds—all of the things the Bible tells us God specifically provided for mankind? Are these but temptations to be avoided on pain of death and damnation?"

Jim was listening intently. He had not anticipated such an intellectually stimulating dialogue in an art history class. At least not something *he'd* find intellectually stimulating. The obviously bright young co-ed responded.

"Professor Singh, I see the flowers and the birds and the fruits as symbols or, um, or metaphors. Sort of like the things that make us perpetual prisoners of our insatiable appetites; in other words, of our Original Sin." "Is there no hope, then? Are we all doomed to eternal damnation according to Bosch, or at least according to this work?" Singh asked forcefully.

"I'm afraid so," Renee Smalley said softly, as if she were expressing her own personal, and sad, belief.

"Well," Professor Singh said as he paced back and forth before the students. "That is certainly one view of the meaning of this work. And I would tell you that it *is* the prevailing view. But it is not necessarily the *only* view. Does anyone see anything different in this painting? And please remain standing, Miss Smalley."

Jim hadn't participated all semester in this class and had always slouched down in his seat whenever Professor Singh, as he often did, looked for some reluctant student to call on to answer a question. But this piece of art was different. It touched something within him. And besides, he *did* disagree with his classmate's interpretation and felt compelled to say so. For the first time that semester, Jim Donovan raised his hand in Art History 101. And he got called on.

"Yes. The young man with the blue and white sweatshirt. Oh my, there are so many blue and white sweatshirts," Singh said, chuckling. "This man over here"—pointing—"with the dark hair. Please stand and state your name."

"My name is Jim Donovan."

"And Mr. Donovan, you have a different interpretation of Mr. Bosch's work than Miss Smalley does."

"Yes sir."

"Well, Mr. Donovan, please explain."

"Professor Singh, I don't think the center panel is necessarily a natural progression from the left panel to the right, at least not the way Miss Smalley reads it. For one thing, it's much bigger than the other two panels. That may be a particular style of Bosch's or of this type of work—what do you call it? A triptych?—I don't know. But it doesn't require the conclusion that it necessarily follows from the left panel and leads to the right panel. For another, it has a very similar landscape to the left panel, which is the Garden of Eden, God's creation of the perfect place."

"So, Mr. Donovan, you do not agree with Miss Smalley that the central panel depicts our insatiable carnal and sinful appetites leading us straight to Hell?" The professor was obviously relishing the debate.

"No sir."

"Well, what *do* you think it is?"

"I think its Paradise. He might have created an unusual view of it for his time, but I think Bosch was depicting that we can have our own Paradise and that its opportunities overshadow those of Hell, just like the size of the center panel dwarfs the panel of Hell."

Singh turned towards Renee Smalley who, as he had instructed, remained standing. "So, Miss Smalley, this young man thinks the center panel is a vision of Paradise, not your one-way ticket to Hell. What do you have to say to that?" The professor delightedly egged her into the battle.

"I'm not surprised that a male college student would view a landscape of naked men and women gorging on food and drink, romping merrily and openly making love, as Paradise. But I don't believe that was Bosch's intention and it's certainly not God's view."

Renee Smalley's tone as she served her biting riposte made it difficult to tell whether she was lobbing a serious grenade or engaging in good-natured debate. In either event, at this shot the class issued a collective "Oooh" at the co-ed's one-upmanship.

"Well, whatever Miss Smalley's view of college men may be," Jim parried without waiting for the professor to moderate, "I also view everything in the painting as a metaphor. Only I have a much more optimistic view of God's attitude towards us, and I think Bosch did too." He didn't know where his ideas or words were coming from, but he ran with them. "Good, healthy food, beautiful flowers, animals to serve mankind, the beauty of our own bodies and the ecstasy and intimacy of lovemaking are all part of the joys of being human, the opportunity to experience the pleasures God created for us. Bosch utilized those joys and pleasures to depict Paradise or, if you wish, Heaven. As you have told us, Professor Singh, Bosch uses weird and irrational imagery to convey his message. If you accept Miss Smalley's interpretation, that would go against what we know of Bosch because there's nothing weird or irrational about the imagery if it's meant to depict the road to Hell."

He had even surprised himself. He looked smugly at his female adversary. By now both students had stopped looking at their professor in the front of the classroom and were fixed on each other, as if determined not to take a shot from the other unaware. Renee Smalley did not miss a beat.

"I think Mr. Donovan's interpretation is nonsense. There is nothing in the art or religion of fifteenth and sixteenth century Europe which would support an argument that images of naked men and women cavorting and fornicating freely and openly could possibly be intended to symbolize Heaven, or even Heaven on earth. It was just the opposite. It was a very strict time in the life of the church and these activities were viewed as sinful. Nothing in the Bible or in church teachings of the time could support a view that fornication, even as a symbol, could be viewed as part of God's Paradise."

"Whoa! Yeah!" another student called out from the back of the classroom.

"True, perhaps, in the church and among the common people," Jim responded. "But we're talking about *artists* here. Artists have always thought and acted differently. Just because Michelangelo's religious work was limited to pious renditions doesn't mean that's what everyone else did. The very nature of Bosch's work shows he was a different type of artist—a free thinker. Everything points to this being his view of Heaven—a happy optimistic view of life and the human condition. Not the pessimistic and hopeless view that we're all doomed to damnation." He kept his eyes fixed on his adversary. Hers remained fixed on him as well, with a look of obvious disdain for his point of view. "What Bosch used to depict his view was ironic symbolism. He was saying that what God condemns in otherwise faithless and immoral people, He provides as reward to those who believe in Him and follow Him. Actually, when you think about it, it's brilliant."

"What you fail to understand, Mr. Donovan . . . "Renee Smalley was interrupted by Professor Singh before she could complete her comeback.

"I'm sorry Miss Smalley, but we're just about out of time. This has certainly been a spirited debate. Let us see what the rest of the class thinks. Those who agree with Miss Smalley's analysis of *The Garden of Delights*, please raise your hands."

Less than half the class raised their hands.

"And those who support Mr. Donovan's interpretation?"

The remainder of the hands went up accompanied by foot stomping and hoots and hollers from most of the male students in the class.

"Certainly an unscientific poll," the professor noted with a smile, "but contrary to most art historians, this class appears to support the thesis that *The Garden of Delights* uses earthly pleasures as an image of the fruits of salvation rather than the giving in to temptation. Good class students. For Wednesday's class read pages three hundred ten to three hundred thirty in the text and you can compare the analyses you heard today with the author's view. Class dismissed."

Jim and Renee had remained standing while Professor Singh dismissed the class. As the students filed out of the classroom Jim's eyes followed her. He had truly enjoyed their *tete-a-tete*. It was the first time he had ever felt so intellectually stimulated by a woman and he wanted to let her know it. As he worked his way towards her, he began to feel attracted to her, despite the fact that he had yet to take particular note of her physical attributes. There was something different, and special, about this woman.

He caught up to her on the sidewalk just outside the building and began walking alongside her.

"Pardon my saying so, but you sure seem to have a jaded view of people," he challenged her, still stimulated by their debate and looking to keep it going.

"And you, Mr. Donovan, seem to have a very crude view of people, and apparently of God," she responded icily. She picked up her pace.

He had viewed their clash of ideas like it was a sporting event and expected her to continue it in the same good-natured spirit as he. But her response was anything but good-natured, and he realized that if he had any hope of getting to know her, he needed to shift their conversation away from the heavy subjects of religion and philosophy.

"Look, we've never been properly introduced." He quickened his pace to keep up with her. "My name is Jim Donovan. I'm a senior psych major."

"I already know your name, Mr. Donovan, and you know mine. There is no need for introductions. Nor is there a need to continue this conversation."

Thus, without once looking at him, Renee Smalley brushed Jim Donovan off and quickly walked away as he stood stunned at her total and cold indifference towards him.

Now there's an odd woman, he thought. *And bullheaded, too.* The challenge quickly intrigued him. He was determined to get to know this woman who had so rudely blown him off.

That night Jim told Nikki that he wasn't ready for the more involved relationship she was looking for. Unlike most of his other relationship breaks, this one didn't end in Nikki respecting him for his honesty and agreeing to still be friends. His mind was dominated by thoughts of Renee, and he didn't choose his words carefully. He couldn't even recall what he said to Nikki immediately after saying it. But whatever it was, it caused her to get angry and scream something at him about treating her like a whore. He tried to feel disappointed about how it turned out, but all he could feel was relief.

He eagerly anticipated Wednesday's class, and the opportunity to see Renee again, and melt the ice. He was sorely disappointed when he realized that she wasn't in class that day. He did see her in Friday's class. She was sitting in the back of the room on the far side. When Professor Singh dismissed the class he immediately turned to follow her out. But her seat was already empty. She must have left early.

By now, his frustration at being unable to talk to Renee had grown to massive proportions. He began to wonder whether she was intentionally avoiding him. He laughed at himself for his arrogant presumptuousness in thinking she would tailor her schedule around him. He thought about how he could get her phone number to give her a call. But it would be too easy for her to hang up on him. Besides, it seemed clear that breaking this stubborn woman would require face-to-face interaction.

The weekend dragged. Jim sleepwalked through his normal weekend activities, his mind fixated on what had become this girl of mystery. He found himself in the unusual situation of wanting the weekend to end so he could get to class.

When he arrived at class on Monday, Professor Singh was just calling the students to order. Jim looked around the lecture hall for Renee. On this day, luck was finally running with him. Not only did he find her, but there was an open seat right next to her. He quickly went over to it and sat down. She turned and looked at him.

"Hey," Jim greeted her.

Remaining true to form, she didn't respond and turned her attention to the now lecturing professor.

A few minutes into the lecture, Jim leaned over and whispered. "Look, Renee, I'd really like . . ."

"I really intend to listen to Professor Singh's *entire* lecture without interruption from you, *Mr.* Donovan," she quietly snapped. Rebuffed again, he sat quietly through the remaining forty-five minutes of class lecture. He didn't hear a word the professor said. He was too busy trying to figure out just what kind of approach was going to work with the first girl in a long time who showed absolutely no interest in him—who, in fact, was being downright hostile towards him. But he wasn't about to give up. Her attitude was challenging his pride. Not only that, it was rekindling old and troublesome memories and feelings, which he was determined to keep buried forever.

After what seemed to be hours rather than minutes, Jim heard the welcome words of Professor Singh concluding the class. "That will be all for today class. Read pages three hundred eighty to four hundred nine for Wednesday."

As Renee gathered her notes and book to get up and leave, Jim softly placed his hand on her forearm. He spoke with as much civility and respect as he could muster.

"Look, Renee, I don't know what I did or said to get you so upset with me. But whatever it was, I apologize. If you'd give me a chance, I think you'd see I'm not such a bad guy."

"Mr. Donovan . . ."

"Please, call me Jim. It sounds too weird to be using Miss and Mister."

"Okay. . . Jim. I'm sure you're not such a bad guy. But your ideas are just a little too far out for me. And besides, I'm not looking for a relationship at this point in my life. I'm sure you can understand that and respect my wish to be left alone." She got up and began to leave.

"Wait! Just give me a minute," he pleaded as he got up to follow her. She stopped and looked at him. She didn't say anything, as if waiting for him to continue.

"As far as my way out ideas are concerned, we were talking about one painting. From that you think you know what my beliefs and principles are? How do you know I wasn't just playing devil's advocate to get a rise out of you? Or to brown-nose Professor Singh?"

"Were you?" she asked. It was the first time she showed any interest or curiosity about him.

"Well, sort of. But I think the only way to get to know each other's ideas and beliefs is to get to know each other better."

"I already told you, I'm not interested in . . ."

"Yeah, yeah. I know," he interrupted. "You're not ready for a relationship. But does that rule out friendship? You must have *some* friends. And, you know, it's not healthy to avoid making new friends. I hear it can cause strep throat."

"What?" Her face curled in disbelief at his nonsensical *non sequitur.*

Jim just shrugged his shoulders and smiled sheepishly. She laughed. With this first friendly gesture on her part he finally saw the pleasant beauty of her rounded face framed by her chin-length blonde hair, as well as a spark of her inner warmth. He wasted no time.

"What do you say we go get something to eat?"

She looked at him for a few seconds, as if giving her computer-quick mind time to analyze all of the data thus far inputted about this strange young man to determine whether he could be trusted.

"Sure," she answered. "But just . . ."

" . . . as friends," he assured her. "Just friends."

She looked at him curiously. She then reached her hand out inviting him to shake it. He extended his hand and they shook.

"Renee Smalley," she said. "Senior music and elementary ed major."

He smiled. "Pleased to meet you, Renee Smalley, senior music and elementary ed major."

They did become friends, quickly. Renee repeatedly made it clear that any thought of a "relationship" was off limits. Jim agreed to this. Ironically, this understanding between them had the effect of making their communication relaxed and comfortable, without pretext or ulterior motive. This surprised him. He had fully anticipated making a move on her once he got his foot in the door. But once there, he found himself respecting her and their growing friendship too much to endanger it. She was different than the other girls he had come to know. And their relationship, born of friendship, was different, too.

They talked every day—if not in person, at least by phone. It was only taking days for them to develop a connection which he would have expected to take months. Nonetheless, Renee continued to remain guarded about her inner self. She didn't speak much about her family. He did learn that she was from Wheaton, Illinois, and that her father was a Methodist minister. She said she had no brothers or sisters, although he noticed that when he asked that question it seemed to cause her some distress. He sensed there was a deep sadness within her that she wanted to exorcise, but she didn't know how. Her mystery served as a magnet for his attention as his mystery had so successfully drawn women to him since his days with Dr. Pe're.

Chapter 18

DECEMBER IS A COLD MONTH in State College, Pennsylvania. Bundled completely under his blankets, Jim didn't hear the phone ringing at first. When he did, he slid the blankets just low enough to expose his head and one arm. He had left his curtains open for some reason, and out the window he could see large snowflakes gently passing by on their descent to the ground below.

The phone kept ringing. Finally, he stretched his arm out and fumbled with the receiver before getting it placed against his ear.

"Hello," he mumbled, groggily.

"Hello, Jim? Jim Donovan?"

The voice sounded familiar, but in his still half asleep state, he couldn't quite place it.

"Yeah, this is Jim Donovan. Who's this?"

"Jim, how are you?" the voice on the other end of the line said cheerfully. "This is Dr. Pe're."

Jim shot up in bed. He hadn't spoken with Dr. Pe're since he had left the psychiatric hospital and he was very surprised to hear his voice now.

"Dr. Pe're . . . uh . . . hi. Hello. I'm fine. How . . . how are you?"

"I'm doing just fine, son. I just thought that it was time for me to check up on how you're doing and what's going on in your life. Therapeutic follow-up, I guess you could call it."

"Everything's good . . . fine. Thanks."

Jim couldn't put his finger on why, but for some reason he felt very conflicted about hearing from Dr. Pe're just now. Equally disturbing was the fact that as soon as he realized it was Dr. Pe're, the image of Father McTighe flashed across his brain. It was the first time he had even thought of Father McTighe since leaving the institution.

"School's going well I trust?" Pe're inquired.

Jim stood up. For some reason, sitting on his bed made him feel like he was in a therapy session with his former therapist.

"School's great, Doc. Right on target to graduate in June."

"Any black moods, episodes of depression since you left us?"

"No. None at all. Things have actually been . . . great."

This was the man who had brought him out of the depths of despair. Probably saved his life, Jim thought. Yet, for some reason, talking to him now made him feel uneasy, uncomfortable—just as it always had during his psychotherapy.

"And what about your relationships?" Pe're asked, his voice lowering on the word "relationships," which he drew out slowly. "Especially with . . ." Pe're paused.

"Women?" Jim said, filling in the blank.

"Yes, women," the doctor responded.

Jim could swear he detected a tinge of the voyeurism Pe're had exhibited when listening to his tales of female woe.

"No complaints, Doc. I've . . . let's just say the last year has been . . . well, it's been more than I could have ever imagined, ever even hoped for."

"And is there a special someone, or are you still playing the field?"

Still playing the field? Jim felt that Pe're said it as if he had been keeping track of him for the past sixteen months. But how could he? *Why* would he, Jim wondered, without just calling before this to find out directly from the horse's mouth?

"No one special," he answered, despite the fact that it crossed his mind to tell Pe're about Renee. But she was just a friend, not a relationship.

"Are you sure? Not even a good . . . friend?"

Jesus, Jim thought, *what is this guy? A mind reader?* No sense in holding back, he decided. Besides, what was there to be afraid of?

"Well, there is this girl I've gotten to know pretty well. Her name is Renee."

"Tell me about her."

It was as if he was back at the institution and undergoing therapy again. Pe're asked, and Jim felt obligated to answer. He sat down on the edge of his bed.

"Well, first off," he began, "it's not a 'relationship' relationship. From the get-go she made it very clear that any thought of a relationship was off limits. I said, you know, 'sure, sure,' figuring that as soon as I got my foot really in the door I'd make my move. Funny thing happened, though. Starting out with no 'relationship'—just as friends—our communications were real . . . relaxed, real . . . you know, comfortable. I found myself respecting her . . . and respecting our friendship too much to mess it up. She's different, Doc. And this relationship—or whatever we call it—is different, too."

"What do you know about her, Jim?" the doctor asked. It was a question Jim would have expected his father to ask, if he were still alive.

"Not a lot, Doc. She's still pretty guarded about herself. She doesn't speak much about her family. Just where she's from, what her dad does. He's a minister. Says she doesn't have any brothers or sisters. But, you know Doc, when I first asked her about that, just asking the question seemed to cause her some . . . some kind of distress, or upset or something."

"Do you think she's lying about having a brother or sister?"

"I don't know. Don't know why she would. But, you know, there seems to be some sort of deep sadness inside her, something that needs healing. But she doesn't know how, maybe. Maybe it's that mystery about her that attracts me."

"So you *are* attracted to her."

"Sure," Jim responded. "Real attracted. But she's insisted that it can't be anything more than friends."

"And you've accepted that?" Pe're quizzed him.

"Doc, I have to admit, this deepening friendship with Renee is having an effect on me. I find myself wanting to place my trust in her. That really scared me at first—you know, given my history with trusting women. So I moved real slow in opening up to her. But with each step, every time I've shared my feelings or thoughts, I've felt a . . . this strengthening bond with her. And worst of all, or maybe best of all—I don't know—while I don't have a physical relationship with her, I'm not looking to lay every good looking woman I can coax into bed with me. Sex stopped for me when I met her. And shit, I hate to say it, but I haven't missed it that much."

"Sounds like Father McTighe has come back into your life."

Jim couldn't tell whether Pe're said this as a mere statement of fact, or as an accusation. Either way, it was not until this phone conversation that Father McTighe had worked his way back into his consciousness. He began to believe that the teachings of the persistent priest must be working on him at some level. He was confused as to whether this was good or bad. He had no doubt that the equally determined doctor would consider it a setback.

"No," he lied, wishing not to displease the man who, after all, had saved his life. "She's just . . . she's a special girl. I'll . . . it'll happen, some day. I'm sure."

"Of course it will, Jim." Pe're said it as if there could be no doubt. "Just remember, my boy, you're in control. You're the boss. You're *always* the boss."

"Yes, sir. I remember."

"Good. Good. Then it's time for me to go. *Au revoir.*"

"Excuse me?" Jim didn't know a lick of French.

"*Au revoir,*" the doctor repeated. "Until we see each other again."

"Oh, yeah. Sure. Okay. Bye Doc."

He hung up the phone. He didn't know what to make of the call or the conversation. He suspected that if the call had come before he met Renee, he would have been glad to hear from Pe're. Now, for some reason, he almost felt guilty for not having bedded her. At the same time, he felt guilty for feeling guilty about it. Pe're and McTighe. Together again in his mind. And for him, confusion anew.

Only one way to deal with it, he decided. He slid back into bed, pulled the blankets over his head and went back to sleep.

Chapter 19

FALL TERM WAS COMING TO an end. During the last couple of weeks, Jim noticed a definite darkening of Renee's mood. He asked her about it, several times. She shrugged it off as stress about her final exams. There was nothing wrong, she assured him. Uneasily, he let the matter drop, until the last day of the semester.

He waited for Renee inside the Sparks Building where she was finishing an exam. The Cellar was holding an end of the term beer blast and they were going to meet Billy and Cory there for a final night of partying before Christmas break.

It was a bleak day. All day it had looked like it would snow at any minute. But it didn't. It was just windy and cold. And now that it was getting dark, it was getting colder. He had walked to the campus building from his downtown apartment. He had been in the relative warmth of Sparks for at least five minutes, but his feet were still cold. This was the fourth winter he would be spending at Penn State, walking to and from the school's expansive campus in often windy and bitterly cold conditions. It was one thing he knew he wouldn't miss when he graduated.

Students began to drift out of Renee's classroom, one, sometimes two at a time. Renee was one of the last to come out.

"Hey. How'd it go?" he asked her.

"Okay, I guess," she said.

He took her hand and headed towards the exit doors.

"Well, let's get to The Cellar and put this term behind us, once and for all," he said.

She stopped before they reached the door. She turned and looked up at him.

"Jim, I'm really tired," she said. "Would you mind if I just went home?"

"Are you feeling okay?"

"Yeah, sure. I'm just really beat. You just go ahead and join the guys. Have a good time. I think I just want to go lie down for a while."

"Well, sure," he said. "If you don't feel like it, I understand. Maybe after you rest awhile you'll feel up to joining us."

"Maybe." She leaned up and kissed him lightly on the cheek. "Thanks for understanding."

Jim walked her down to College Avenue. She turned and walked up the street. He crossed College and headed to The Cellar. They hadn't talked much, but there was something in her voice that concerned him. Something that told him she shouldn't be alone that night. He decided he would have a couple of drinks and then go check on her. He left The Cellar at seven-thirty.

Renee was among the few seniors who still lived in a dorm. She actually claimed to have enjoyed dorm life the entire three-and-one-half years she had been at Penn State. Jim had never been in her room, but was well aware of where it was from occasionally walking her home.

It was a good fifteen-minute walk from The Cellar—a cold fifteen-minute walk. When he got there, he noticed that the dorm was quieter than usual. Many students had already left for home. As he approached her room he could hear the sounds of soft jazz coming from the other side of her closed door. He knocked gently.

"Who is it?" she called out.

"It's Jim."

"Just a minute."

He could hear her closet door opening. She was probably getting some clothes to throw on, he figured. A moment later the door opened and Renee invited him in. Her reddened eyes betrayed tears.

"Hey, kiddo. How are you doing?" he asked lightly.

"Fine," she said. "What are you doing here? I thought you were out celebrating."

"I was but, well, I just wasn't in the mood. So I thought I'd come and see this great bachelorette pad you've been hiding from me." His attempt at levity managed a slight smile from her. "Has your roommate already gone home?"

"Yeah. Her last exam was Tuesday and she left right after it."

She turned off her stereo and sat down on the edge of her bed. The only chairs in the room were two desk chairs that didn't look particularly comfortable. He walked over and sat next to her.

"So, where are you flying out of?" he asked. "Pittsburgh?"

"Flying?"

"Yeah. Your flight home. You're flying, aren't you?"

She looked down at her hands sitting in her lap.

"I'm not going home for Christmas," she said.

"You're not going home?" he asked with curious disbelief. "Then where are you going?"

"Nowhere. I'm staying here."

"You've got to be kidding," he said. "Why? Why wouldn't you go home for Christmas?"

"It's . . . I . . ." Renee's eyes were tearing up and she struggled for words. He could see that there was something very wrong and that she was hesitant to talk about it. It was also clear to him that she very much needed to.

He softly laid his hand on her knee and drew his face closer to hers. "Renee, there's been something bothering you and it seems to be getting worse. Now this thing about not going home for Christmas. Why don't you tell me what's wrong."

He began to hear a voice creeping into his mind. *Okay, Doc,* he thought to himself. *I know what you're going to say—"sounds just like Father McTighe." I need you to bug off right now. This is important. Let me handle it, my way.* His mind cleared. He focused intently on Renee.

A few seconds passed. She lifted her downcast eyes to meet his. The dam burst. Her body began to tremble violently. Then, a loud wail of grief one might expect from a mother who has just lost her child. Jim was stunned. After a few seconds he put his arms around her and drew her to him. Her head was buried in his chest, involuntarily bobbing up and down from her uncontrollable crying. He held her and said nothing.

It was a good five minutes before her near hysterical outpouring reduced itself to a whimper—more from exhaustion, he thought, than self-control. He still remained silent. He figured it was best that he let Renee decide when, and if, to talk. He continued to hold her, gently caressing her hair, and seeking only to comfort her.

"I'm sorry," she finally said, wiping the tears from her eyes with her hands while her head remained resting on his chest.

"Shhh," he said. "Don't be silly. A good cry is healthy. It can keep you from getting strep throat."

She laughed a slight laugh. *Thank God*, he thought. He was grateful that she didn't consider his corny effort to cheer her up as crude or insensitive. Or at least she didn't appear to.

She lifted her head from his chest and sat up.

"Thanks for being here," she said.

"Sure," he answered with an empathetic smile. Then he cautiously ventured forward. "Do you feel like talking about it?"

She nodded, and stared across the room at the wall as if she was watching a movie of the story she was about to share with him.

"When I told you I didn't have any brothers or sisters that was the truth. But it's only partially true. I . . . I used to have a sister, an older sister. Her name was Sheri. She was two years older than me. And a lot prettier."

"I doubt that," Jim said.

"She was. *Much* prettier. And boy were guys attracted to her. When she walked into a room, every male head turned to look at her. Sheri and I were real close, but we were very different. I've always been someone who pretty much follows the rules, who doesn't make waves. My father being a minister, I never wanted to do anything that would embarrass him, or disappoint him. And being a minister's daughter never . . . never really bothered me. I've never felt too restricted by it or anything—probably because I'm a lot like him."

Renee got up and walked over to her desk where there was a box of tissues. She pulled one out and blew her nose. She brought the box back to the bed and sat back down next to Jim. She pulled another tissue out of the box and held it balled up in her hand.

"But Sheri," she continued, "God how Sheri *hated* being a minister's daughter. She loved Daddy, but she hated his rules. And she despised the fact that she felt she always had to be a goody-two-shoes so she wouldn't *embarrass*—she'd say it with just that kind of sarcastic tone and face—so she wouldn't *embarrass* the Reverend Bob Smalley. And when Daddy would drive us or push us to do better, and to be the best we could be, Sheri would complain that nothing she ever did was good enough for him—that she had to be perfect for him to be satisfied."

She paused. She blew her nose again. She took another tissue out of the box and placed it in her hand.

Always prepared, the stray thought popped into his head.

Renee went on. "Sheri was really smart, and Daddy expected her to go to college. He had saved money for it since she was little which, you know, isn't so easy on a minister's salary. But she didn't want to go to college. At least not right away. They fought a lot about it. But Daddy couldn't really make her go, so he finally gave in. He told her he wouldn't give her the money he had saved—that she could have it if she changed her mind, or he'd just use it for me.

"So when she graduated from high school, Sheri got a job in the city . . . in Chicago. She was a receptionist in a doctor's office. It wasn't a lot of money, but it was more than she had ever had before. She got an apartment in the city with one of the other girls in the office. It wasn't a great place. They didn't have enough money for anything fancy. But it was hers. And . . . and she was really happy."

Her voice was trembling again. She paused to collect herself.

"Sheri's problem was that she trusted people too easily, especially men. She really enjoyed the nightlife. She and her roommate would go to bars and clubs almost every weekend. They'd meet guys. All kinds of guys. Sometimes, they'd just drink and dance and brush the guys off. But, sometimes, she'd go home with them or take them to her place."

"How do you know this?" Jim asked, more to just give her a chance to breathe than from a burning need to know the answer.

"When she would come home she would tell me all these stories about how exciting her life was and how it was '*sooo*' good to feel '*sooo*' free. I was scared for her. I tried to tell her to be careful, that she was putting herself in danger. She'd just laugh. She'd say, 'Little Sis, you're sounding just like Daddy, and I'm not going to just trade his rules for yours.'"

She dabbed her eyes with the tissue in her hand.

"Last New Year's Eve," she continued, "Sheri went to a party in a fancy apartment down by the lake. Her boss got her the invitation. There were a lot of doctors and lawyers and investment bankers—you know lots of pretty well-off people. When she was home for Christmas she told me about it and said it would be a really good chance for her to get in with some high class kind of people. She was really looking forward to it.

"Anyway, she went to the party. Sometime after midnight, she left with some guy. Strange thing is, no one seems to know who he was. They don't know if he was invited, or came with someone, or maybe just crashed the party, or what. Can you believe that? Over a hundred people there and not one of them knows who the guy was. And no one could even describe him. The only thing anyone noticed was that he had some kind of tattoo on one hand. Some kind of lizard, or snake or something."

Renee stared ahead for a moment. She swallowed hard, turned her head towards Jim and slowly continued.

"Did you ever see the movie *Looking for Mr. Goodbar*?"

Her story was leading directly to where he feared it was headed. "Oh, no," he said softly, and sympathetically.

She nodded her head. Tears welled up in her eyes again. Her voice cracked.

"They found her in her bed the next morning. Her roommate found her when she came home. Sheri had been . . . had been raped and murdered." Renee buried her face in her hands and began to cry again. Jim put his arms around her and held her. She was able to stop more quickly this time.

Cradled in his arms, she said softly and ominously, "Have you ever felt that it wasn't worth going on anymore? That life just isn't worth living?"

She was in a very fragile emotional state. He realized that he needed to weigh his words carefully—to neither diminish the significance and brutal reality of her loss or her feelings, nor exaggerate his ability to empathize with her, even given the loss of his best friend to violence. Yet she was clearly looking to him to help her out of her deep depression, to help her retain the will to live—a place he knew all too well.

"Yes, Renee, I have felt that way once." He proceeded cautiously. "I lost someone very dear to me, someone I felt I couldn't live without. Not the same way you did, not violent." Funny, he thought, how the example that came to mind was Katie, not Tony. "And not a brother or sister. But what happened was like a death . . . a death to me. All I can tell you is that you never forget. Sheri will never be out of your mind or your heart. But with time, you can move on. You *do* survive. And life can even become meaningful and joyful again. You have friends and family who love you, who will always be there to support you. You just have to be willing to use us, to call on us whenever you're in that dark mood, whenever you feel like you just can't handle the grief anymore. Trust me, Renee. It works. It *does* work. It *does* get better."

Jim thought of recommending therapy to Renee. For a second he even thought of recommending Dr. Pe're. The thought caused a reaction he couldn't quite describe to himself, except that he noticed it created a very negative feeling within him. He abandoned the thought immediately.

He kissed Renee on the forehead. "You've done that for me," he said, "and you didn't even know it. Let me do it for you."

She looked up at him. There was a different look in her eyes, a look of renewed hope and of something, something deep—respect? love?—for him. *If this was a movie,* he thought, *this is when the tender kiss would happen.* But he wasn't going to take a chance on shaking her fragile emotional state right then. He didn't have to. Renee gently raised her lips to his and tenderly kissed him.

When their eyes opened he noticed a slight smile. She collected herself, and pulled away from him. "Thank you, Jim," she said. "I will always love you for this moment."

It was like Cupid's arrow pierced his heart at just that second. For him, the close, relaxed friendship exploded into love—real love—the love he had thought he had with Katie. Now, having been truly stricken, he could finally see the enormous difference between adolescent love and the real thing. It was the difference between the infinitesimal atom and the vastness of the universe. If only he could know what lay in Renee's heart. Until he did, he knew that he would have to keep his true feelings to himself, even at the risk of it becoming an unrequited love.

"What about going home for Christmas?" he asked, purposely avoiding a direct response to her comment.

"No. I can't," she said. "Not this year. It would be . . . too hard. It'll be the first Christmas of my life without Sheri. The reminders at home would be . . . would be too hard for me to handle."

"But what about your parents?" he asked. "Don't you think they'd want you there? They've lost one daughter. Without you there it may feel to them as if they've lost two."

"I've already talked to them. They want me home, but they understand. Daddy and Mom will keep busy at the church and visiting. You know, like nursing homes and sick people and stuff. They'll be okay."

"But *you'll* be alone, and that's not good," he insisted. "Why don't you come home with me? We've got plenty of room and my mom would be cool with it."

"That's sweet, Jim. But I don't know that that would be any better."

He reflected for a moment. "Then I'll stay, too."

"No. No way," she said. "You're not missing Christmas at home for me."

"Subject's closed," he said firmly. "I'm staying with you. Besides, you can't stay in this dorm room over break. You'll stay at my place, in Billy's room. I'll even straighten it up for you. And we'll get our own little tree . . ." He stopped. There was a look of concern on Renee's face.

"I'm sorry," he said, reining in his enthusiasm. "I know how that might sound. I promise, it's all on the up and up. No ulterior motive. No bad intentions. I just don't think you should be alone."

He realized that the image of her sister alone in her apartment with the killer must have danced through Renee's mind. Facing her, he put his hands on her shoulders and with as much sincerity as he had ever said anything, half whispered, "Renee, you *can* trust me."

She looked deep into his eyes, as if drawing into herself every ounce of his sincerity and protectiveness.

"Okay," she said, simply.

<hr />

Jim had worked part-time as a waiter at a small restaurant on College Avenue, across from campus, for almost a year. The owner of the restaurant was glad to keep him on over the holiday, since most of his employees were students and most of them went home for the break. During the couple of weeks leading up to Christmas, Jim worked almost every day. Renee stayed home, at Jim's place. She spent much of each day reading and playing her two favorite instruments, the violin and the clarinet. She also brought a woman's touch to the apartment. It had never been so clean and neat. He didn't know how he would be able to handle Billy's return, and the resulting return to chaotic normalcy.

They bought a small tree and a few lights and decorations to create some semblance of holiday spirit. Jim's mother told him she was very disappointed he wasn't coming home for Christmas. She did everything she could to make him feel guilty about it—pleaded, whined, yelled, accused him of loving "that girl" more than his own mother. He withstood it all and told her it was time to realize he was an adult—and to let him go.

Renee stayed in Billy's room. True to his word, Jim was the perfect gentleman. They played the parts of platonic roommates, though the emotional undercurrent of their relationship was unmistakable. On Christmas Eve they had a candlelight dinner with good wine. They exchanged small gifts. She gave him a handsome sweater. He gave her a book of inspirational and uplifting poetry by a new poet neither of them had ever heard of. They took a walk in the chilled air of the late December night. And when they got home, they said good night and retired to their respective rooms.

A few minutes after Jim got into bed, his door opened. Framed within the doorway, against the dim yellow cast of the hallway night-light, he could make out the silhouette of Renee. She was dressed in a floor-length nightgown made partially transparent by the background light. Without saying anything, she closed the door, walked over to his bed, crawled under the covers with him, kissed him, and softly whispered, "I love you."

Jim said nothing. The way he held her would tell her all she needed to know. They didn't make love that night. He was determined that he wouldn't touch Renee sexually until the night of their wedding.

Somewhere, he thought, Father McTighe must be smiling.

⊱─◦─⊰

Jim's eyes opened. He turned to see if what he thought had happened the night before really had. Sure enough, Renee was lying next to him. She slept so beautifully, so angelically, he thought.

He was awake now. No use trying to go back to sleep. He got up and looked out the window. Dawn was coming. And even though the sun hadn't risen yet, there was a brightness all around. Overnight, several inches of snow had fallen, and it lay on the ground as yet undisturbed by human activity. He was not ordinarily one to go out into the pre-dawn wintry cold, but something drew him to the idea of a walk in the freshly fallen snow. He quietly dressed and slipped out, making sure he didn't disturb Renee.

There was no wind blowing, making the air brisk but not biting. As he walked up Beaver Avenue, it was so still and quiet that the sound of his boots pressing into the snow was almost deafening. He felt a child-like satisfaction in making the first footsteps this snowfall would see in this limited part of the world. He looked up at the trees, snow clinging on all of the branches, and realized that it had been a long time, a very long time, since he had truly appreciated the simple but enormous beauty of a new snowfall the way he was appreciating it now. He couldn't remember the last time he felt so contented.

He had walked a few blocks when he stopped. It was a little brighter now. He was enjoying his walk, but he decided he should get back home before Renee woke up to an empty apartment. As he turned to head back, he realized that he was standing in front of a church. It was a relatively small church, built of stone, with no outward indications of what denomination it was. While it certainly wasn't Catholic, the cross on the door clearly identified it as a Christian church. Jim realized that he must have passed this church dozens of times over the years, but he had never really noticed it. He stood and looked at it for a minute. Then, not knowing why, he walked up to the front door and tried the doorknob. It was unlocked.

Jim opened the door and stepped into the church. A few lit candles near where he would consider the alter to be provided just enough light for him to see most of the interior. It was as simple on the inside as it was on the outside. On either side of him in the back of the church were tables with literature on them. There were six rows of pews on either side of the center aisle. At the far end of the church was a large cross. Several feet in front of the cross and to the left of the center aisle there was a speaker's podium. Other than those features, Jim could see nothing else.

He slowly walked up the center aisle. As he reached the second row of pews, he reflexively genuflected, crossed himself, and entered the pew on the left. He knelt down, folded his hands, and bowed his head.

Thank you, God, he prayed silently. *I know I don't deserve it, and I don't know why you sent her to me, but thank you for Renee.*

He remained motionless, hands folded, head bowed. He heard no sounds, other than the silent thoughts that were entering his mind—thoughts that no longer seemed to be his own, though they sounded in the first person.

Renee is the sign, the inspiration, for what I'm supposed to do with my life. It's not all about me. It's about helping others, serving others, serving God. Renee is God's messenger to me. She is God talking to me. She was sent to me to show me the way. I see it, God. I see the way. I know what I'm supposed to do, supposed to be. I know, for the first time, I really know You. Thank you, Lord. Thank you, God.

"Amen," Jim said out loud, momentarily startling himself. He raised his head and opened his eyes. He could swear there were twice as many candles lit as there had been when he first entered the church. He looked around to see if there was anyone else there—a minister or parishioner perhaps—who might have lit more candles. There was no one. But Jim had the distinct feeling he was not alone. In fact, he had never felt so un-alone in his life, nor so safe and secure.

He unfolded his hands and slowly stood up. He stepped out into the aisle and looked at the cross. He nodded his head, turned and walked to the back of the church and out into the winter morning. The sun had risen and the snow was sparkling. It was the most beautiful morning Jim had ever seen. And, Jim knew, the most profound day of his life.

Chapter 20

JIM PICKED UP THE RECEIVER of the wall phone mounted just inside the doorway of the small kitchen. He leaned against the counter top next to the sink and looked at the kitchen table, where Renee was seated.

"This is fruitless," he said.

"You have to give it one more try," Renee said. "She's your mother."

"She didn't even come to our wedding," he said. "She's not going to come to witness my ultimate heresy."

Mr. and Mrs. James Donovan lived in a small, two-bedroom bungalow a block from the railroad tracks in West Palm Beach, Florida. They had been married the October after their graduation from Penn State in a picturesque gazebo on the dune overlooking the Atlantic Ocean just down the road a few miles, in the quaint seaside town of Ocean Ridge. It was a small wedding—only friends and family. But Mrs. Donovan wasn't there. "Father McTighe made it very clear," she had said. "The Church will not recognize the marriage. I cannot sanction your decision to live in sin."

She had pleaded with Jim to convince Renee to convert to Catholicism, and to marry in the church. She had even had Father McTighe call him. But Mrs. Donovan had no idea the extent to which her son was breaking his ties to her beloved church.

The service was conducted by Reverend Smalley. Billy was the best man. Renee honored her sister by considering Sheri's spirit as her maid of honor. The wedding was also attended by a handful of uninvited, but welcome guests, strolling along the beach and sunning themselves on the sand, taking a few moments to witness the romantic ceremony taking place on the dune above them, in nature's own chapel. The music was provided by the cries of delight of the seagulls winging over and around the wedding party, accompanied by the soft percussion of the waves breaking gently over the shore.

They had chosen Ocean Ridge as the site of their wedding because it was a beautiful spot to get married, and it was close to the Westin Bible College. The second big blow to Jim's mother was when he told her he had enrolled in the Bible College—a school not affiliated with any of the major Christian denominations—to study for the ministry.

He had tried to explain to her that not only had he found in Renee his future wife, but in consoling and counseling her, he had found his calling. Her love for him, and his deep love for her, had rekindled his faith in God. The self-satisfaction and sense of unselfish accomplishment he felt in helping Renee overcome her grief and depression over the loss of her sister, inspired within him the desire to make helping others his life's work. He thought about medicine, social work, psychotherapy. None of them seemed sufficient. It was the ministry which drew him, to do the work he felt called to; maybe even to atone for his past sins. But it would not, could not, be in the Catholic Church. This, she could not understand. And he realized it was something that mere words could never adequately explain.

No matter how devastating it was to his mother, Jim knew he had made the right decision. The past two years had been good ones. Renee was teaching second grade, and was deliriously happy with her work. They were in love. And in his studies for the ministry, he had found that purpose in life; a reason for living that went beyond himself. This he attributed, in large part, to Dr. Robert Westin—theology professor, and founder and president of the small college and seminary which bore his name.

From the very beginning, Jim had been particularly inspired by Dr. Westin. Dr. Westin likewise seemed to take an immediate shining to him—a young, eager student with a sweet, petite fiancée who was to become his wife within weeks of the start of school.

As a mentor, Jim felt he could have found none better. A morally upright, inspirational leader, Dr. Westin challenged his students to be more than what he sneeringly called "mere Bible readers." He challenged them to think, and question. He even encouraged them to question *his* biblical interpretations in order to arrive at a better understanding of the Bible's true meaning and its clear direction and relevance to their present lives. "Only in that way," he demanded, "can you truly *lead* a congregation, and not just preach to it."

Two years of study and learning had passed. It was time for graduation, and ordination. He had written to his mother asking her to come. He knew she wouldn't, but Renee had insisted. Graduation was the next day, and he still hadn't heard a word. Renee, bless her heart, wouldn't give up.

"Call," she said, directing her eyes to the receiver still sitting unused in his hand.

Jim dialed 1, the 412 area code for Pittsburgh, and his mother's number. He hoped she wouldn't answer. But on the third ring he heard her voice.

"Hello."

"Hi, Mom. It's me."

"Oh, hello Jimmy," she said. She spoke the words with an air of formality one would not expect from a mother who was talking to her only son for the first time in months.

"Mom, I'm . . . I'm . . ." He looked at Renee. She waived him on with the back of her hand. "I'm graduating tomorrow."

"Yes, I know," his mother answered. "I got your invitation."

"Mom, I know you aren't happy about me becoming a minister. But . . . but I'd really like you to be here tomorrow. You can catch a plane and be here by tonight. It would mean . . ."

"You know how I feel, Jimmy," she responded coldly. "Your father and I raised you the right way, but ever since you met that woman . . ."

"Mother! That's not fair. She had nothing . . ."

"Protestants have always perverted the word of God. And it's only weak Catholics that get led astray, like you have. Until you come to your senses, I don't think we have much to talk about."

"Mother, I don't want to get into an argument."

"Well, you called me . . ."

A loud rumbling noise began to grow and the small house began to shake as a freight train motored by. The train would take a few minutes to pass, and talking on the phone would be almost impossible. Jim viewed it as a welcome sign from Heaven that this conversation was over.

"Can't hear you, Mom," he said loudly. "Train's going by. Do what you want. Good-bye." He hung up, not waiting to hear if his mother said anything else.

Renee stood up. She walked over to him and put her arms around his waist. She reached up and kissed him lightly.

"You had to try," she said.

"Yeah," he answered. "But not anymore."

⊷—◦—⊶

Dr. Westin, at six foot one, struck an imposing figure as he stood at the lectern at the front of the modest-sized chapel. His dark blue suit highlighted an already distinguished head of white, wavy hair. In his early sixties, he had the look of a handsome, well-aged leading man, *a' la* Cary Grant or Gregory Peck.

"Your families have much to be proud of," Dr. Westin said as he looked out over his audience. "*You* have much to be proud of. But as each one of you knows all too well, today is not the end of your journey. It is just the end of the first step, and the beginning of a life-long trek that will deeply affect every person you come in contact with, and will bring *you* ever closer to God and to life everlasting."

Dr. Westin's stature, together with his silver-tongued oratory, demanded the attention of Jim, the nine other graduating divinity students and their families and friends gathered together for the school's modest commencement and ordination exercises.

"And now it's time to present our graduates with their diplomas—their licenses to preach, if you will," Westin continued, smiling broadly. "As is our tradition, the first diploma will be presented to the student who has earned the highest grade average in the post-graduate divinity program. To recognize this accomplishment"—Dr. Westin reached into the back of the lectern and pulled out a book-sized, finely crafted wooden box-—"we present the top graduate not only his diploma and credentials, but also"—Westin opened the box and pulled out a Bible—"this Bible and this carrying case." Westin held the bible up in his left hand and the wooden case in his right. "And for those of you who can't see the face of the carrying case, engraved in gold are the words, 'Go Forth, in the Name of the Lord—Westin Bible College and Seminary.' "

Westin placed the Bible back in its case and picked up a diploma from a table situated behind him.

"It is my distinct pleasure to present this year's Westin Bible and *summa cum laude* diploma to . . . James Donovan—that is, the Reverend James Donovan."

The assembled guests applauded. Renee squeezed Jim's hand and kissed him. He stood up and began to make his way to the front of the chapel. As he approached the lectern he couldn't help but marvel at the strange path he had taken to get to this point—from the depths of depression, to a wildly enjoyable (if now guilt inducing) hedonistic college life, to meeting Renee and now, of all things, becoming an ordained minister. He turned briefly to look at Renee again, because he knew it all began with her. Her beaming smile showed her pride in her husband.

When he reached the lectern, Dr. Westin reached out his right hand and took Jim's in a firm handshake.

"Congratulations, Jim," Westin said, handing him the Bible and his diploma. "I'm very proud of you."

"Thank you, sir," Jim replied. "Thank you for everything."

⊢·⊕·○·⊕·⊣

The rest of the graduation ceremony was equally simple, and short. It lasted all of fifteen minutes. The small crowd filed out of the chapel in an orderly fashion. At Dr. Westin's direction the students and their families and friends headed towards the student union building next door for a reception in honor of the graduates, stopping in the courtyard between the buildings only long enough to take the obligatory graduation photos.

The refreshments being served were in keeping with Dr. Westin's penchant for simplicity and humility. The punch was spiked with nothing stronger than ginger ale. The hors d'oeuvres consisted of cheese and crackers. In an unaccountable fit of extravagance for the Westin Bible School and Seminary, the cheese plate included three different kinds of cheese –cheddar, gouda and muenster—and two types of crackers—Ritz and some kind of snack crackers Jim didn't know the name of.

No matter. Jim was hungry. And cheese and crackers and punch would tide him over until the full lunch his in-laws would be treating him and Renee to right after the ceremony. They would be going to Chuck & Harold's Restaurant in Palm Beach. "Enjoy it," he had joked with Renee when her parents made the offer. "On a minister's salary, it's probably the last time in a long time we'll be eating somewhere like that."

Despite his mother's absence—her disowning him as he saw it now—Jim considered it a very good day. He was proud of what he had accomplished. And he enjoyed being in the limelight, however briefly, for his accomplishments. Renee was proud of him. And so were her parents. That, and the fact that he had met Dr. Westin's high expectations, was more than enough for him. He looked around at the small gathering of proud and happy students and guests as they talked, and laughed and "broke bread" with each other. *Yes,* he thought, as he sipped on his punch, *I couldn't ask for a better day.*

"Dr. Westin seems like a very impressive man," Mrs. Smalley said as she daintily picked up one cracker and one piece of cheese from a plate on the hors d'oeuvres table.

"Yes, he is," Jim said. "I'm sorry I haven't had an opportunity to introduce you yet."

"You're going to get the opportunity right now, honey," Renee said, nodding to Jim's right. Dr. Westin was at that moment walking towards them. He was accompanied by a gentleman in a brown sport coat and tan trousers. Jim had never seen him before.

Dr. Westin reached out his hand to Jim and shook it firmly.

"Congratulations again, Jim." He took Renee's hand gently in his. "And to you, too, my dear. You are a big part of his success."

"Thank you, Dr. Westin," Renee replied.

"Dr. Westin," Jim interjected. "I'd like to introduce you to my in-laws. This is Reverend Robert Smalley," he said, holding his hand out in the direction of his father-in-law, "and his wife, Jane."

"It's my extreme pleasure," said Dr. Westin. He firmly shook Reverend Smalley's hand and bowed in a gentlemanly fashion to Mrs. Smalley. "What is your denomination, sir?" he asked. Jim knew that Dr. Westin knew Reverend Smalley's denomination, because Jim had told him more than once. But it was the measure of the man that he would express his interest in knowing directly to Reverend Smalley and allow his colleague to provide his own biographical information.

"Methodist," Reverend Smalley answered.

"Ah, Methodist. Wonderful. Wonderful," Dr. Westin responded with a smile that evinced genuine pleasure.

"Excuse me. Where are my manners?" Westin said as he took the arm of the man accompanying him and gently pulled him forward into the group. "I'd like you all to meet Reuben Conrad. Reuben is an old friend of mine from Alabama—from my first parish."

They all shook hands.

"Jim, I particularly asked Reuben to come today to meet you." Westin looked at Renee and the Smalleys. "Would you mind terribly if I borrowed a few moments of Jim's time?"

"Not at all, Dr. Westin," Renee said.

"Great. Great. Enjoy the food and drink. And Renee, don't forget to show your parents the religious art hallway upstairs."

"Of course," said Renee.

"Great. Great. Jim. Reuben. Why don't we step outside," Westin said, turning to the two men who were now standing next to each other. "The Lord has blessed us with a gorgeous day, so let's take advantage of it."

They stepped outside into a small side courtyard. Dr. Westin closed the sliding glass door behind them. The three men were alone.

"Jim," Dr. Westin said, draping his left arm across Jim's shoulders, "Reuben and I go way back."

"Don't say how *far* back," Conrad interjected with a laugh.

Westin laughed, too.

"Let's just say it was far enough back that I wasn't much older than you are now," Westin said, looking at Jim and tugging slightly at his shoulders before removing his arm from them.

"My first church as a preacher was the Pleasant River Christian Church, in Pleasant River, Alabama," Westin continued. "A great little church and a great little town."

"Still are," Conrad said proudly.

"No question about it—none at all," Westin agreed. "Reuben here was just a young buck himself at the time. Had just come back from the University of Alabama. Started his own investment counseling business. First one in town to offer that service."

"No one had seen a need before," Conrad added, again with obvious pride in himself.

Westin stepped over to Reuben and put his hand on his friend's shoulder. "I decided smart young fellows like Reuben here ought to be teaching Sunday School—not just leave it up to the . . . the mature ladies of the parish. All I had to do was ask. Reuben said yes immediately. And we became fast friends."

Jim remained silent. He wasn't quite sure where this conversation was going. But given Dr. Westin's fondness for him, he expected it to be something good.

"Now," Westin continued, "Reuben is one of the most respected men in Pleasant River. In fact, not just Pleasant River. Has clients coming all the way from Montgomery—not to mention all the politicians he's helped get *to* Montgomery. Now what's all this got to do with you, right Jim?"

"Well . . ."

"Reuben's the president of the church's Council of Elders. And I've asked him to come today, Jim, to meet you, and get to know you a bit, because I believe you and the Pleasant River Christian Church are perfect for each other."

"Robert has spoken very highly of you, Jim," Conrad said. "In fact, he called me several months ago to tell me about this prize pupil of his. We didn't even have a vacancy. We were very happy with our minister. Then, just two weeks ago he took a position in Birmingham. I don't know how he does it," Conrad said, nodding towards Westin, "but somehow he just seems to make things happen."

Jim finally understood. "Are you recommending me for this position, Dr. Westin?"

"Indeed I am, Jim," Westin answered. "With your credentials and ability, I have no doubt you could obtain a good position as an assistant pastor at a large church. And you could do very well. But Reuben's church gives you a real opportunity to develop leadership skills right away—in a less pressurized and stressful environment."

"We're a small church," Conrad added. "Only about four dozen regular church-going families. We don't have significant needs beyond someone to conduct services, weddings and funerals—and occasionally counsel folks through periods of grief or family discord. And, of course, oversee the Sunday School and its two teachers."

"In other words, a great place for a young minister to start," said Westin. "It was for me, and I know it would be for you, too. That is, unless you've already committed elsewhere."

"No. No, sir. I haven't."

"I knew that, of course. I would have expected you to have asked for a recommendation or two," Westin said. "Well, I'm going to go back into the reception while you two talk a bit. Take as long as you like." Westin patted both men on the back and went inside leaving them alone in the courtyard.

The two men talked for another half hour. They would have continued for hours more if the reception hadn't started to break up. Jim genuinely liked this older, soft-spoken Southern gentleman. And Conrad seemed to like him, too. He made the small town atmosphere of Pleasant River sound as appealing as Andy Griffith's fictional Mayberry. By the end of the conversation, Jim was ready to accept an offer, if one was forthcoming. And it was.

"Certainly, Mr. Conrad. I . . ."

"Please, call me Reuben."

"Of course . . . Reuben. I accept."

He was so excited at the prospect of his first position being as a full minister that he never even asked what his salary would be. Nor did he think of waiting until he talked to Renee before deciding to accept the offer.

⊷•◦•⊶

Renee was already in bed under the covers as Jim crawled in. He was wearing nothing but his briefs. As usual, she wore her ankle length, cotton nightgown. That didn't make much sense to him given the South Florida weather. It was particularly out of sorts since they needed to lower the air conditioning so Renee wouldn't be too hot.

"I'm just saying that you didn't have to say yes on the spot," she said, continuing the discussion about the job offer that had begun as soon as Jim told her about it, and had been *the* topic of conversation on and off the rest of the day. "I'm sure Mr. Conrad would have understood if you asked for a day or two so you could talk to me, and maybe get my father's advice."

"I know. I know, Honey," Jim responded, apologetically. "But Reuben was so nice, and so persuasive. And not many new graduates get their first church right out of the chute. And think about it. This was Dr. Westin's first church. And look where he is now."

"But it's such a small town, Jim. I'm sure they can't pay much. And what will we do if I can't get a good job?"

He was getting a bit annoyed at her very practical questions which he felt were taking some of the excitement and luster off of his unexpected good fortune.

"We'll do fine," he said. "God will provide. Can't you just be happy for me—for us?"

Renee was silent for a few seconds. She turned and looked at him. "I am, Honey. I am," she said. She kissed him lightly.

Jim reached back and turned off the lamp on his nightstand. He turned back onto his side facing Renee. He placed his hand on her breast.

"How about tonight? Can we try it tonight?" he asked.

"No, Jim. I . . . I just can't."

He took his hand off her breast and left his arm lying across her midsection. There was a silence between them. His thoughts drifted back to that first night they had spent in bed together. He had kept his promise to himself, and the silent one to her, not to make love until their wedding night. She was a virgin—a pleasant surprise to him despite Renee's "good girl" aura. His experience with Katie had dashed any expectations he had had of being his wife's first lover.

Renee's virginity became part of what made their early sex more exciting. He introduced her to experiences she had never known. And being her teacher and mentor in the art of lovemaking brought him more satisfaction and pleasure than the carnal, impersonal sex of his wilder, pre-Renee college days.

It didn't last, at least not the way he had hoped it would. Before Renee, he had experienced seductive, experimental sex. He now looked to her to make it as playful and varied as he knew it could be. After all, monogamy required one's wife to be a partner in sexuality and the delivery of physical pleasure and joy (whatever Father McTighe might have said about it being for procreation, and *only* procreation).

But for Renee, inexperienced, a minister's daughter, naturally reserved, it was different. It was a gift of God, to be experienced with reverence and, to the extent possible while naked, writhing and groaning, with dignity. To treat sex as nothing more than a game was irreverent. She made it clear that to primp herself and seduce him made her feel like a whore, and she considered it disrespectful to herself.

By this, their third year of marriage, these differences had begun to eat at him. What concerned him as much as her reticence to "loosen up" was the fact that it bothered him so much. Why was sex so important to him? Why, he wondered, had sex—his sex, others' sex, the consequences of sex—played such a large role in his life, and in the development of who he was? It had brought him great joy and ecstasy, and also tremendous grief and lingering bitterness. And now it was affecting his relationship with his wife, with whom he was deeply in love.

He didn't want it to be so important to him. In fact, the ten months he spent with Renee before their wedding were ten months of ecstatic love, with no sex. Looking back, those ten months were the happiest time of his life. But now . . . now that he could be closer, more intimate, more open and less inhibited with that same wonderful, lovely person, he was less happy, less fulfilled, less able to focus entirely on the qualities he so loved in her—because sex, *sex damn it,* was getting in the way.

"If not tonight," he asked, "then when, Renee? When?"

"I . . . I don't know, Jim," she said. "I don't know."

She turned onto her left side, her back to him. He left his arm hanging over her side, but made no further effort to initiate lovemaking. His exchange with her saddened him. Before finally falling asleep, he managed to put it out of his mind, by thinking of the new adventure they were about to set out on.

Chapter 21

"**I**'LL HAVE THE *CRÈME BRULEE*."

"Very good choice, sir." The formally attired waiter—black tuxedo pants, white shirt, white jacket, and white gloves—took the dessert menu from Jim's hands.

"And for you, Mr. Leigh?" the waiter said turning his head to the other side of the table.

The distinguished, impeccably dressed, fifty-something gentleman seated across from Jim studied the menu intently. As he did so, Jim looked over his shoulder and out the window of the exclusive Governor's Club. The club was located on the twelfth floor of the tony Phillips Point office building in downtown West Palm Beach. From the top floor of the East Tower of the two-towered pink complex, Jim had a clear view of the Intracoastal Waterway and the Palm Beach Marina, where many of the world's wealthiest people docked their yachts. During his days at the Bible College, he always wondered what it would be like to eat at such a fancy restaurant, and now here he was.

"I'll have the Chocolate Death," his host told the obsequious waiter, selecting a dessert with four different types of rich, dark chocolate intended only for those whose arteries are entirely incapable of becoming clogged, or those who feel that death is a fair price to pay for total self-indulgence.

"Yes sir. The usual," the waiter said as he took the dessert menu from the hands of the obviously well known, and important, club member.

"So, Reverend Donovan, tell me, how have you enjoyed your experience at the Pleasant River Christian Church?"

Jim had received some background information about his host from Dr. Westin, but he already knew he would be in the presence of a very influential and powerful man. Richardson Leigh was a wealthy and powerful West Palm Beach lawyer. He had founded one of Florida's largest law firms. He wielded tremendous influence in the state's business and political circles and was on a first name basis with virtually every significant political official in the state. And when the President of the United States came campaigning and fundraising in South Florida, it was at Richardson Leigh's home that he spent the night. While Jim had never met the man during his time in Palm Beach County, he had certainly heard and read about him, often.

Leigh was also largely responsible for the establishment of the Church of the Light of Christ of the Palm Beaches. A life-long Southern Baptist, Leigh had left his church as a result of a vicious and virulent schism, purportedly over the fate of the church's minister. In truth, as told to Jim by Dr. Westin who seemed to know everything about everything, it was over a power struggle for control of the church's board. The power struggle was between Leigh and Dr. Joseph Wellman, Palm Beach County's pre-eminent plastic surgeon. The dispute led to the election of two competing boards and eventually ended up in court, where Leigh presumed his clout and that of his firm would carry the day.

Leigh had miscalculated. He and his faction lost the court battle, a rare and humiliating defeat for this civic and legal giant. Not willing to accept the defeat, he turned his fury on the minister, castigating him for "improper deviation from the teachings of Christ as revealed in the words of the Holy Scripture." He then simply led his followers out of the church, and started a new one.

Since Richardson Leigh put up most of the front money to start the new church, he pretty much got his way with it. He insisted that it not align itself with any single denomination. This way, he had argued, the congregation (meaning Richardson Leigh) would have total independence in managing its own affairs, including the selection of its pastor. It had been made clear to Jim that this was the reason he had been flown down to the Palm Beaches to meet with Leigh.

"I've enjoyed Pleasant River very much," Jim said in response to Leigh's question. "The congregation is hard working and devoted. The town is great. The people are so friendly and nice and . . . and, just real down to earth folks. We've both enjoyed it—me and my wife, Renee."

"I would have expected that," Leigh said. "I've been to Pleasant River several times. Reuben Conrad was my college roommate."

"Really?" Jim responded, truly surprised. "I didn't know that."

"Yep. Went to Alabama. Majored in political science. But I'm a Florida boy, and to make it—really make it—in Florida, your best bet is to go to the University of Florida. So, I came home and went to law school there. But I loved Alabama. And I got to visit Pleasant River many times with Reuben."

Jim sensed that they finally seemed to be heading towards discussing what had caused Leigh to fly him down to West Palm Beach. All through dinner he had, for the most part, listened uncomfortably and awkwardly to Leigh extolling the beauty and virtues of the Palm Beaches. While he suspected what Leigh was getting at, his host had yet to come right out with it.

"Is that how you heard of me?" he asked. "From Reuben?"

The waiter set the desserts in front of the two men.

"More coffee, Mr. Donovan?" the waiter asked politely.

"That's *Reverend* Donovan," Leigh stated sternly to the waiter.

"I'm so sorry." Jim noticed definite fear in the waiter's voice and demeanor. "Reverend Donovan. More coffee, sir?"

"No. Thank you."

"Mr. Leigh?" the waiter asked timidly.

"Yes, Rinaldo. I'll have more."

There was a definite shaking in Rinaldo's hand as he replenished Leigh's cup. When he finished, the chastised waiter walked away with a definite, though silent, sigh of relief.

Probably thankful to God that he didn't spill the coffee while pouring it, Jim thought.

Both men began to eat their desserts.

"Where were we?" Leigh asked, his mouth full of Chocolate Death.

"I had asked whether Reuben had spoken to you about me."

"Oh, right. Well, yes and no. Since our split with the Baptist Church, we've had two different ministers. Both experienced—been around a while. But, maybe because of their long experience, neither one was right for our church. They were both too . . . too rigid; too set in their ways. We're a new, young, *dynamic* church. We need young blood to lead us. Someone not afraid of change. Someone creative, ambitious."

"And you just knew of this incredible young minister in a small town in Alabama whose fame had spread far and wide?"

Leigh laughed.

"There. See? That's perfect," Leigh said. "An irreverent sense of humor. Even when you're talking to someone who can change your whole life. Anyway, what I did was I went to Westin College and asked to see the records of their last three graduating classes."

"But those records are supposed to be confidential," Jim said, surprised.

"Perhaps," Leigh responded. "But when I want something, I can usually get it. So, in looking through the files, your credentials jumped right out, above all others. Then, when I asked about your whereabouts and Rob Westin told me you were at Reuben's church—well, it was obviously Kismet."

"Excuse me?"

"Fate, son. Fate. Haven't you ever seen *Kismet*? The play?"

"No sir."

"Never mind." Leigh wiped the remaining Chocolate Death from his lips and placed his napkin on the table. "I called Reuben and asked about you. He wasn't thrilled about the prospect of losing you. But he would never stand in the way of someone advancing in his career. And Reuben had nothing but praise for you."

"So, on the basis of that you asked me to come for this . . . what? I guess this is an interview, then."

"Yes and no. Yes, this is an interview. No, I didn't bring you down on Reuben's word. I do more due diligence than that."

"What did you do?" Jim asked. "Like a criminal background check?"

"Not yet. But I will. What I did do is I went to Alabama and spent a week there. Watched you preach twice. And otherwise, just hung out and watched you go about your daily tasks."

"How could you do that without me knowing?" Jim asked in disbelief. "It's such a small town. I would have had to have seen you, or heard something."

"You forget. I know that town. The people know me—even all these years later. It wasn't too hard to blend in, and ask old friends for a little discretion."

"So, what has your due diligence told you?" Jim swallowed the last of his *crème brulee*.

"That you're just the person to lead our church. Spiritually, that is."

Jim placed his napkin on the table next to his dessert dish. He leaned forward, folded his hands and rested his elbows on the table before him. "I'm very flattered, Mr. Leigh," he said. "But as good as I may be—and I feel I'm very good at what I'm doing—I still have only one year of experience at a small town church. I'm not sure I'm ready for something this . . . this big."

"Listen, Jim. May I call you Jim?"

"Yes, of course. Please do."

"I'm confident you're just the man we need," Leigh continued. "At this point, we're still somewhat small—only a hundred or so families— and we're meeting in an old bingo hall in a strip shopping center which I bought. But because of who we are, and who I am, we're already a very influential church—much more influential than our size would suggest. What we need now is to grow in numbers. And that's where you come in. I've watched you preach. You're very inspirational and charismatic. I know you can draw people in who I can't reach. The people who are looking for the right spiritual leader, with the right words said in the right way—with an uplifting message of hope and love. You're that man, Jim Donovan."

Jim knew the effect Leigh's flattering words were intended to have. And they were succeeding.

Leigh continued.

"I have big plans for this church, Jim. I intend to build a magnificent new sanctuary and community center. When you see the plans and the location they'll blow you away. I want our church to be the largest church in the county—and then to grow beyond the county, beyond the state. I've made a lot of money, Jim. And I have a lot of influence. I have no question of our ability to make this vision a reality. I'd like you to be my partner in bringing Jesus to the masses in a spectacular fashion." Leigh took a sip of coffee, never taking his eyes off of Jim. He put his cup down. "What do you say?"

Jim's head was swimming. Here he sat, in an exclusive private club, the likes of which he had never experienced, with an incredibly wealthy and powerful man—the likes of which he had also never experienced— who wanted to use that wealth and power to build a large and influential church to spread the Gospel of Jesus Christ. And he wanted Jim Donovan to be the spiritual partner, the spiritual leader, in achieving that vision. It was all he could do to maintain even a sliver of perspective. But, remembering Renee's reaction the last time he accepted a job without consulting her, he tried.

"Mr. Leigh," he said, "not only am I flattered, but I'm . . . I'm intrigued by the possibilities. Excited actually. But I'll need to talk to my wife . . ."

"How much are you making right now, Jim?" Leigh interrupted.

"Excuse me?"

"How much are they paying you?"

"About twenty thousand, with extra money, you know, for funerals, weddings . . ."

"And your wife is a part-time substitute teacher, right?"

"Yes, that's right."

"I'll start you at seventy-five thousand. And, of course, you can keep all of the wedding and funeral tips—tax free, if that's what you choose. I need an answer now."

Jim was floored. Seventy-five thousand a year?! How could he say no? Renee would understand. Besides, they would be right up the road from where they were married. Only fifteen miles or so. Close to where he went to school—to Dr. Westin. Renee would understand. She'd even be happy. How could she say no?

"You've got a deal, Mr. Leigh," he said, extending his hand across the table. Leigh took it and shook it firmly.

"Great, son. You won't regret it."

Chapter 22

THE FIRST SIX MONTHS BACK in West Palm Beach were pretty much a blur to Jim. The move from Alabama had been easy enough. Richardson Leigh saw to that.

And Renee had been no problem at all. When he reported to her that he had accepted a position in West Palm Beach for seventy-five thousand a year, she made no complaint about not having been consulted. In fact, she was ecstatic. She had never really adjusted to life in a small southern town.

As soon as they arrived in Florida, Leigh instructed them that for the first few months their main task was to circulate in the community and become well-known, and well-liked. He had offered Jim enough money that it wasn't necessary for Renee to work. And Leigh made it crystal clear that he expected her to be a full-time minister's wife.

"Why can't I just substitute teach part time?" she asked Jim when she heard of Leigh's expectation.

"Because Mr. Leigh has big plans for this church," he answered. "And we're supposed to play a major role in those plans. I need you to do this, Renee."

Renee agreed. It was, after all, a tremendous opportunity for them. Jim was making more money as a second-year minister than most pastors with ten to twenty times his experience. If she had any reservations about things being too good to be true, she didn't express them to her husband.

Their first six months was a whirlwind of activity. Much of it involved attending community and social events, meeting community activists, social and financial bigwigs and government leaders. Every week they seemed to attend at least two high society events or parties in the wealthy enclaves of Palm Beach, Boca Raton, Jupiter Island and, several times, at the Leigh's' oceanfront mansion in Manalapan, the wealthy seaside town just north of Ocean Ridge. They quickly learned high society's niceties, and they seemed to be received well. It was a lifestyle that neither of them had ever expected to be a part of when Jim decided to go into the ministry.

At the same time, Jim worked hard at tending to his new flock. He took great care in preparing his services and sermons, and delivered them with great emotion and flair. He was proud of the reputation he was quickly earning for leading inspirational services. And, he was getting results. In those first six months, church membership doubled, much to Richardson Leigh's pleasure. He was generous with his praise of Jim, both in private and publicly. And he never missed an opportunity when in Jim's presence to express his pride in making such a wise selection for his young church's spiritual leader.

Six months to the day after his arrival in West Palm Beach, on a rainy Friday afternoon, Jim sat at his desk working on his Sunday sermon. His office had originally been a small shoe repair shop next to the bingo hall. With a little redecorating, directed by Renee, some decent furniture and the installation of a door leading directly from the former bingo hall, which was now the church's sanctuary, the former shoe repair shop had been transformed into what he considered a comfortable place to work.

As he put the period on the last sentence of the sermon, the phone rang. He put his pencil down and lifted the receiver.

"Reverend Donovan," he answered.

"Jim," the voice on the other end said. "This is Richardson."

"Hello, Mr. Leigh," he answered. "What can I do for you?"

Leigh coughed. It was something Jim came to expect almost every time he talked to his new mentor. Leigh was an unapologetic two-pack-a-day smoker. Even a constant smoker's hack wasn't enough to make him quit.

"I'd like you to come over to the office," Leigh said once he cleared his throat.

"When?"

"Right now."

"Is it important Mr. Leigh? I was just about to head home." Jim and Renee had rented a nice home a few miles west of the church. Leigh's office was several miles east, in downtown West Palm. Jim didn't relish going in the opposite direction from home late on a Friday afternoon, especially since he and Renee were expected to attend a charity event in Palm Beach that night.

"Very important, Jim," Leigh said with undisguised excitement in his voice. "The architect just dropped off the finished plans for our new church. I think it's time you got a first-hand look at our future."

That was different, Jim thought. It was even worth going out of his way for. For six months he had listened to Leigh talk about his big plans for new church facilities; but he had been given no details about what it would look like or where it would be. He would have liked to have had input into those decisions, but it wasn't to be. This was Richardson Leigh's baby, and Leigh was keeping total control of it. Now, finally, he was ready to show his minister their future home, and Jim was anxious to see it.

"I'd very much like to see the plans, Mr. Leigh," he said. "I can be there in about fifteen minutes."

"Great. Great. See you shortly."

Leigh hung up.

Jim laid the receiver back in its cradle. He placed his finished sermon in the leather folder he used just for that purpose, made sure all the lights were out in both the sanctuary and his office, grabbed his umbrella, stepped out onto the front sidewalk and locked the office door.

The rain was falling hard. Strong gusts of wind made it difficult for him to control his umbrella as he tried to navigate the minefield of puddles in the parking lot between his office and his car. As he approached the car, through the driving rain he saw a man standing in the middle of the parking lot, about twenty feet beyond his parking space. There was no car parked anywhere near the stranger. The man was wearing what appeared to be black dress shoes, black dress pants, a trench coat and an old style fedora hat, which hung low over his eyes.

The man stood there, making no apparent effort to move or get out of the rain. It seemed very odd to Jim. As he wove his way to his car, he began to feel an uneasy sense of danger. Nonetheless, he felt compelled to offer his help.

"Do you need a lift?" he yelled out to the man.

There was no response. The man didn't move. Jim tried again.

"Can I take you somewhere? At least get you out of the rain?"

This time the man lifted his head, as if to look at Jim. Even with the low hung hat, the man's entire face was directed straight at him. But he could see nothing—no features at all. He squinted hard to see through the rain. Still, he couldn't make out any of the man's facial features.

Danger and fear swept over Jim. He wasn't sure if it was for himself or for the stranger. He decided to give it one more try and if he received no response, he would go back to the office and call 9-1-1.

"Sir?" he called out.

The man slowly raised his left hand and held it palm forward towards Jim. He then turned and slowly walked through the rain in the direction of the highway. In a moment, he was gone. Then, the rain stopped.

Jim turned his attention back to his car. *That was one weird guy*, he thought as he inserted his key into the door lock. He got in, started the car and drove off. Despite the umbrella, his clothes and his shoes were wet. Together with the eerie thought of the strange man in the rain, it made for a damp, chilly and uncomfortable drive to Leigh's Phillips Point office.

Traffic was heavier than usual. It took him a few minutes more than the normal fifteen to get into town. He expected Leigh would be upset. Leigh was almost maniacal about punctuality, his own and others'. He brooked no excuse for tardiness, no matter how minor the infraction.

When Jim got to the upscale office building, he left his car with the valet parking attendant. He ran across the complex's open plaza to and through the main doors, walked rapidly past the security desk with a quick wave to Seymour, the septuagenarian security guard, and entered a waiting elevator. He pressed the 10 button and hoped he was lucky enough to not have the elevator stop at any intervening floors. He knew how silly that was, being so concerned over the possibility of being delayed the few seconds it would take for the elevator to take on another passenger or two. But not displeasing Richardson Leigh had become a big part of Jim Donovan's life. And, as he saw it, a big part of his future success.

He got to 10 without a stop. The elevator doors silently slid open. He stepped out, turned to his left and walked towards a set of ornate mahogany doors with gold lettering announcing that he was about to enter the offices of Leigh, McLaughlin & Hall, Attorneys at Law.

He opened the door and stepped into the firm's lavish reception area. Leigh had once told him that the top law firms had to have expensive offices and their lawyers had to dress well and drive expensive cars in order to convince their well-heeled clients that they were worth the several hundred dollars an hour they charged for legal fees. By that standard Jim figured that Leigh, McLaughlin & Hall must be the best firm in town—or at least the highest paid. To his right was a couch, two chairs and a coffee table, all of which looked like they could have come directly from the palace at Versailles. They sat on a large Persian rug which he knew was the most original and expensive rug the firm could find. Not that most people would know that, but that it might be known by only one client, or better yet, one potential client, was enough to justify the cost. In keeping with the French motif, on either side of the setting, there was placed a sculptured bust. One was of Napoleon, and one was of King Louis XIV, the Sun King.

To Jim's left was a semi-circular reception desk. It was modern in design, yet somehow tastefully complimented the period pieces on the other side of the room. Seated behind the desk was the firm's pleasant and outgoing receptionist, Nancy Gilchrist.

"Hello, Reverend Donovan," Nancy beamed. "How are you today?"

"Fine, thank you, Nancy. And how are you?"

"I'm just *great!*"

Nancy was always great, he thought. He wondered whether she was one of those rare people who managed to go through life blissfully ignoring all that was bad and unpleasant in the world, and even their own lives, or if she was a volcano suppressing all of the pressures of her life and hiding them behind a façade of joy and happiness, just waiting to erupt at a time and for a reason no one would expect, or ever understand. It was an interesting question, but one he didn't have time to dwell on right at that moment.

"Mr. Leigh is expecting . . ."

"Go right in," Nancy interrupted, nodding to her left.

Directly opposite the entry doors was a glass encased conference room with windows overlooking the Intracoastal Waterway, the Town of Palm Beach and the Atlantic Ocean beyond. Jim hadn't noticed him when he first came in. But now he could see Richardson Leigh in the conference room, standing with his back to the reception area, cigarette in hand. He appeared to be poring over some documents spread out over the extremely large and expensive marble conference table.

"Thank you, Nancy," he said to the still smiling receptionist. He turned and headed towards the conference room.

"Don't forget to let me validate your parking ticket before you leave," Nancy called after him.

Jim answered with a wave of the hand as he opened the glass door to the conference room. He entered and began to make his way to the opposite side of the table from Leigh.

"Hello, Mr. Leigh," he said. "I'm sorry I'm late. The traffic and the . . ."

"No. No. Come over here," Leigh said. "Next to me. You can see better if you're not looking at it upside down."

Leigh had ignored both his lateness and his effort to explain and apologize. *This must be really important to him,* Jim thought.

He moved to Leigh's side of the table and stood next to the engrossed lawyer. Spread out on the table there two sets of plans. At the top of the first page of one set—the one immediately in front of Jim—was the heading CHURCH OF THE LIGHT OF CHRIST OF THE PALM BEACHES—SITE PLAN. The other set—the plans Leigh was studying intently—were architectural blueprints.

At first glance, neither set of plans made much sense to Jim. He had no background or experience in architecture or development. But Leigh had plenty. And he knew that Leigh was chomping at the bit to show and explain it all to him.

"Beautiful. Just beautiful," Leigh said, seemingly more to himself than to his guest.

Leigh pulled back the large page he had been viewing and began to study the next page of the blueprints. Jim looked at it but couldn't decipher what it represented.

"Magnificent," Leigh said softly. "Absolutely magnificent."

He pointed to the plans.

"Look at that altar, Jim. It's a stage. Big enough for singers, a piano, an organ. And look. That's where the large video screen will be. Can you imagine? Can you just imagine?"

"Mr. Leigh, I . . . I could probably imagine if you describe all of this to me. I'm . . . well, I don't think I'll get much out of looking at these drawings. I'm afraid I'm somewhat architecturally challenged."

Leigh chuckled, what to Jim seemed to be a self-satisfied chuckle. One of the things he learned quickly about Richardson Leigh was that he always liked to be in a superior position to those around him. And he worked hard to make it so.

"Of course." Leigh turned the drawings back to the first page. "These are the plans for our new church, Jim. Had Russell Stack draw them up. Best architect in the county—probably the state if you ask me. I told him I wanted a sanctuary that would seat at least three thousand, with a large stage to give you plenty of room to work the crowd and to fit however many singers, readers and assistant pastors you would need. And high tech. The most modern sound and video system available."

As he talked, he turned the pages of the plans again, pointing to what was apparently the rendering of the specific item he was talking about. The drawings still didn't mean much to Jim, and wouldn't have even if he were paying close attention to them. But he wasn't. His mind was still reeling from Leigh's first description. *A sanctuary big enough to seat three thousand!*

"And in a separate building," Leigh continued, "we'll have our community center. Here. See?" he said, pointing. "But not just *any* community center. It'll be big enough for our Sunday School, a counseling service, a lay ministry program, day care. It'll have a banquet hall that'll seat at least seven hundred fifty. We can rent it out to help cover our overhead. And . . . and get this . . . look here. A gymnasium! We'll have the best youth program, and best church basketball team, in all of South Florida!"

Leigh was silent for a moment, as if waiting for a reaction from Jim. He put his cigarette out in an ashtray and lit another.

"Well?" Leigh asked finally. "What do you think?"

Jim tried to measure his words carefully.

"Very impressive, Mr. Leigh. But . . . but it's kind of . . . big, isn't it?"

"Big?"

"I mean . . . three thousand people? We're only a couple hundred families. I know we're growing fast, but . . . "

"But nothing, son." Leigh's almost child-like enthusiasm gave way to the stern countenance of the powerful man he was. "I didn't get where I am today by thinking small. Don't you think I've planned this out?"

"Well . . . I guess . . ."

"Damn right I have." Leigh may have been a life-long Baptist, but he didn't hesitate to sprinkle his speech with cursing. "First step was getting a young, charismatic, ambitious minister—someone like you—to lead this church. Start growing it. Appeal to our youth and through them to their parents. That's your job. And you're doing it. Damn well, too. We've doubled our size in just six months. And most of that is because of you."

"Thank you, Mr. Leigh."

"Forget thank yous," Leigh said, waving his hand at Jim. "I'm not buttering you up. Besides, you're part of my plan, and I picked the talent. Next step—a great building. Or, more accurately, a great complex. A religious complex like no other. Not only for praying together. But for *playing* together, and learning together. And programs that will draw people from all over, and from other Christian churches—Protestant, Catholic, and Orthodox, all of them. Big? No, Jim. If anything, maybe not big enough. That's why I've had Russell design it so it can grow even larger if necessary. Now, can you dream that big Jim? Can you truly believe in such a vision?"

Leigh's enthusiasm was infectious. It was as if Leigh was the charismatic evangelist and Jim the lost soul waiting to be led to the Promised Land.

"Yes, Mr. Leigh," he answered. "Yes, I can."

"Good. Because that's the easy part. Let me show you the hard part."

Leigh nudged him to the left until he was standing in front of the site plan. Leigh put his finger on it.

"There," he showed Jim. "Right there. *That's* going to be where the battle is."

Jim looked closely. He could tell that the site of the new church complex was a large, triangular piece of property. At the base of the triangle was a road and on the other side of the road was the Intracoastal. His eyes moved to the point of the triangle where three roads converged. The road leading due west from the point was named on the plan—Clematis Street.

He understood what Leigh meant when he said this was where the battle would be. He intended to place his church on the choicest piece of property in downtown West Palm Beach—the large waterfront parcel at the end of the City's main street—the center of the downtown's dining and entertainment district. It was where the City's library had sat for a hundred years—a piece of property considered inviolate by most of the City's residents and most of its officials.

Jim believed in having vision but, to him, this seemed like pure fantasy.

"But, Mr. Leigh," he said, "how could you possibly hope to get the City to ever let you build *anything* there, much less a project so . . . so big, and so . . . so private?"

"What do you mean private?" Leigh shot back. "This will be a benefit to the entire community. It'll be *great* for downtown. Not only for its morals, but for business, too."

"Mr. Leigh," Jim countered, " I haven't been here nearly as long as you, but even I know that getting the City to move the library, and then transfer that land, and then allow development on it, well . . . well, I just can't see it happening."

"Why? Because it's waterfront? Because of the library? The library can be moved. In fact, my plan is to offer the City my property on Dixie Highway in trade. They can put a new, improved library there. One that's big enough to serve everyone and that doesn't leak every time it rains. And as far as its use as a church complex, there are churches all up and down Flagler Drive. There's the Baptist Church right up the street. Look right next to this building, the Christian Science church. There's the Greek Church down at the South bridge. Hell, there's even a synagogue just a few blocks north of here. There's plenty of precedent."

Jim turned and faced Leigh, who was still looking down at the plans on the conference table. "You know what I mean, Mr. Leigh," he said. "This is *the* prime piece of real estate in the City. And the City owns it. How could you ever get the City Commission to work a deal for it? It would be political suicide for them."

"Ah, my boy," Leigh said, turning to face him. "That's the fun part. Taking on a challenge that seems nigh on to impossible." He could see a gleam in Leigh's eyes saying the powerful lawyer really *was* looking forward to taking on this challenge.

"How are we going to do it, Jim?" Leigh asked rhetorically. "Persuasion. Simple persuasion." Leigh poked his finger into Jim's shoulder. "You and me are going to go talk to the mayor and commissioners. And we're simply going to persuade them."

"You and *me*?" Jim asked, with obvious trepidation. "But . . . but I don't know anything about . . . about lobbying."

"Lobbying? Who said anything about lobbying? I don't lobby. I educate, and persuade. And as the spiritual leader of the church, you need to be there by my side."

"What about the board?" Jim asked. "Has the board approved this plan?"

"The board approves whatever I tell it to approve. Surely you've figured that out by now."

"Well, yes."

"Of course you have. So, for now, put aside all of your misgivings about how we're going to get this done. What do you think of the plans?"

He couldn't deny that what Leigh envisioned was spectacular—a great edifice on a fantastic piece of property that would put their church in the very center of a booming metropolitan area. He began envisioning outdoor waterfront services and group baptisms in the Intracoastal—right outside their very own doors. The more he thought about it, even in these very few seconds after Leigh's question, the more excited he became. And, with some guilt, he realized that no small part of his excitement came from knowing that being the minister of such a church would elevate his stature beyond all of his peers in the area. It hadn't taken long for Richardson Leigh to land his first convert.

"I think the plans are great—no, *incredible*," he gushed.

"Good!" Leigh said with enthusiasm, slapping his hand on the table. "You've got to be a complete believer to help me make this happen, because as you've so aptly described"—he looked down at the plans and sighed softly—"this ain't going to be easy, no matter how much influence I think I've got in this town." He turned and looked at Jim. "Reverend Donovan, we've got a lot of hard persuading to do. Are you ready?"

"Yes, sir," Jim lied. "I'm ready." He was enthusiastic, but he was anything but ready to jump chin-deep into Richardson Leigh's power game. It was clear to him that he was about to be schooled in the art of bare-knuckle local politics. What wasn't clear was how he would feel when the battle was over—win or lose.

Chapter 23

I T WAS ONLY SIX OR seven blocks from Richardson Leigh's Phillips Point office building to City Hall. But Jim had learned early on that nobody in South Florida—at least no business person—walks six or seven blocks to a meeting.

He arrived at Leigh's office at five-thirty sharp. Right on time. Their meeting with the mayor was scheduled for six, in the mayor's office. An odd time and place, he thought. Leigh's normal manner of winning friends and influencing people was to wine and dine them at the Governor's Club or the Palm Beach Yacht Club. But, for some reason, Leigh wanted this meeting to be in an office, and after hours.

He was ushered into Leigh's office suite by Leigh's secretary, Mildred, a frumpy, middle-aged woman who was a crackerjack legal secretary and who had worked for her boss for over twenty years.

"Have a seat, Reverend Donovan," Mildred said in her typically pleasant manner. "Mr. Leigh will be with you in a moment."

Jim sat down on one of two very comfortable leather chairs in front of Leigh's oversized executive desk. He had been in the office several times before. But each time he entered it, he was newly impressed by the room's testaments to Leigh's power and influence—the exquisite furnishings, the plaques and awards for outstanding achievements and service to the community, and the photos of the influential attorney with various celebrities and politicians, including the last three presidents and four governors. Looking around the office, Jim could certainly understand Leigh's confidence that he could sway the mayor and enough of the city commissioners to get what he wanted.

He waited ten minutes before Leigh arrived.

"Hello, Jim," Leigh said as he spryly bounced into the office, his right hand already extended to take Jim's in his usual firm handshake.

Jim stood and let his hand be taken in Leigh's strong grip.

"Hello, Mr. Leigh."

Leigh stepped around his desk and sat in his high-backed executive chair. Jim followed suit. When he sat he noted, as he had before, how much lower he was in his chair than Leigh was in his. He was sure that Leigh's chair was set intentionally higher than the guest chairs—to place him in a more physically dominating position than whomever he may be speaking to. It was an old trick, and a still effective one.

"Well, Reverend Donovan," Leigh said with undisguised enthusiasm. "Are you ready to begin selling our grand Christian vision?"

He must really enjoy the political arena, Jim thought. For him, it was something he had never paid much attention to. And he wasn't particularly overjoyed at the prospect of getting involved in it now.

"As ready as I'll ever be, I guess," he said, obviously much less enthused than Leigh at the prospect of trying to convince the mayor and city commission to back a project that easily ninety percent of the city's residents would oppose.

It had been three months since Jim had been shown the grandiose plans for the new church. In that time, another sixty families had joined the church. There was no doubt that the Church of the Light of Christ was the fastest growing church in the county, probably the region. But, he still felt it was an incredible leap of faith to believe they could get this project approved.

"So, Jim," Leigh said, "let me tell you a little bit about our illustrious mayor, for background information."

"I've met Mayor Winslow," Jim answered. "On several occasions."

"Yes, I know you have. And I know that you know he's a lawyer; and that when he was elected last year he was the youngest person ever elected mayor of West Palm Beach." Leigh waived his hand dismissively. He reached into his shirt pocket and pulled out a pack of Marlboros. He took one out, put the pack back in his pocket and lit the cigarette before continuing. "That's just his bio. Let me tell you the *most* important thing to know about Terry Winslow."

Leigh drew deeply on the cigarette. He held the smoke in for several seconds and then began to blow smoke rings. Like his elevated chair, he would use pregnant pauses at key points in his conversations as a manner of control over those around him.

Jim felt awkward in the silence. He finally decided to break it.

"What is that?" he asked Leigh, who was still admiring the fruits of his creativity as the smoke rings drifted up and dissipated in turn.

The attorney smiled and leaned forward, as if he was ready to disclose a state secret.

"Terry Winslow wants to become the youngest governor ever elected. And *that's* our hook."

"I don't understand," Jim said.

"You will, Reverend. You will."

Leigh stood up. "I'd say it's about time to head over to City Hall," he said.

Jim looked at his watch. It was five fifty-five. By the time they got the car from valet, drove to City Hall, parked and made their way to the mayor's office, they would be at least ten minutes late. *Keeping the mayor waiting—just another of Leigh's control tactics,* he thought as he turned and followed his newly minted mentor in the art of politics out the door.

⊷━◦━⊷

City Hall was pretty much deserted when they got there. Usually by now the doors would have been locked, but the mayor had obviously made sure they would be open for his after-hours appointment. They entered the empty lobby of the drab, aging government building and took the elevator to the fifth floor. The doors opened on an empty waiting area bordered by empty work stations. Without hesitating, Leigh walked through the unoccupied outer rim of the building's top floor and entered the inner sanctum leading directly to the mayor's office. Jim followed.

The door to the mayor's office was open. As they entered, Jim saw the mayor sitting comfortably with his feet up on his desk talking on the phone. Without interrupting his conversation, Mayor Winslow motioned for them to take the seats located across from him. Before sitting, Leigh closed the door.

"Great Kim! Great!" the mayor spoke into the phone's mouthpiece exuberantly. "Bring this baby home and you'll be a hero! Got to go. Talk to you tomorrow."

The mayor hung up the phone, stood up and shook both men's hands.

"Richardson. Reverend Donovan. How good to see you," he said with the same enthusiasm and affectation Jim imagined was so successful for him on the campaign trail.

"You, too, Mayor," Leigh responded for both of them. "Sounds like something hot's happening."

"Yes, yes," Winslow said as he re-took his seat. "That was Kim Barker, Executive Director of the Downtown Development Authority. They think they're just about to close a deal with an outfit from Chicago that's interested in buying and redeveloping the old Burdine's Department Store building. I can't tell you right now what their plans are. But if it comes through, it'll be very exciting for the entire downtown."

"That's great," Leigh said.

Jim couldn't believe the perfect segue' the mayor had provided for the purpose they were there. Leigh immediately seized on it.

"In fact, Mayor, that's what Reverend Donovan and I are here to talk to you about. An exciting downtown development project."

"Sounds like an exciting day all around," Winslow said, beaming.

Jim was struck with just how young Winslow was to be the mayor of the largest city in the county. He was only thirty-one years old. Never having held office before, he had defeated the incumbent mayor on a platform of getting the city moving again. He had run a surprisingly tough campaign—his opponents called it dirty—and had taken firm control of City Hall almost immediately after he was sworn in. His appeal seemed to come from his ability to portray an almost naïve innocence combined with, at the same time, a tough and steely resolve.

Leigh picked up the plans he had placed on the floor next to his chair.

"Let me show you our plans," he said.

"Of course. Of course," the mayor said as he came around his desk and motioned his guests to a small conference table on the other side of the room.

Leigh spread the building plans out and went through the project— the large, state of the art sanctuary, the community center with banquet facilities, meeting rooms and gymnasium, the availability of the facilities not only for church programs, but for community activities as well. Every once in a while he would ask Jim to describe or explain some routine aspect of the project—to Jim's way of thinking just to get him involved so it didn't look like he was just there for decoration.

Winslow asked a few questions, but mostly just let the men make their presentation. He appeared throughout to be duly impressed, even mildly excited. Then, when Leigh finished showing him the building plans, he asked the key question.

"This is really a beautiful project, Richardson. Really great. Where are you going to put it?"

Leigh looked at Jim as if he was expecting something. At first, Jim didn't understand. Then he got it.

"The site plan's right here," he said, turning the plans to the page showing the buildings situated on the property and identifying the adjacent roads. Leigh's look had made it clear to him that the unspoken plan was for him to present the location issue to the mayor. It would be the man of religion, not the power broker who would invite the mayor to walk with them into the tiger's den.

He stepped back from the conference table as the mayor began to review the site plan. Neither Leigh nor Jim said anything as the mayor pored over it.

Then, finally, it hit Winslow.

"This . . . this is . . . shit, Richardson! This is the library site!"

"Yes. Yes it is," Leigh said.

"You can't be serious," Winslow said.

"Dead serious," Leigh responded. "Can you think of a better, more beautiful site?"

"Hell yes!" the mayor exclaimed. "*Anywhere* but *there*! I'd be crucified if I proposed, or even supported, a church on that site. And you *know* it."

"What I *know* is that putting a church and community center of this caliber on that site will not only make this one of the finest religious edifices in the country, it'll put West Palm Beach on the map."

Jim was just a bystander now, watching and learning how the game of power politics is played.

"Be serious, Richardson. Even if I could support this, I don't make the zoning decisions. The city commission does. And they'll never go for this. Besides, this is city-owned land. That means we'd have to sell it to you. There's no way, Richardson. No way."

"I'm not naïve, Terry." Jim noted that Leigh had now gone from addressing the mayor formally to calling him by his first name.

"I know it'll be tough. And I know you don't have a vote. But you're the *mayor*. The leader of the city. What you say carries a great deal of weight."

Leigh and Winslow were standing toe to toe in front of the conference table. Leigh was about three inches taller than the mayor and he was using every inch of that difference to his fullest advantage in trying to make Winslow bend to his will.

"You know, Terry," he continued, "this could just be the test of leadership that sets the stage for bigger and better things for you."

"What do you mean?" Winslow asked.

Leigh turned his back on the mayor and stepped a few paces away. Then he turned and faced him again.

"Look, Terry. You and I both know where you want to be in three years."

"I plan on being mayor for . . ."

"Don't give me that shit," Leigh interrupted. "You have your eye on the governor's mansion—and soon. It's your time. You're riding high and you don't know what the future will bring. *Carpe diem* and all that crap."

"Even if that's true," Winslow said, "pushing something like this could kill whatever hopes I have."

"Nonsense! In a statewide race the fact that you may piss off a few folks in West Palm Beach means nothing. Only one thing means *everything*. Money."

Leigh paused to let that comment sink in. Jim had been almost enjoying the show from his ringside seat. But now, the mention of money in a conversation trying to obtain the mayor's support made him nervous.

The word "money" also caught Winslow's attention. "What are you saying?" he asked Leigh.

"I'm saying that for you to get elected governor, you're going to need a lot of money. And it's people like me who raise that money. And what we look for in deciding who to raise money for is who has leadership abilities, and who can win."

"You mean you look for people who will lead in the direction *you* want them to go," Winslow retorted.

"Of course! Do you think I'm going to go out there and raise hundreds of thousands of dollars for someone whose beliefs are different than mine? Someone who supports things I don't want?"

Winslow walked back to his desk and sat down—slumped down actually.

"And for you to raise money like that for me, I need to support this project," he said, more than asked.

"Not only for me to raise money *for* you," Leigh answered, "but for me *not* to raise money *against* you."

There it was, Jim thought. A blatant *quid pro quo*. Winslow's support for Leigh's money. He knew there must be something unethical about this. Probably illegal, too. But there he was. Right in the middle of it. A part of it, even. One side of him hoped Winslow would reject Leigh's heavy-handed proposition. But another side hoped Winslow would go for it. He had bought into Leigh's vision of a grand waterfront church that could help him bring the Word of God to so many more people in such a brilliant and convincing way. If this is what it took to get it done, maybe that's just how politics had to be played to make good things happen. Besides, what was going on in that office that very minute was creating within him an adrenalin rush like nothing he had felt before, at least outside sex.

"How much could you raise?" Winslow asked.

"At least two hundred fifty thousand," Leigh answered. "And there are others around the state I can get who can do just as much."

"And all I have to do is support this?"

"Not just support it," Leigh said. "I need you out front on it. Pushing it. Using the bully pulpit and persuading people this is a good thing."

The mayor looked out the window. He had the look of a man with a great deal on his mind.

"And what if I do that and I work against something else that's important to you? Are you going to threaten to pull your support?"

"No. You do this for me, you've got a free ride on anything else as far as I'm concerned," Leigh said as he stood in front of the mayor's desk looking down at him. "This is the most important thing to me. If you support this, you've got my word I'll give you one hundred percent support in the governor's race."

Winslow and Leigh had appeared to forget that Jim was in the room with them. Now, Winslow turned and looked at him.

"And what about you, Reverend?" the mayor asked. "Are you going to be able to keep this conversation quiet?"

Jim knew what he was asking, and why. The mayor was concerned that Jim's conscience might get in the way of this secret, illegal political deal or, worse yet, might expose it. Jim knew that Winslow was specifically asking him if he was a willing party to this conspiracy.

He remained conflicted, but he knew that unless he gave the right answer, Richardson Leigh's vision would go up in smoke. And right with it would go Jim's position, if not his career.

"What's between us stays between us," he said to the mayor.

"Render unto Caesar what is Caesar's, eh Reverend?" Winslow responded. He then turned and looked at Leigh. He stood up and extended his hand. Leigh took it in a firm handshake.

"Okay, Richardson," Winslow said. "You've got a deal. I'll do my best to get you your church on the waterfront."

Leigh broke out into a broad smile. "Thank you . . . Governor," he said.

As Leigh and Winslow sealed their deal, Jim couldn't help but feel that he had just taken the first step into uncharted waters which would either raise him to a level of glory he could never have imagined, or plunge him into the depths of despair and destruction. His mind was taken back to his first encounter with Renee, when they debated the meaning of Bosch's *The Garden of Delights*. Like the painting, to him there were two starkly contrasting interpretations of what he had just observed-—and participated in—in the mayor's office. One was good, the other bad. He prayed that he had chosen the right one.

Chapter 24

RENEE REACHED UP AND TURNED off the lamp on the bedside table. She turned and laid on her left side, her body pressed snugly against Jim's, whose back was turned to her. She softly laid her right arm over his side and across his stomach.

"You were very quiet at the party tonight," she said. "You've hardly said two words since you got home from work." She pressed her hand against his stomach in a loving hug. "Is something bothering you?"

"It's nothing," he said.

She removed her hand from his stomach and began stroking his hair.

"Come on, Jim. Something's bothering you. You'll feel better if you talk about it."

Jim didn't think it would help, but he did want to talk about it. Maybe by doing so, he thought, he could get some moral clarity. Renee was never in doubt about what was and wasn't moral. Yet he knew he couldn't disclose to her the details of his and Leigh's meeting with the mayor earlier that day.

He turned over onto his right side facing her, his left hand softly coming to rest on her hip.

"Richardson and I finally went and talked to the mayor today about the new church." The only time he referred to Leigh by his first name was when he was talking to Renee.

"It didn't go well?" she said as she lovingly stroked his cheek.

"At first, no. He said just what I thought he'd say—basically, that we're nuts."

"At first? You mean he changed his mind?" she asked.

"He said that he would support us. Even as to the location."

"That's great, honey! With Terry Winslow's support that'll give you a better chance at getting the Commission's support. So, what's the problem?"

While Jim could only see Renee's silhouette in the darkness of their room, he could picture her furrowed brow questioning why such good news should be causing him such apparent distress.

"To get Winslow's support, Richardson made . . . a deal," he said.

"A deal? What kind of deal?"

"A political deal."

Renee stopped stroking his cheek.

"What *kind* of political deal?"

"I . . . I can't go into the details . . . "

"Jim, are you telling me Richardson *bought* Winslow's support?"

"Well, not exactly."

"There's no such thing as 'not exactly,'" she said. "He either did or didn't."

Jim didn't answer. He didn't know what to say. Though Renee had never raised her voice, he felt like he was being scolded by his mother for not knowing better.

"Where were *you* when all of this was going on?" she asked.

"With them. There, in the room. I didn't really say anything."

"Jim, baby,"—she started stroking his cheek again—"you can't let yourself become a part of Richardson's politics. You're a minister. Maybe he can afford to take the risk of getting caught up in political hardball or scandal. You can't. Besides, you wouldn't be acting the way you have tonight if something inside you wasn't telling you that it was wrong."

She had hit the nail on the head. Something inside, or more accurately, some*one*, had been telling him that his participation in the meeting with Leigh and the mayor was wrong. Father McTighe—in full throaty force—had started preaching to him the moment they had left Winslow's office. Worse yet, through all the chatter in his head, Jim could also feel the disapproving presence of Dr. Westin. This was most troublesome to him. Both the spiritual guide of his youth and his adult mentor seemed to be speaking to him on this. And now they appeared to be doing it through Renee.

"But Renee, this church . . . this church could mean so much—to our ministry, to the city, and . . . and yes, to us, too. And to do great things, sometimes you *have* to play the political game. I'm a minister. I preach the Word of God, and I promote our church. That's my calling. And those are my talents, what I have to give.

"Richardson . . . well, Richardson has the money and the influence. And he knows how to use them to get things done, including good things like this church. Those are *his* talents. And maybe his calling. How can I say that his use of those talents to do God's work is wrong?"

Even as he talked, he sensed he was trying to convince himself as much as Renee.

Renee lifted herself up on her left elbow and looked down in the direction of Jim's head.

"Jim," she said her voice firmer and even stern now. "It's *wrong*. It's just wrong, and I don't think you should be a part of it. That's all there is to it."

He didn't respond, and Renee said no more. To her, everything was clear—black and white, good and bad, right and wrong. He envied that, caught as he so often was in a world of gray, a world of uncertain choices.

He closed his eyes. He knew she was right. He just had to find a way to make Richardson Leigh's dream—which had become his dream—come true, without letting himself become too big a part of Leigh's manner of making it come true.

><del>-+-+>-0-<>-+-+<</del>

Jim looked out the window of the smoke-filled car as it moved south on Flagler Drive through the south end of the city. The homes were exquisite and well-manicured. They were neither as big nor as expensive as the mansions on Palm Beach. But while so many who lived in Palm Beach had concluded their immensely successful careers or had inherited great fortunes, the well-off of West Palm Beach, many of whom lived in this part of the city, tended to be the successful and still working lawyers, businessmen, doctors and professionals who made up the city's elite—and its powerbrokers.

"Are you ready?" Richardson Leigh said as he controlled the steering wheel while cruising a good ten miles per hour over the posted speed limit of thirty.

"Uh . . . yeah," Jim said. He turned and looked at Leigh. "Why has it taken two months since our meeting with the mayor to set up another one?"

"Had to lay the groundwork, Reverend. You don't just go in to elected officials and say 'this is what I want you to do' and expect them to say 'okay' just because of who you are. Had to do my due diligence."

"Weren't you concerned word would get out, once you talked to Winslow?"

"No. Not at all. The only people who know about our plans so far are those who drew them up—and they won't *dare* say anything—you, and Winslow. And I feel pretty secure about Winslow."

Leigh slowed the car down to the speed limit and nodded up ahead. Jim looked closely and could see a motorcycle traffic cop almost hidden by a royal palm pointing his radar gun in their direction. *Richardson doesn't miss a thing,* he thought.

"Why Commissioner Leyton next?" Jim asked.

"Because I need one more vote and he's the most likely," Leigh said, shifting his gaze from the road to Jim and back.

"But I thought you hadn't talked to anyone else yet?" Jim asked, confused.

"I haven't. But I put Matter and Krajeck in their seats. When push comes to shove, they owe me. I'll get their votes."

Leigh turned right on a street called Santa Lucia. It was a pleasant neighborhood of modest, old style Florida homes; worth much more than one would think by their size due to their proximity to Flagler Drive and the Intracoastal. He turned right into a driveway a few houses down the street and turned off the motor. Jim started to open his door.

"No," Leigh said. "You wait here. I'll call you in, if I need you."

Jim didn't understand but he did as he was told and closed the door to wait in the car until called.

"Sure, Mr. Leigh. Whatever you say."

Leigh opened his door. Before getting out, he reached in the back and retrieved a bulky envelope from the back seat. As he started to get out, Jim noticed that he hadn't grabbed the plans which were also on the back seat.

"Mr. Leigh," he said. "The plans."

"I'll call you if I need you," Leigh replied. He closed the door without retrieving the plans, walked up to the front door and rang the bell. Within seconds, Commissioner Andy Leyton opened the door and invited Leigh in.

Jim sat in the silent car. The neighborhood around him was equally still and quiet. He wished he had asked Leigh to keep the keys in the ignition so he could listen to the radio while he waited. As it turned out, it didn't really matter. It was less than five minutes before the front door opened. He saw Leigh and Leyton shake hands and bid farewell. Leigh returned to the car, got into the driver's seat, closed his door and placed the key in the ignition. He didn't have the envelope that he had taken into the house with him.

"Is that it?" Jim said, bewildered.

"That's it," Leigh said, smiling and obviously satisfied.

"And?"

"And he'll support us."

"But . . . but how—you were only there five . . ."

"We came to an understanding." Leigh started the car, looked at Jim and began to pull out of the driveway.

Jim didn't need Father McTighe, Dr. Westin or even Renee to tell him what had just happened. Leigh had given Leyton a bribe to get his vote. That's why he didn't need to take the plans in. And that's why it took another two months to set the meeting up—so Leigh could find out if Leyton was bribable, and how much it would take. He realized that he had been brought along for cover. By saying that he and Reverend Donovan had gone to see the Commissioner, the idea was to remove any suspicion. He knew he had been used. And he was angry. The only thing he could say for Leigh was that he kept Jim away from the actual act of bribery. But that was little consolation. In every other way, Leigh all but had him count the money.

Renee was right. Getting involved in Leigh's "business dealings" could only bring him down eventually. This was the last time—the last time he would participate with Richardson Leigh in anything that wasn't directly related to his role of ministering to the people. Even if it meant his job.

☙

Jim was still fuming when he got home that night. He wasn't about to tell Renee what happened. He didn't need the lecture that it would be sure to bring. He knew that what he did need to do was begin preparing himself— and Renee, but without her knowing it—for a move to a new position somewhere where he could practice his ministry without feeling so dirty. Even if it meant making a lot less money, which it invariably would.

When he walked into the house he noticed that all the lights were out except for a dim, flickering light coming from the dining room on the other side of the living room from the front door foyer.

"Renee?" he called out as he closed the door behind him.

"In the dining room, honey," she responded.

He walked through the living room and turned to his right at the entryway to the dining room. He stopped. His eyes were first directed to two lit candles on the dining room table, each set in formal silver candleholders which they had received as wedding gifts—from whom he didn't remember anymore.

There were two full place settings of their finest china and silverware, one at his end of the table and the other at the left side of the table directly next to his. And seated at the table was Renee, pouring wine into two silver goblets—their wedding goblets.

The setting was surprising enough for him. What was particularly stunning, though, was Renee. She was dressed in a beautiful black dress with a plunging neckline that left little to the imagination. He had never seen it before, so it must be new he thought. The dress was perfectly accompanied by a pearl necklace and matching pearl earrings. Renee was beautiful. *No,* he thought, *she's drop dead gorgeous!*

"Hello, sweetheart," she said, holding up a glass to him. "Wine?"

He was speechless. He was still trying to process what was going on. Her love for him was total, but creating this type of romance was not something he would expect from her.

"Well, are you going to join me in the magnificent dinner I've prepared?" she asked saucily. "Or do you just want to take me to McDonald's?"

Jim snapped out of his trance.

"Yes . . . yes, of course," he stammered as he sat down. Renee handed him his glass of wine.

"What . . . what is . . . "

"To us," she interrupted him, raising her glass in a toast.

"To us," Jim said, not knowing what they were drinking to. He raised the glass to his lips, as Renee did the same, and sipped the rich red wine. He was not a wine connoisseur, but he knew by the taste that this was a very fine wine.

"Do you mind having a glass or two of wine before I bring out the stuffed flounder?" she said. There was almost a sultriness in her voice and expressions. It was something Jim had never really seen from her before.

And there was obviously an ulterior motive. Candlelight, sexy dress, fine wine, and his favorite dish. Yes, she was up to something all right. Whatever it was, he decided he liked her strategy. He decided he might as well go with the flow.

"No," he said. "Wine is . . . wine is fine."

"Good." She took another sip from her glass. He followed suit.

"So, how was your day?" She asked the one question that could kill the mood. He was determined not to let it happen.

"Great! A perfect day," he lied. "How about yours?" Not only was his question designed to change the subject, but he hoped it would lead to a clue as to what might be behind Renee's sudden transformation from straight-laced, moralistic—almost prissy—minister's wife, to sexy, almost vamp-like, temptress.

"It was great, too," she said. She placed her empty glass down and poured more wine into it. "I had a doctor's appointment today."

"A doctor's appointment? Why? Are you okay? What's wrong?"

She took another sip of wine.

"Nothing's wrong. They just needed to run some tests. But everything came out okay. I just can't drink any more wine after today."

"Why not?" Jim asked. He had put his wine glass down. He was no longer interested in the fine wine, the candle lights or stuffed flounder. Renee was being evasive about a health issue and his concern overrode everything. It also seemed incongruous to be hearing about medical tests in such a purposely-created romantic setting. "If you can't drink anymore, there must be something wrong!"

For a moment Renee was silent. She just looked at him, fingering the lip of her wine glass and smiling. She put the glass down and folded her hands on the table.

"Nothing wrong, honey," she said. "Just . . . different."

"Different? Different how?"

Then it hit him like a bolt of lightning. How could he have been so blind, he thought.

"You're not . . . Are you . . . are you . . . You can't be . . ."

"Yes, I can."

"You're . . . you're . . ." He couldn't get the word out.

"Yes, I'm pregnant," Renee said, her face flushed with the joy of a first time expectant mother.

"We're going to have a baby?" Jim beamed at the thought of it.

She nodded quickly, smiling. He stood up, grabbed her out of her chair, lifted her in the air and twirled her around. Then he thought better of it. He put her down and apologized. "I'm sorry, honey. That was stupid. I could hurt the baby."

"Don't worry," she said, reassuring him. "I'm only six weeks. I'm not at the fragile point yet."

Jim was elated. He was going to be a father. For the moment, every problem, at work and at home, seemed very, very far away.

They had a beautiful, romantic dinner. Afterwards, Renee having convinced him it wouldn't harm the baby, they rendezvoused in their bedroom for one of the most passionate lovemaking sessions they had ever had together. When it was over, and Renee had softly fallen asleep, Jim lay in bed, exhausted and spent, thinking about the events of that day. At one point, it had seemed to be one of the worst days of his life—at least his adult life. Then, just like that, it turned into one of the best. As he thought more about it he realized these two major events converged in a way that placed him in a very difficult position. He so wanted to be able to walk away from Richardson Leigh and his questionable machinations. But he was going to be a father now. And that meant family obligations. Money. Position. All of a sudden, these were more important—things that couldn't just be tossed aside or ignored. He had to think of his child now. He would have to find a way, he decided, to come to terms with what was expected of him. And to come to terms with Richardson Leigh.

Chapter 25

J IM SAT AT HIS DESK. It was Monday evening. The day before he had given the sermon which marked his first anniversary as pastor of the Church of the Light of Christ. Now it was time to begin work on his sermon for next Sunday's services. Renee was upset that he would be late for dinner. But Richardson Leigh had called late that afternoon and asked to meet with him in his office at seven o'clock. And saying no to Richardson was not something easily done, at least not by Jim.

At precisely seven, the door to his office opened. Richardson Leigh walked in guiding his reluctant seventeen-year-old daughter, Melanie, by the arm. Jim had never met the girl, but he had seen pictures of her. The many times he had been to Leigh's home he had seen family photos of her throughout the house, from birth until maybe thirteen. When he asked about her, Leigh and his wife, Gayla, both explained that their daughter attended a very exclusive private school in New England. Then they would change the subject.

Leigh and his daughter sat in the two chairs facing Jim's desk, neither of them saying so much as hello. Jim was surprised to see Melanie. Leigh had indicated that he wanted to speak with him but had made no mention of bringing his daughter.

"Good evening, Mr. Leigh," Jim said, trying to melt even slightly the obvious chill that existed between parent and child. "And you must be Melanie. It's a pleasure to finally meet you."

She said nothing. She kept her eyes fixed on him as if to ignore the presence of her father.

"What can I do for you?" Jim said.

At this invitation, Leigh finally spoke up. "Reverend, I'd like you to have a talk with Melanie. She's been acting . . . well, kind of strange lately. And she has me and her mother worried about her."

"Acting strange? How?"

"Well, for one thing, she absolutely defies us. Won't do anything we tell her to do. Always argues with us, using foul and profane language." Leigh spoke with a mixture of anger and parental worry. Jim wondered when all of this strange behavior was supposed to have occurred if she had been away at school for the past year.

"Mr. Leigh, with all due respect, that may be disrespectful and inappropriate, but it's not exactly strange for a seventeen-year-old in this day and age."

Melanie looked at him and smiled.

"That's not all," Leigh said.

Melanie looked at her father. "Daddy, why don't you quit fucking around and tell the pastor what you're *really* upset about."

Leigh turned towards his daughter and raised his hand in anger. "Watch your mouth or I'll smack that filth right out of it!" he yelled threateningly at his cocky teenager.

"Please, please," Jim pleaded. "Let's just settle down and tell me why you're here."

Leigh pulled a pack of Marlboros from his shirt pocket, took a cigarette out and lit it knowing full well that Jim did not allow smoking in his office.

"She's in some kind of cult, some kind of devil worshipping cult," he said, scornfully. "We found her and a bunch of her strange friends late last night on the beach, just up a bit from our home."

Jim knew where he was talking about. Leigh's home was on the west side of State Road A1A, the beach road that runs the length of the State. His back yard fronted on the Intracoastal Waterway. Across A1A from Leigh's home was the beach portion of his property on the Atlantic Ocean. The dune was covered with sea oats, sea grapes and typical Florida native dune vegetation. It was very thick, but there was a narrow path cut through the vegetation that went down to the beach from the top of the dune.

"They were dancing around a bonfire and chanting stuff, stuff we couldn't make out," Leigh continued. "They had crosses in the sand, upside down, and they were burning them. They were all dressed in black, except one guy. He seemed to be the leader. He was dressed in a robe and hood, like the Klan, but all red. He, he . . ."

"Okay. Okay. Settle down, Mr. Leigh." Jim tried to calm his increasingly agitated benefactor. He noticed that Leigh hadn't smoked any of the cigarette since he lit it. Half the cigarette was now burnt ash. He cringed as Leigh flicked the ashes on the carpet. "What did you do?" he asked as Leigh finally took a drag on his smoke.

"I went up to the circle where they were dancing," Leigh said. "I grabbed Melanie by the arm and pulled her away. I told her she was going home right away."

"Then what?"

"Then what? She said no, she was going to stay. She called out to the rest of them for help. When they started to close in on me I could see many of them were older. So I told them Melanie was only seventeen"—he slammed his left fist on the desk—"and if they tried anything to keep me from taking her home I'd have them arrested!" The cigarette had burned down to the filter and Leigh looked around for someplace to put it out. Hoping to save the office carpet, Jim slid his half-full coffee mug towards Leigh. Leigh dropped the butt in the cup. Jim cringed again at the attorney's disgusting habit and listened as he went on with his story.

"They backed off. I dragged Melanie home. She was kicking and screaming the whole way. As we left, they all began to chant, over and over: 'From our eye, you will die. From our eye, you will die.' And then Melanie began to chant it, looking at me like she really wanted me to die."

Leigh looked at his daughter. She sat expressionless, her gaze fixed on Jim.

"Jim, Gayla and I are worried about Melanie. We love her dearly, but something's terribly wrong. We'd like you to talk to her, counsel her. Help her get these fiendish thoughts and beliefs, whatever they are, out of her head."

"What about her school?" Jim asked. "They must have a good counseling program at a school like that."

Leigh looked down at his lap. He raised his head and looked at Jim.

"Melanie . . . well, she hasn't been at a prep school in New England. She's . . ." He paused. It was clear to Jim that this was very difficult for a man as powerful and proud as Richardson Leigh. "She's been in Ocala. Staying with my brother. We just couldn't handle her anymore. So we sent her up there to stay with Randall. Randall raises horses and we thought a change of environment and . . . and maybe working with the horses would help . . . help settle her down. Give her some kind of purpose."

"And?" Jim said.

"Didn't help. Randall called two weeks ago. Said we had to go get her. He just couldn't do it anymore."

Jim noticed that Melanie's eyes remained fixed on him. "Have you considered taking her to see a psychologist or psychiatrist?" he said.

"Jim, this isn't mental illness," Leigh protested. "She's just gotten caught up with the wrong crowd and they've put notions in her head. Talk to her. She might listen to you. You can make her understand the danger she's putting herself in and the pain she's causing her mother and me."

Melanie turned and looked at her father with an angry scowl on her face. "Quit talking like I ain't even here!" she shot out at him.

"When did you want me to start?" Jim asked, quickly stepping in to prevent an escalation of the antagonism between father and daughter.

"Right now," Leigh said. "I'll leave and you can start right now. I'll come back . . . when? An hour? Hour and a half?"

Jim didn't know what he could do on such short notice, without enough background on the young girl or time to prepare. Even with time and preparation he wasn't sure he was equipped to handle a situation like this. But Leigh was obviously desperate and needed someone to try something, anything.

"Why don't I just call you when we're done," Jim said.

With that, Richardson Leigh, West Palm Beach's penultimate powerbroker, mover and shaker, left his daughter, over whom he appeared to have lost all control, in the hands of his handpicked spiritual leader and the full breadth of that leader's two years of ministerial experience. *Lord help me on this one,* Jim thought as he watched the anguished father walk out the office door and close it behind him.

"Why don't we move over here," Jim said. He got up and motioned towards a couch and a leather easy chair on the other side of the room. Melanie rose and ambled over to the couch. As she did, he noticed for the first time how provocatively she was dressed. Before, as was usually the case when Richardson Leigh was in a room, attention was mostly centered on him.

But now Jim's attention was focused on the young teenager. She wore a white halter-top with no bra allowing the nipples on her fully developed breasts to protrude noticeably. Her midriff was fully exposed revealing what appeared to be an onyx stone implanted in her navel. Her black denim skirt was extremely short showcasing long, elegant legs ending at sandals which gently wrapped around petite ankles and feet which seemed incongruously childlike anchoring, as they did, an otherwise fully developed woman's body on a seventeen-year-old child. Her dishwater blonde hair was cropped short and her fingernails and toenails were polished black. The only jewelry she wore, aside from the onyx navel stone, was a large ring on her left hand consisting of a silver band and another black onyx stone. *How,* Jim wondered, *can the daughter of such a powerful and righteous—well, at least publicly righteous—man get away with dressing like a vixenish tart?*

Melanie turned and sat on the couch. She expertly crossed her legs in a well-bred, non-revealing manner that was no small trick given the minimal amount of fabric she had to work with. Jim sat in the easy chair that faced the couch and rested about five feet away. It would be a struggle, he knew, to keep his eyes focused on her eyes and not on her body.

"You've obviously got your parents worried," he said, stating the obvious because he wasn't quite sure how or where to begin.

She shrugged her shoulders. "They worry about everything," she said matter-of-factly.

"Do you think your father's concerns about the incident he described are unwarranted?"

"He has no right to tell me who I can hang out with," she answered in a mildly defiant, yet still respectful tone.

"Well, actually Melanie, he does. You're seventeen and he's your father, and he *does* have the right to tell you what you can and can't do."

She didn't answer. He sensed that his defense of her father on legalistic grounds was a mistake. He shifted his focus.

"Tell me something about this group you were with last night."

Melanie's head was down. She was looking at her hands on her lap as she played with the black ring on her finger. She lifted her eyes to look at him without lifting her head. "What do you want to know?" she asked.

"Your father feels it's some kind of cult. Is it?"

"What do you mean by cult?" she responded coyly.

"Good question," he admitted. "Instead of us characterizing it, why don't you just tell me something about these people and what you all were doing last night down on the beach."

She hesitated, as if trying to decide how much to tell him. Then she spoke. "They're friends. Friends who share common interests, common beliefs."

"Interests and beliefs in what?"

"In honesty, brutal honesty. And loyalty. Things people like my father could never understand."

"You don't feel your father is honest or loyal?"

"Are you kidding?" she said, the scorn freely oozing from her pores. "How do you think he got so powerful and rich? By being honest and loyal? He did it by screwing people, by walking all over those who got in his way. My father demands loyalty to him, but he'd stab his best friend in the back to get what he wants."

"That's not my experience of him," Jim said. While in truth his recent experience of Melanie's father was similar to hers, he felt it was not appropriate and figured it would do no good to join her in her trashing of Richardson Leigh. "Your father is a very dedicated, religious man. He worships regularly. He gives money and time to good causes. He founded this entire church."

"Hah! He's sucked you in too, Reverend." She was starting to get animated now. "My father is a hypocrite. He puts on a good face. The *honorable, distinguished, devout* Richardson Leigh." She sneered as she venomously spewed out the adjectives describing her father. "That's how the community sees him, how he wants the world to see him. It's all an act, a lie! Don't you see? He's a power hungry manipulator. And he's a bigot. He hates niggers and money hungry Jews and spics!" She was yelling now. "And he uses this church and its so-called God to cover it all up!"

She had hit a nerve. "So-called God?" Jim repeated. "You don't believe in God?"

"We believe in the True One," she said. Her anger had immediately given way to a new-found mellowness.

"And who is this True One?"

"Let me ask *you* a question, Reverend. Have you ever heard God?"

"Of course. I've heard Him many times. That's why I became a minister."

"I don't mean that inner voice people are always talking about. I mean actually heard him—heard his *actual* voice."

"That's not how God works," Jim said. He knew when he said it that that was precisely the response she would have expected.

"And *that's* dishonest!" she exclaimed. "If God really exists, and if he truly *talked* to Moses, and Abraham, and Jesus, why doesn't he talk to me, or at least someone like you? What's his game?"

"His game as you call it, is faith. He judges us on our faith. Faith depends on what is in our heart, not what we can see, hear or touch."

"I know the company line, Reverend. It's been force-fed to me since I was a baby, by Daddy and Mommy Hypocrite. And I believed it, too. Until I heard the True One."

"And who is the True One, Melanie."

Jim knew that he was getting to the crux of her issues. He also had begun to realize that despite her young age, she was bright and quick-witted. It would take more than ministerial technique to reach this troubled teenager.

"The one who tells the brutal truth," she said. "The one who doesn't play games, or ask for blind faith. The one who speaks so you can hear him." Her tone was reverential, and her eyes had a faraway look in them.

"And what is the brutal truth?"

Melanie looked at him and grinned. She kicked off her sandals. She placed both hands on the couch and pushed her butt slightly up from the cushion. She lifted her feet from the ground and folded her legs under her, crossed Indian style. She showed no self-consciousness about the fact that she was fully exposing her private area to the minister opposite her. Jim unavoidably noted her red-panties and immediately diverted his eyes upward to her face. She had caught him looking. Despite his full authority and obligation to tell her to sit like a lady, he said nothing.

She placed her elbows on her knees, cupped her chin in her hands and leaned forward. "The brutal truth," she said, "is that your God game is a fake. It's phony. This whole thing about suffering in *this* life to get to a better life is crap. *This* life *is* the better life. Everything we need to create paradise exists *here* and *now*. And we're supposed to use it and enjoy it. The sin ain't in enjoying the great things that are available to us. The sin's in *not* enjoying them. They're gifts. To ignore them is just . . . just rude!"

Jim was reminded again, as he had been during his meeting with Leigh and Mayor Winslow, of his first encounter with Renee when they debated the meaning of *The Garden of Delights*. Why, he wondered had his encounters with the Leigh family continuously raised that image? Of immediate concern was that Melanie's beliefs appeared to be his long-ago arguments taken to their absurd conclusion. He now understood why Renee was initially so wary of him.

"And what if you're wrong, Melanie? What if this so-called True One is the one feeding the crap? What if he's just holding out to you those temptations God has spoken to us and warned us of—the temptations that test our faith? What if God *is* real and you fail his test of faith? Have you considered that?"

"Sure Rev. I've considered it. But he's not. And if he is, then at some point some real holy man, like you, will be able to make me see it. Right? God reveals himself in one way or another to all of us. Ain't that what you preach? And if he's real, and if he reveals himself to me, then all I've got to do is ask for forgiveness, and mean it. Right? And I'll tell you Rev, if he really reveals himself to me, I'll be the first to ask for forgiveness. And real sincere, too."

"Is that what the cult has taught you?"

"I thought you weren't going to characterize it?"

"Listening to what you claim to believe, I think cult is the right characterization."

He now realized that he wasn't simply dealing with a rebellious teenager who needed guidance and counseling. He was dealing with something far more dangerous, a force, something evil. And if he was going to save Melanie from it, he didn't have much time.

"Melanie," he said, "this isn't some sort of game. What's at stake ultimately is your soul. And you don't just get to thumb your nose at God and then someday say, 'Oops, made a mistake. Sorry God. Forgive me,' and have it all be okay. It's not that simple. There can come a time when your soul has been so corrupted that it can't be redeemed. No matter what."

"And when is that, Reverend?"

"What do you mean?"

"When have you so corrupted your soul that it can't be redeemed? How do you know when that time is?"

"You certainly know when you die—when you face God's judgment."

"Aha! Another one of God's great mysteries!" she exclaimed mockingly. "Tell me Reverend, have you ever given in to your temptations?"

"Of course I have. We're all sinners and we've all been weak."

"More than once?"

She had now turned into the interrogator and he was beginning to feel uncomfortable. And he knew that she knew it.

"Of course," he said.

"And have *you* reached that point of no return?"

"I hope not. I don't believe so. I've sinned, but I have faith in God and in His mercy."

"But what if your sins keep getting worse?"

She was pursuing him now, like a hunter closing in on her prey. He was on the defensive and knew he had to get control of the direction of the conversation. But, for reasons he didn't understand, he didn't know how.

"What do you mean?" he lamely asked.

"What if your sins keep getting worse? Does that make it harder to obtain God's forgiveness?"

"Obtaining God's forgiveness doesn't depend on the degree of sins," he said. "It depends . . ."

"So the fact that I'm seventeen and you've been sitting there looking at my titties and my pussy and wanting to fuck me won't make it any harder for you to get into heaven now than it was fifteen minutes ago?"

She had him where she wanted him and she wasn't going to let him go now. Flushed and embarrassed all he could come up with was, "I think we can do without that kind of talk. And sit right."

Ignoring his direction, Melanie continued. "Don't you see, Reverend? Look how uncomfortable and guilty you feel now. Just because looking at me turns you on. Why does it get you excited? Because our creator, whoever that is, made us that way. And made sex feel good. And we have this whole religion crap built around telling us if it feels good, it must be bad. And that it's our creator who made that rule. That's bullshit! And that's what the True One has come to tell us. That the *true* plan is that we enjoy the gifts our creator has given us—all of them, and to the fullest extent possible."

She sounded like no seventeen-year-old Jim had ever known. He was feeling despondent, because of the convoluted belief system she was expressing as well as his inability thus far to counter it.

"So," he said, trying to regain control, "the True One has told you its okay to give in to temptation, do anything you want to do, and you and your friends believe that?"

"You call it giving in to temptation. We recognize it as experiencing all life has to give. The rules preventing that don't further God's will, they frustrate it."

"Melanie, that's a twisted logic."

"Is it, Reverend Donovan? Then let me ask you this."

Melanie stood up facing him. She crossed her hands at the bottom of her halter-top and pulled it over her head revealing her youthfully firm, fully matured breasts. On the inner side of her left breast, just below the nipple, was a strange tattoo—a black circle with a snake's head in the center, mouth open and fangs bared, ready to strike. There was a glimmer of recognition in his mind, as if he'd seen it before. As he tried to remember, he realized that he was staring, staring at the seventeen-year-old girl's naked breast.

"Melanie, put your . . ."

She abruptly interrupted him. "Wait! Let me finish! Right now you're feeling upset and scared, and angry, because you feel this is wrong, it's against the rules. *I* feel free, and happy, and excited."

He hadn't noticed as she spoke that her right hand had slipped behind her skirt and unzipped it. It fell to her feet revealing red bikini panties. Before he could even mouth his protest they had also come off.

Every cell in his brain screamed for him to stop her immediately. But neither his body nor his lips would move. He was paralyzed by the beauty of her near perfect body. She was no longer the seventeen-year-old child of his parishioner and mentor. She was a naked woman coming on to him and every fiber in his body wanted her.

She stepped towards him. "And right now," she said, "we're both feeling turned on, dreaming about being naked in each other's arms."

She was right. That was exactly what Jim was feeling. She was exuding all of the seductive charms of a fully developed child-woman and the intensity of his desire was beginning to overwhelm his moral compass. He continued to fight the temptation. But she knew exactly what was happening.

"The difference is," she continued, "you're feeling all torn up inside, conflicted, guilty. I'm feeling thrilled and excited about what's to come, about making you feel good and you pleasuring me."

As she talked she moved towards him so that she now stood right before him. Her legs were on either side of his legs, straddling him. He didn't resist. His crossed legs reflexively uncrossed. She bent over and kissed him—a long, delicious kiss that further filled his already confused mind with lascivious thoughts. When she was done, she leaned back and looked in his face.

"According to your rules," she said, "even though you're fighting to resist this so-called temptation, and I'm enjoying every minute, we'll both be punished, right? Just the same. Does that make any sense?"

His mind was spinning. A fire was burning within him to have her. She was promising him a kind of risk and excitement, and intense passion, he could never get with Renee that he hadn't had since Veronica Taylor. Yet not only was he married, and her minister, she was a teenager. Not only was this morally wrong, but he could ultimately lose everything— his job, his wife and his future. At the same time, what she was saying was beginning to make sense, to ring true to him. For an instant he believed he heard a voice, a low voice murmuring, "I made it for you. Take it."

Lost in this kaleidoscope of thoughts, feelings and sounds, Jim hadn't noticed that Melanie had deftly started to unzip his pants. He suddenly realized what was about to happen. Drawing on every ounce of faith and willpower within him, he loudly yelled, "NO! NO!" and pushed her away.

She turned and sat down on the couch. There was a look of pity on her face. Then she smiled. It was a wicked smile.

"Your loss," she said with a shrug.

Jim was trembling. He had stopped her, but he remained mesmerized by this young, not yet woman-child sitting naked before him. He began to gather himself when he heard a knock at the office door. In a panic, he realized he hadn't locked it.

"Get up! Get dressed," he whispered frantically.

Melanie slowly stood up. As she stood naked before him, she made no effort to get dressed or cover herself in any way. *What is she doing!* he screamed to himself .

He was startled out of his thoughts by another knock on the door. "Reverend, can I come in?" It was Richardson Leigh.

Before Jim could get anything out of his horror-stricken mouth, Melanie turned her head towards the door and called out, "Come on in, Daddy. We're almost done."

Jim leapt out of his chair and clumsily fumbled with his partially open zipper as Melanie casually reached down to pick up her panties from where she had deposited them on the floor. It was at that moment that Richardson Leigh entered the office.

For a split second Leigh stood frozen, mouth agape, aghast in utter disbelief. His mind couldn't comprehend the picture which had unfolded before him—the pastor of his church, in whom he had entrusted the well-being of his young daughter, struggling to get his zipper up while that seventeen-year-old child—*she's a child, for God's sake*—stood naked before him slowly starting to get dressed with a look of smug satisfaction on her face.

When his brain caught up to his eyes Leigh erupted, spewing forth the accumulated anger of over half a century of every slight, every wrong ever done to him, all of which, put together, couldn't equal the magnitude of disgust and ignominy visited upon him at this single moment. He shot across the room and grabbed Jim by the lapels of his jacket. He drove him several feet slamming him into and up against the far wall of the office. He screamed, as loud and blood curdling a scream as Jim had ever heard. "WHAT THE HELL DO YOU THINK YOU'RE DOING, YOU PERVERTED SON OF A BITCH!" Leigh drew has right arm back, fist clenched, and prepared to administer the whipping of a lifetime on the befuddled and hapless minister. "I'M GOING TO . . ."

"Oh Daddy, you're so melodramatic."

Melanie's quietly sarcastic remark stopped her father in mid-sentence, and mid-air. He forgot Jim for a moment and let him go. Leigh turned to see his daughter. She was in no apparent hurry to get decent, still clad only in her panties and slowly arranging her top right side out.

"GET DRESSED! NOW!" he commanded her, his face so red with anger that the image of blood splattered all over the minister's office from Leigh's exploding head didn't seem so far-fetched to Jim, and seemed to mildly amuse Melanie.

"All right. Don't have a conniption," she said. She looked over at Jim and winked at him. He had taken advantage of Leigh's diverted attention to slip away from the wall and retreat behind the flimsy security of his desk. Her wink obviously intended for her father's benefit and designed to infuriate him even more, caused Jim to cringe.

Even at her snail's pace it didn't take her long to put on what little clothing she had come in. When she was finally dressed Jim again marveled at Leigh's incongruous laxity in what he let his daughter wear. He wondered if Leigh failed to see a connection between the way she dressed and her antisocial, rebellious behavior, or if this otherwise giant of a man in the community really had so little control over his teenage daughter. Whatever the case, Jim understood that his main concern had to be with *his* problem with Leigh, not Melanie's.

"Go to the car and wait for me there," Leigh ordered her through clenched teeth once she had pulled herself together.

"Yes Daddy. But don't be long. I've still got homework to do," she taunted as she left the office.

Leigh turned and looked back at Jim. A desk was now standing between Jim and the enraged father.

"I should kill you with my bare hands," Leigh said.

"Mr. Leigh, it's not how it looks." Jim knew how lame that sounded as soon as it escaped his lips.

"Not how it *looks*? Not how it *looks*? My seventeen-year-old daughter is naked and you're pulling up your zipper when I walk in and it's not how it *looks*? Then what *was* it, Reverend Donovan?" The sarcasm literally burst from every pore as he addressed Jim by his formal title. "A new kind of child *therapy*? Some kind of . . . of parental *shock* therapy?"

"Of course not, Mr. Leigh. But . . ."

"But *shit*! Look, I know my daughter. I know she probably came on to you. But for Christ's sake man, you're the adult! You're a *minister*! What kind of fucking minister can't control himself with a child?! I brought her to you for help, God damn it! Not so she could play Lolita with you!"

Jim wanted to defend himself. But he knew Leigh was right. There was no excuse for how far he had let the situation go. Yet, he *had* ultimately resisted her. Despite her incredible seductiveness and his overpowering urges, he *had* done the right thing in the end. He had said no. He had tried to make her understand how wrong she was being. Somehow, he thought, that must count for something. But he knew it didn't. Not for Richardson Leigh. There was nothing he could say in his defense that would mean anything to Leigh, at least not now. So he said nothing.

"I want you out of here tomorrow," Leigh said. "I want you out of Florida. I don't ever, ever want to see your face again? You understand?" The hard look of a powerful man had replaced the pained and angry face of a distraught father.

"No," Jim said..

"No?"

"No."

"You have the nerve to say no?"

"I'm willing to leave, Mr. Leigh, but I'm not willing to be fired."

"I don't see as you have much choice Donovan."

"Yes I do sir. If you just fire me you'll have to have a good explanation. I've been good for this church. You know it and so does most everyone else. I know you control the board, but you'll still have to tell them why you're getting rid of me. And there's nothing you can point to, other than tonight."

Jim knew he was a goner at this church. After this, there was no way he could co-exist with Richardson Leigh even if he could somehow save his job. But he had to find a way to avoid being fired—for the sake of his good name, his future and to avoid having Renee find out what had happened.

"And I know how you've gone about getting political support for your new church project," Jim went on. He decided to play his trump card up front and early.

"Then you'll just resign," Leigh shot back. "That is, if you don't want everyone, including that pretty little wife of yours to find out what a pervert you are."

"No Mr. Leigh, I won't resign. And I don't think you'll spread the story around. It would humiliate you as much as it would hurt me."

Jim was right and he knew that Leigh knew it. They were at a standoff. Silently Leigh stared at him, appearing to be searching his mind for a way to get rid of his former golden boy in a way that didn't risk his own embarrassment or worse, his grandiose plans for the future. He turned and walked towards the office door. He stopped and turned again to face Jim.

"Alright. You don't get fired, and you don't just resign. But you leave anyway."

"How is that?"

"Missionary work."

"What?"

"Missionary work. You're going to leave to do missionary work."

"Where?"

"Togo."

"Togo? Where's Togo?"

"In Africa. I visited there a few years ago with a delegation of businessmen and health care professionals. It's a very poor country in western Africa. I've contributed some money to the missionary work being done in some of Togo's poorest villages. They have very little health care and some of their children wouldn't have any education at all if it weren't for the mission schools. In a twisted way maybe your little perversion here can lead to some good."

"How?"

"I'm going to create a foundation, to fund missionary work in Togo. And you're going to be my champion. The energetic, charismatic minister who has done so much for our church will now go to one of the world's poorest countries to teach the children and bring Christ to the hinterland." Leigh's sarcasm was barely disguised.

"You mean you want to send me into some kind of exile."

Leigh walked back to the desk and stood directly opposite Jim.

"Look Donovan, I want you as far away from here as possible. I'm willing to work something out to save some portion of whatever dignity you have left, but I'll be damned if I'm going to just let you leave at your pleasure expecting some sort of grand going away party and a good recommendation. So here's the deal. You announce that you've decided, you've gotten the calling, to do missionary work with the poor. It just so happens that I've been contemplating setting up a foundation to support missionary work in Togo. I went there a few years ago with a group of local muckety-mucks—one of those "hands across the sea" goodwill tours. Lord knows they could use the help. And that's going to make it possible for you to do what God has asked you to do. And so that's where you're going to go."

"For how long?"

Leigh pulled his ever-present pack of cigarettes out of his pocket, took one out and lit it. This was a sign to Jim that Leigh's anger was sufficiently under control for the business side of his mind to take over. Leigh took a long drag and blew the smoke directly into Jim's face.

"Two years, minimum," he said.

"Two years in . . . in . . ."

"Togo."

"Togo?"

The deal was not sounding particularly attractive to Jim.

"Yes asshole! Two years! How long do you think missionaries serve their missions? A week?"

"No, but . . . but Renee's pregnant, and two years somewhere like what your describing Togo is. . . well, that's liable to be too hard on her."

"Look," Leigh said, "I'll make it worth your while. The foundation will pay all of your living expenses. We'll see that all of your wife's health needs are taken care of too."

"And one hundred thousand dollars," Jim said. He was surprised how quickly the words jumped out of his mouth.

"And what?!" Leigh said, incredulously.

"And one hundred thousand dollars. If you expect me to take my family to Africa for two years, I want some additional security."

Jim knew he was pushing the envelope. They both had a lot to lose, but if he pushed too hard he knew Leigh might just decide to suffer his own embarrassment if it meant destroying him. Once Leigh described what had happened between Jim and Melanie, who would believe his stories of political chicanery regarding the church project? Who would care? Nonetheless, he felt he needed to get as much out of the situation as he could.

"That's fucking blackmail!" Leigh shouted.

"It seems to me Mr. Leigh, that we're both in the same situation. It's now just a matter of jockeying for position. You want me gone. I don't want to leave, but I realize it's not realistic for me to think I could survive long here with you as an enemy. Your only hold on me is the damage that you could cause me by revealing what happened tonight. But that would cause just as much damage to you, or at least public humiliation that you can't bear the thought of. And, if I tell all I know . . . well, not only will you go down, but you'll take some of your political friends with you. You want me banished, and I want protection. Mr. Leigh, now it's only a matter of negotiating the details."

Jim was playing hardball and speaking a language Richardson Leigh understood. It was the language that had gotten Leigh to the level of power and prestige he now enjoyed. Even though it put him directly into Leigh's element, he had managed to shift the conversation from confrontation to business negotiation.

"One hundred thousand dollars is a lot of money," Leigh said.

"Not for you. And I'm sure living in Togo for two years won't be easy for Renee and the baby. I think it's a fair amount. Only fifty thousand a year. You pay the young associates in your law firm a lot more than that. And it's less than what you're paying me now."

"You're a minister. You shouldn't be comparing your income to lawyers'."

"I'm a man, with a family that I have to provide for."

Leigh's cigarette had burned down to the filter. He looked around for an ashtray. Not seeing one, he threw the butt on the carpet and snuffed it out with his foot. He immediately pulled out another one and lit it.

"Well, I'm not going to just turn over a hundred thousand dollars to you and have you skip out on me after a few months."

"I wouldn't do that."

"Don't tell me what you would or wouldn't do. You don't have much credibility here mister." Leigh looked up at the ceiling. He took a drag and blew the smoke upwards. He continued to stare as if he was expecting inspiration to form in the artificial cloud he had created. After a few seconds he went on. "Here's what I'll do. I'll place twenty-five thousand in an account set up for you that you can't access until you get to Togo. The other seventy-five I'll put in a trust for your kid. If you stay the full two years, the trust becomes irrevocable. If you don't, the trust dissolves and the money comes back to me. That should take care of your security concerns."

Jim contemplated Leigh's offer for a moment. It was actually more than anything he could have hoped for at the beginning of their negotiations. He had to admire Leigh's ability to put this most personal of incidents into a business context. He also knew that Leigh was a very tough deal maker, but one who kept his word. He decided he had pushed him as far as he was likely to go. He nodded his head. "It's a deal."

"I'll have the documents drawn up," Leigh said. "Get me an account number to wire the twenty-five grand. I want your announcement to be made this Sunday. And I want you on a plane within two weeks."

"That's too soon. I don't even know who to contact about where I'll be going or . . ."

"Don't worry about that. I'll take care of everything. You just get yourself ready to go."

Leigh turned to leave. When he reached the door, he looked back at Jim, who was still standing behind his desk.

"And when you come back from Togo, Donovan, I would strongly suggest that you stay as far away from Florida as you can." With that, Leigh stormed out slamming the door behind him.

Chapter 26

As they flew over the Atlantic Ocean approaching the west coast of Africa, Jim looked down at the water. It was as still and blue as the sky above. He turned and looked at Renee. Her seat was back and she was napping. He thought about how shocked she was—as shocked as anyone—at his sudden decision to do missionary work for the next two years. She was certainly proud of him for his dedication and humanitarianism. But the timing of the decision was difficult for her to accept, given the upcoming birth of their child.

He had assured her that all would be well. "Mr. Leigh's foundation will take care of all of our medical needs," he had told her. "And it's giving us a twenty-five thousand dollar stipend in addition to paying for all of our living expenses. We'll be able to set up a college fund for the baby." Of course, he told her nothing about the trust Leigh was establishing. To do so would have caused the entire story to unravel. He figured he had about eighteen years to come up with some sort of explanation.

He knew that despite all of his reassurances, Renee remained worried, and unsure of the wisdom of his decision. But he also knew that she would support him, as she always did. And she did. And she promised to make the best of it. And he knew she would.

The brightness of the blue sky above and the blue sea below contrasted sharply with the darkness of Jim's mood. *How has it come to this?* he thought. *I did the right thing. God, Melanie's temptation was stronger than anything I've ever experienced before. She's only seventeen, but that body, her sexy come-on. I did want her . . . as wrong as it was . . . so much. But I did the right thing, the Christian thing. I did resist her. Still, I lost my position, my status, my ministry. All the good I did for my church, my congregants. And I'm being sent into some kind of exile, like some deposed monarch who plundered his country and his people—who deserved their righteous indignation. But I didn't. I don't. I did the right thing.*

He tried to convince himself that this too was all part of God's plan, that he was meant to minister now to the poor in Africa rather than the well-off in Palm Beach County, Florida. No matter how he looked at it though, he could not escape the sense of being sent away, being shunned, despite doing the right thing.

He turned and looked at Renee. Her seat was tilted back and she was sleeping peacefully. She radiated beauty and goodness. She was the one woman who truly loved him—loved him for who he was. She treated him with all the kindness and compassion a man could ever hope for. She was the one right choice he had made in his life when it came to the opposite sex. At that moment he felt great love for her. And a great need—a need, alas, that for reasons he did not understand, she could not fully satisfy.

He turned and looked out the window of the plane. He looked up into the infinity of the sky above, hoping to see God's face, reassuring and comforting, ready to pull him back from the edge of the emotional abyss he seemed to be falling into. All he saw was blue sky. He turned and looked again at Renee, still sleeping peacefully, unaware of the inner turmoil going on within her husband.

He reclined his seat, lay back and closed his eyes. His mind drifted back to his college days, to the days after Katie and Veronica. It was a time he had focused on his own needs and desires, not those of others. A time when he didn't worry about following rules or doing the "right" thing all the time. He thought about how much more pleasurable his life seemed then.

He knew what Dr. Westin and Father McTighe would have said to that. That's how the devil works his wiles, how he lures and captures his prey. By making the wrong seem right. By making the bad feel good. Isn't that what he had tried to tell Melanie? How Satan would zero in on your greatest weaknesses and how masterfully he would exploit them? Is that what Satan was doing to him now? Exploiting his weaknesses? Taking advantage of his inability to let go—of his pain, his disappointments, and his anger?

He looked out the window again. The sea below was no longer visible. They were flying over a layer of clouds. He looked up at the vast expanse above, and prayed.

The plane hit an air pocket that caused a brief, jarring jolt. Renee's eyes opened and settled on Jim who was staring out the window, his head tilted, looking upward into the sky. Since he informed her of his decision to go to Africa to do missionary work, she had sensed within him a troubled heart and mind. She had thought it strange that having experienced such a calling, he would remain so unsettled about it—or about something, something that he wouldn't, or couldn't, share with her. She wouldn't press him about it. He knew that she was there for him, whenever he needed her. She always was, and always would be.

She continued to look at the man she loved. It seemed like he was praying. *Good,* she thought. *Whatever it is, he's talking to the right guy about it.*

Chapter 27

JIM WALKED OUT OF ONE of the two ramshackle buildings that all too inadequately served as the village's hospital. He looked up at the bright yellow sun, squinting his eyes and unconsciously stroking his newly grown beard. The sub-Saharan African heat had added to a long, hard day sapping all of the energy from his body.

His daily rounds always exacted a heavy psychological toll on him. This was a poor village of mostly subsistence farmers. The scarcity of good land and the primitive farming methods that they still used limited the opportunities to grow cash crops like coffee or cacao to supplement the food they could grow for themselves. And even that was often insufficient. Poverty, lack of education and malnutrition were the predominant characteristics of this small corner of western Africa. Combined with the lack of adequate facilities and medical supplies, even with the assistance of benefactors like Richardson Leigh, and missionaries like Reverend Jim Donovan, these factors and the growing scourge of AIDS kept the small clinic (it would have been a farce to call it a hospital) very busy—far too often, Jim lamented, with young children with distended stomachs, haunting eyes and parents who had already died.

Jim stepped out onto the dirt path that served as the main road to the clinic. He pulled a handkerchief from his back pocket and wiped the sweat from his brow. From his left a young African boy raced up to him.

"Pastor Jim! Pastor Jim!"

It was Charlie. That wasn't his real name, of course. Jim had been told what it was, but he had already forgotten it. Charlie so loved everything about the westerners who had come to his small village to help that he wanted to know everything he could about the United States, Great Britain and any other country of the western world that sent its people to his part of the world. And he wanted to be as much like them as he could. When they first came to open the clinic and teach the villagers about Christianity, the first thing he did was find a western name that he liked. How and why he chose "Charlie" Jim never learned. But Charlie it was.

When Jim and Renee first arrived at the village it was Charlie who first ran up to them and offered, for a small price, to show them to the mission house. Jim estimated that Charlie was no more than ten years old, though there were no records in the village to verify that. Not even his father was certain of his birth date. His mother, who Jim suspected would have known, had died a year earlier of AIDS. With her death, Charlie and his father were viewed by the other villagers who had so far escaped the epidemic, as being cursed by the gods—or God, for those who had converted to Christianity. The ignorance about this new epidemic was one of the battles that Jim and the other missionaries fought on a daily basis.

"Yes, Charlie, what is it?" Jim said.

Charlie always had a wide, infectious smile on his face. Jim had grown very fond of him in the six weeks since he arrived, as he had of most of the people in this dirt poor African village far from any semblance of civilization as he knew it.

"Post! Post!" Charlie shouted. He was holding up a business size envelope in his right hand.

Jim reached in his pocket and found a quarter. He took the envelope from Charlie's hand and gave him the dull silver coin.

"Thank, Pastor Jim. Thank. Thank." Charlie clutched the quarter firmly in his fist and ran off down the path, his swift bare feet kicking up a cloud of dust behind him.

Jim looked at the envelope. The return address bore the distinctive raised green printing of the firm of Leigh, McLaughlin and Hall and its prestigious 777 South Flagler Drive address in West Palm Beach.

Finally, he thought, *the trust documents from Richardson*—although the envelope seemed to be somewhat thinner than he would have expected. He shrugged his shoulders, placed the envelope in his back pocket and began the half a mile walk from the clinic to the mission house.

⊢•◄•─○─◄•⊣

The mission house, though quite modest by western standards, was by far the largest and most modern house in the village. Unlike the villagers' homes, which were built of sun-dried mud with roofs of grass, the mission house was a two story wooden home. It had a covered front porch with two ceiling fans, a rocker and a glider. Since the house wasn't air conditioned, the porch was often the coolest place to be.

Inside there was a comfortable sitting room, a large dining room, a kitchen and a powder room on the first floor. On the second floor there were four bedrooms and two bathrooms.

Jim and Renee, being the newest arrivals, at first had the smallest bedroom. It was cozy, and big enough for the two of them. Renee, of course, was concerned about what would happen when the baby came. A month after their arrival, her concern doubled when a routine check-up revealed that she was carrying twins.

"Don't worry," Les Mendelson, the director of the mission, told Renee when they first arrived. "By the time the baby arrives, you will have moved up the pecking order at least once. You'll have a bedroom big enough for all of you. I guarantee it."

"How can you be so sure?" Renee asked. Neither she nor Jim was all that comforted by Les's assurances.

"I've run this mission for five years," he answered. "I've been here so long the villagers have begun to call me Father, even though I'm neither a priest nor an ordained minister. I just know how things turn around here. Trust me. You'll have your bigger bedroom in time."

Sure enough, Les was right. Only three weeks after they got there, a young couple—teachers who had come to Togo only three months earlier to run the village school—informed Les that they couldn't cope any longer with the severe deprivation—the villagers' and their own. With only two days' notice, they up and left. Within two weeks, the ever-industrious Les Mendelson had managed to replace the couple with a seasoned, middle-aged Briton from London who said he had had enough

⊷ 210 ⊶

of trying to teach hooligans who didn't want to learn. He was ready to teach children who were starved for education and who would appreciate what he had to offer.

With that, not only did Jim and Renee now have their larger bedroom, but the mission was again complete. It consisted of the minister and his wife from Florida, the teacher from London, a doctor and his nurse wife from Minnesota, and Les, the director, an engineer by training and a Peace Corps veteran. Jim felt that this was where he was meant to be, at least for the next two years, and whatever the circumstances that brought him here.

As he walked in the front door of the mission house, Jim was greeted with the hearty odor of Irish stew simmering on the stove. *Perfect,* he thought.

Out of the corner of his eye, to his left, he saw Renee walking down the stairs. She was now twelve weeks pregnant and was definitely showing. When she reached the bottom of the stairs she reached up and kissed him.

"Hi honey," Renee said. "You look tired. Tough day?"

"Yeah," he said. "We lost a six year old little girl today."

"AIDS?" she asked, already knowing the answer.

Jim nodded his head despondently. He headed up the stairs to change, Renee following slowly behind.

"Her mother died some time ago," he said over his shoulder.

"Same thing?"

"Yeah."

As they reached the top of the stairs, Jim felt something being removed from his back pocket.

"What's this?" Renee asked as they walked into their bedroom.

Six weeks earlier Jim would have done everything he could to keep Renee from seeing the trust documents he was expecting from Richardson Leigh. But he felt different now. He felt like a real minister again—truly doing God's work as it was meant to be done. Not that he would have gone out of his way to come clean with her about the whole Melanie escapade. But he no longer felt he needed to hide it. He could tell Renee the whole truth and he knew that it would all work out.

"Some papers Richardson Leigh was going to send to me, I suspect," he answered, taking the envelope from her hand.

"What kind of papers?"

He didn't answer. He figured he would just show her the documents. After she had read them he would explain how it all had happened. But when he opened the envelope there were no trust documents. What he found in the envelope shocked and frightened him. Instead of trust documents, there was a newspaper article from the front page of The Palm Beach Post dated two weeks earlier. The headline read: PROMINENT ATTORNEY AND WIFE FOUND SLAIN. As Jim began to read the article, he slumped onto their bed, his mind swimming in utter disbelief.

> Prominent local attorney Richardson Leigh and his wife, Gayla, were found brutally slain in the master bedroom of their Manalapan estate early Friday morning. They were found by their housekeeper when she reported for work at about 8:00 a.m. according to police sources.

"What is it honey?" Renee asked, her concern evident in the tone of her voice. Jim waived her off, expecting her to understand that he needed to finish the article first. She sat next to him and said nothing as he continued to read.

> Homicide detective Ernest Rankin of the Palm Beach County Sheriff's Office called the double murder one of the most brutal killings he has seen in his twenty-three years as a police officer.

> Leigh, 52, and his wife, 45, were found naked and spread-eagled on their nineteenth century antique bed with their wrists and ankles tied to the bedposts. They had each been stabbed at least fifteen times in what authorities say appeared to be a ritualistic slaying.

> In a scene reminiscent of the 1969 Los Angeles murders of actress Sharon Tate and several others by followers of Charles Manson, informed sources have stated that messages and symbols were scrawled on the walls and mirrors of the victims' bedroom and bathroom in what was apparently their own blood. Officials refused to comment on a report that one of the messages read FROM OUR EYE—ALL WILL DIE.

There are no specific suspects at the present time, according to Rankin. The police are searching for the Leighs' seventeen-year-old daughter, Melanie, who has not been seen nor heard from since the discovery of her parents' bodies. It is believed that Melanie Leigh, who reportedly belongs to a Satanic cult, may have information regarding the slayings. According to Rankin she is not a suspect and is being sought only as a material witness.

Jim read on, still in shock, as the article described Richardson Leigh's life, community activities, power and prestige in the most glowing terms. The Post made it quite clear that Palm Beach County had tragically lost one of its leading citizens.

The pit of Jim's stomach went hollow. Leigh had been right to worry, really worry, about his daughter. He had come to Jim for help. Jim had failed him, and now Leigh and Gayla were dead.

Jim handed the article to Renee without saying anything. As she began to read it, her face expressing her shock and dismay, he opened the letter that accompanied the article. It was from Leigh's partner, Brandon Hall, who was the attorney who was to draft the trust documents.

Dear Reverend Donovan:

As you can see by the enclosed newspaper article, my partner, and your benefactor, Richardson Leigh, has met an untimely death. Prior to his death I had, at his instructions, prepared certain documents for the creation and funding of an education trust for you. Unfortunately, Mr. Leigh passed away prior to executing the trust documents and funding the trust.

As a result of Mr. Leigh's premature death, the trust he had intended to create will not be established and the anticipated funds will not be provided. The Leigh Foundation has decided, however, that you may keep the $25,000 stipend previously provided to you and that it will honor its commitment to pay your living expenses, including health care for you and your family, for the duration of your two year mission in Togo.

Please be advised that any attempt to challenge the decision of the Foundation with respect to the trust will be vigorously resisted by all legal means available and will result in the withdrawal of all payments and benefits, as well as a demand for the return of funds already paid to you.

PLEASE GOVERN YOURSELF ACCORDINGLY.

Sincerely,

Brandon Hall, Esquire

He had been betrayed again. This time by simple delay and cruel fate, but betrayed and frustrated nonetheless. While he had made the connection between his failure and its consequences for the Leighs, somehow its connection to his own fate didn't compute.

"It's horrible, Jim!" Renee cried. She put the article on the bed and her head on his shoulder.

"Yes. Yes it is," he said, slowly folding the letter and placing it back in the envelope. He put his arm around her and they sat in silence, comforting each other. Renee said nothing more about the papers Jim said he had been expecting. That was good, he thought. There was nothing to be gained now by telling her anything about Melanie Leigh, and the truth about why and how he left Richardson Leigh's church.

Chapter 28

JIM STARED UP INTO THE darkness of their mission bedroom. Renee lay quietly next to him, but he knew by her breathing that she wasn't asleep yet. The twins were fast asleep. At one-and-a-half years old, they would have been in their own bedroom by now if they were living in anything like normal circumstances. But these were anything but normal circumstances, Jim knew—lying in a mission house, in the middle of Africa, with several other people who were just as far away from home and everything they had ever known as he was.

So they made do in their single bedroom, which was now the second largest one due to the departure six months earlier of Dr. Corba and his nurse wife, Martha. They had been replaced by a young doctor, a Dr. Michaels, who now enjoyed the privilege of sleeping in the house's smallest bedroom. The loss of Mrs. Corba had left the clinic without a nurse—a role that Renee tried to help fill when she had time, despite her lack of formal training. When and if a nurse did eventually arrive, the crowded house would become even more so and awkwardly at that, given the absence of any further bedrooms.

Having a larger bedroom, Jim and Renee had divided it into two with a partition made for them by villagers from the small church Jim had established to serve those he had managed to convert to Christianity or who had been converted before he arrived. It at least gave them the illusion of having two rooms.

It was late. As they lay in bed Jim struggled with how to broach the subject to Renee. He turned his head towards her.

"Are you asleep?" he asked, knowing full well she wasn't

He felt her stir slightly.

"Hm, uhm," she mumbled.

"I need to talk to you about something," he said.

She laid her arm across his stomach.

"Sure honey. Is something wrong?"

"No, nothing's wrong," he said. "I just need . . . well, we just need to make some decisions."

She snuggled a little closer to him. "Like what?" she asked.

He wasn't quite sure how to start, because what he was going to ask of her he knew would be very difficult for her to accept, even if she understood.

"I know you're looking forward to going home soon," he said slowly.

"Uhm, hm!" she murmured joyously, neither wanting nor needing to hide her desire to return to a normal life.

"And I know," Jim continued, "that would make things much easier for you and the girls."

Renee removed her arm from around his stomach. She propped her pillow up against the headboard and sat up.

"What are you trying to tell me, Jim? That you want to stay here?"

He remained silent. That is what he wanted to say to her. But the tone of her question made her attitude about that prospect perfectly clear.

"Jim," she said, "this is *no* place to raise a family."

"I know. I know," he answered. "But . . . but Renee, it's . . . it's just that . . . I've . . . *we've* done so much good here." He propped himself up against the headboard so he could look directly into her eyes in the moonlit darkness. "I know this isn't the most hospitable place in the world to be. But the last two years . . . it's made me . . . inside, it's made me feel so useful, purposeful. Even . . . how do I explain it? Peaceful—spiritually peaceful. I mean, these people not only need what we have to offer, they are *starving* for it. And they *appreciate* us for it."

"I know, honey." She softly placed her hand on his arm. "But people everywhere need the Gospel, including—and maybe especially—people back home."

"Of course. You're right. But the difference here is that the deprivation and the suffering are so much greater. I can truly feel, deep inside of me, that I'm making a difference, that I'm truly doing God's work. I've never felt . . . felt so right about it, Renee."

She was silent. He knew what was going through her mind—her desire to return to the states and her concern for the children versus her understanding of her husband's calling, and her role as a minister's wife to support that calling.

"How long?" she finally asked. "How much longer do you want to stay?"

"I don't know."

"Neither do I, Jim. I hear what you're saying. And I know it's important to you. But . . . our children. They're so young, and vulnerable. And this really is . . . it's a dangerous place for them, and for us, to be." He could see the glint of moonlight reflecting in her eyes as she looked fearfully up at him. "I'm scared."

"I know, sweetheart." Jim placed his hand on hers. "But God . . ."

"I know God will provide," she interrupted. "And he protects us, in His way. But when it comes to our children, *we're* the instruments of God. *We* need to make the best decisions for them." She paused, rubbing her hand softly on his chest. "Still, you have your work. I know that, too." She laid her pillow down flat and rested her head on it. She looked up at him. He no longer saw fear written on it, but deep concern remained. "Let me sleep on it, okay?"

"Okay," he said as he readjusted his pillow and laid down facing her. "That's all I can ask."

Renee kissed him softly.

She whispered, "Good night."

"Good night," he said and then kissed her on the forehead. "I love you."

He felt good about the discussion. Renee's concerns about their living conditions and the welfare and safety of the children were his as well. But he had found the place he was supposed to be—at least for a while. And that being the case, he knew they would be safe. Renee would see that too, he was certain. He closed his eyes and quickly fell asleep.

The noise that woke Jim came from his right—from the open bedroom window on that side of the room. He heard voices. They were too hushed and garbled for him to even determine whether they were familiar ones. He reached over to nudge Renee awake before turning to see what or who it was. He felt nothing but the sheets and an empty pillow where his wife should have been.

He sat up quickly and looked around the room, squinting his eyes to see better in the dim light provided by the moon which had by now moved higher in the sky.

"Renee?" he whispered.

No answer.

He called a little louder. "Renee?"

Still no answer.

He got up and went around the partition to the girls' cribs. They were both sound asleep.

He went back to the main part of the bedroom to look again for Renee. When he looked at the window, he saw two protrusions sticking up from the windowsill. He walked closer and opened his eyes wide in horror. The protrusions were the top of a crude, handmade wooden ladder leaning up against the outer wall of the mission house. He stuck his head out the window and looked out onto the mission grounds, the full moon providing enough light for him to see a sight that struck terror in his heart. Three dark-skinned men were running away from the house. One of them had slung over his shoulder a limp, nightgown-clad Renee.

There was no time to get help. If he didn't move quickly they'd be long gone into the savanna and he'd never find them. Clad only in his boxer shorts, he climbed out the window and down the makeshift ladder. On his way down he said a quick prayer for Renee and for God to watch over and protect the twins who he had no choice but to leave alone for the moment.

When he reached the ground he turned and ran as fast as he could in the direction he had seen Renee's abductors go. *Thank God for the moon,* he thought.

Within seconds he was in grass up to his chest. He could neither hear nor see anything up ahead of him. But he kept running anyway, at full speed. Something was guiding him. He didn't know what—or who—but he could feel it, and he knew he was going in the right direction.

He was gaining on them, he was sure of it. He didn't know how he was going to take on three of them alone, but he'd worry about that once he caught up with them. He didn't know he was capable of it, but his speed picked up even more. Then, in an instant, he was sprawled on the ground, clutching at his right ankle in pain. His bare foot had stepped awkwardly on something. A rock. Perhaps a branch. He didn't know. Whatever it was, it threw him down hard.

Jim got up. He had been so close. He couldn't let them get away now. He tried to run. But it was no use. The ankle had throbbed with pain. But he knew he couldn't stop. No matter how slowly, he had to push forward. Renee was in danger and he was the only one who could save her.

Maybe I should have gone for help, he thought. *If something happens to her it'll be my fault.*

He still couldn't hear or see anything ahead of him. But the unknown guidance system kept him moving on a definite path. With every limping step, his ankle swelled and hurt more. But he couldn't afford to stop. He kept moving, painfully, slowly, as precious minutes passed by.

He figured it must have been a half hour or more since he sprained his ankle. As he made his way through the high grass, thanking God as he ambled on for the favor of sparing him any encounters with the continent's exotic and dangerous wildlife, he saw a glow rising above the grass ahead. He couldn't tell exactly how far ahead the source of the glow was, but it didn't seem too distant.

Within a minute or two, as he moved closer, quietly and trying not to noticeably disturb the grass as he moved through it, he began to hear sounds. He quickly recognized them as human voices. He moved closer, and the voices grew louder. They were the blended droning of a choir of voices heard from afar. Soon he could see smoke rising from the glow. It was a fire.

Closer still. The droning became the distinguishable staccato of individual voices engaging in conversation, often talking over each other. There was chanting. It sounded like there was arguing. He could only surmise that from the volume and the tone used by the speakers since none of it was in English. Nor was it the native tongue of the villagers. Jim had come to learn much of that language. This was different. A different dialect perhaps, but it was so different from what he knew that he figured it was most likely a different language entirely. This would make it difficult to communicate, if that became necessary. He hoped it wouldn't.

He couldn't afford to be discovered, but he had to see what was going on, and if Renee was with these people, whoever they were. He moved to his stomach and crawled slowly through the grass towards the fire and the voices. As he got closer he could hear the voices more clearly and distinctly. There were men's and women's voices—several of each. He could hear laughter, too. He couldn't tell yet what was going on. But he was becoming more convinced that this was where he would find Renee.

His urge was to rush forward as fast as he could. He was almost grateful for the injured ankle which kept him from doing something that he knew would be utterly foolhardy, but which he would probably have done anyway if he could. He continued his slow crawl. And then, suddenly, he was there. He had reached the end of the highest grass and was at the edge of a clearing. It was almost perfectly circular and looked to be about two hundred fifty to three hundred feet in diameter. In the middle of it, what appeared to be the *precise* middle, there was a tall, round, wooden pole. Surrounding the pole was a ring of fire, it's radius from the pole being no more than five or six feet all the way around.

In front of the fire, facing Jim, were two black men. Their faces were painted with white paint in matching patterns—starting from the middle of their foreheads making a circle of their entire faces with lines beginning at the bottom of their cheekbones and extending up to the sides of their noses. All they had to do, Jim thought, was draw a line up their noses to the top of the circle and the pattern would be that of the iconic peace sign popularized during the Vietnam War. Each of them was completely naked and held a spear. They appeared to be, or at least looked like, sentries or guards. While activity went on all around them, they remained motionless, and mute.

On both the left and the right sides of the fire there stood about a dozen people. On the left, they were all women; on the right, all men. The men wore animal skin coverings just large enough to cover their genitals. They all carried spears and had their faces painted like the sentries.

The women all wore skirt-type coverings from the waist to the ground. They were bare-breasted. Unlike the men they had no paint or make-up on their faces. Jim could see that each of the women wore a necklace with some sort of figurine (he was too far away to make out what it represented) dangling on the end and extending on each of them precisely to that point between their breasts level with their respective nipples. (Why, he wondered, was he not too far away to notice *that* detail?)

The markings, the dress, the rituals, what he could hear of the language—none of it was familiar to him. *They're not from here,* he thought. *They're not from anywhere around here. Who are they? What are they doing here?*

Jim looked around the entire clearing. There was no sign of Renee.

Within a few minutes, the talking among the natives stopped. The women began clapping in unison, a rhythmic, patterned beat. To the right, the men began pounding the butt end of their spears to the same beat.

From around the right side of the fire came a man dressed like the other men, but wearing a necklace of animal teeth and a mask made of an animal's skull. He took his place in front of the spear-toting men. He stood with his legs spread apart somewhat further than his shoulders and with his hands on his hips. The rest of the natives appeared to look at him with awe, or at least great deference. He was obviously a man of great importance to this tribe, or group, or whatever they were. Perhaps a medicine man of some sort, or their leader, Jim figured. He stood staring at the women for a minute, or a few. Jim was beginning to lose track of time. Then, slowly, the man in the mask removed his right hand from his hip and pointed towards the women.

Jim, following the man's finger, looked at the women. Then he saw. His jaw dropped in horror and it was all he could do to swallow his scream. From the left side of the fire came two men, also wearing animal tooth necklaces and skull masks. Between them they were dragging Renee. She was somewhat limp, but Jim could see she was wide awake, and scared to death.

He didn't know what to do. Every fiber in his body strained to run out there and rescue his wife. But he was hurt and far outnumbered by armed natives. For now, he could only watch and look for an opportunity to make some kind of move.

His eyes stayed riveted on Renee. From his right he heard the leader shout something. The clapping and spear-pounding got louder and faster. The women and the men began chanting in unison. At any other time, and in any other circumstances, Jim would have considered the rhythmic chanting mellifluous. Now it was eerie and frightening.

The two masked men with Renee took her to the two sentries. One sentry took her by the back of her arms, the other by her calves. They lifted her above their heads in a prone position and walked through the fire to the pole. She was putting up no resistance.

She must be drugged, Jim thought.

One of the sentries lifted her arms above her head and placed one hand on either side of the pole. The other one then tied them tightly to the pole with rope. When they were done with her hands, they bent down on either side of her. Through the fire Jim couldn't see exactly what they were doing. But he could see by the movement of her nightgown that her legs were being spread apart. Then the two sentries stood up. He could only guess that her ankles must have been tied to stakes or something on the ground.

Jim was frightened and sickened. He had never felt so helpless in his life. Then, it got worse. As the chanting grew even louder, the two naked sentries walked up to Renee, one on either side of her. Each of them grabbed her nightgown at the neck and, with one violent and efficient movement, they ripped it off her body.

The sight of Renee's naked, exposed body and the fear of what would happen next were too much for Jim to bear. He began to leap up out of his hiding place in the grass to run to her rescue, not knowing or thinking what he would do once he reached the circle of fire.

He had risen no more than six inches from the ground when a heavy force landed on his back and pushed his chest hard onto the ground. He then felt something cold, with a sharp point, pressing against the back of his neck. He had no trouble figuring out that it was the carved stone point of a spear.

"How noble of you, Reverend Donovan," a deep, baritone voice above him said in heavily accented English. "So willing to rush into a crowd of armed natives to rescue his damsel in distress."

"Who are you?" Jim asked through lips eating dirt as he talked. "How do you know my name?"

"As for who I am," the voice responded, "that you will learn in due time. As for how do I know your name, do you really consider that important right now?"

"What . . . what do you want?"

"What do I want? For now, I just want you to watch."

The pressure eased on Jim's back enough for him to lift his head. The spear remained pressed against his neck so that there was only one direction he could look—straight at Renee.

She was alert now and fully aware of her dire circumstances. He could see she wanted to scream, but she didn't. He figured that she understood that no one who could be of any help would be able to hear. She pulled at the ropes binding her hands but he knew she would never get free of them.

The two sentries moved within the circle of fire and began to dance around her. As they came before her, they stopped. They put their hands up to their temples with their index fingers extended from their eyes, pointing at Renee. As they did so, all of the natives followed suit, as if they were playing some kind of children's game in which Renee was "it." After a few seconds the eye pointing stopped. Then they moved within inches of her. They put their hands in the air and moved up and down, from a crouching position to the top of their toes, as if inspecting every inch of their helpless prey. The chorus kept clapping and chanting while the three animal heads stood before the fire, their backs to Jim. The one in the center periodically shouted what Jim could only assume were instructions to the men within the ring of fire.

He was drowning in his feelings of inadequacy and helplessness. Before his very eyes his wife was about to be molested, and maybe much worse, and there was nothing he could do about it.

The ritualistic dance of the naked men continued for several minutes. He couldn't be sure how many. It seemed like hours. His captor remained quiet, obviously content to silently observe Jim's anguish—probably relishing it, he thought. Then one of the sentries crouched before Renee and didn't move. He remained crouched, as Jim squinted trying to get a better view of what was happening. Finally, between the tips of two flames he could see the man's hands stroking her inner thighs.

Renee screamed.

This was too much for Jim. He lifted himself up and yelled out, "NO!" Instinctively, forgetting that there was a spear pointed at his head, he turned around facing his captor. There, standing before him, was a large black man—at least six feet seven inches tall—with several animal tooth necklaces and an animal skull mask, much larger than the ones worn by the men in the clearing. Before Jim could say or do anything, the man's spear came crashing down on his shoulder. Jim fell onto his back, his head hitting the ground with a dull thud.

He lay on the ground, stunned. His head, shoulder and ankle all throbbed with pain. His eyes were open, but his vision was blurred. He could see the outline of the huge man looking down at him, the full moon, made extra-large by his blurred eyesight, situated so as to appear to be resting on the giant's head. The animal skull mask went down only over the giant's nose, so Jim was able to see the broad smile spread across the man's face. It was a cruel smile.

"So, what do you think of our celebration of the moon so far, Reverend Donovan?"

"What are they going to do to her?" Jim asked, trying unsuccessfully to suppress the quiver in his voice.

"You would like to save her from whatever cruel fate awaits her, wouldn't you Reverend Donovan?"

"Yes, of course."

"Because she's your wife, and you love her."

"Yes." As much as Jim wanted to turn and see what was happening to Renee, he stayed on the ground looking up at his captor, not wanting to risk taking another blow, at least not yet. "And . . . and because she's a human being. No one deserves to be assaulted like that."

"Ahh. How chivalrous you are, Reverend Donovan. And not only towards your wife, but to *all* mankind. Isn't that right?"

"Please," Jim pleaded. "I don't know what you want. But I'll do anything, anything you ask. Just let her go. Please."

"Well now," the giant said through his still smiling teeth. "Now we are getting to the crux of—how did you put it?—what I want."

The giant turned and looked over his right shoulder. He raised his spear once and rested it again on the ground. Within seconds, out of the darkness, appeared a young naked woman. Her skin was so ebony black that if it weren't for the full moon, she would have been all but invisible in the night. She was short, so short that when she took her position next to the giant, it made him look even more the Goliath than he was. Her brilliantly white eyes looked down briefly at Jim, and then lifted themselves up to the animal mask. The giant nodded. She nodded back. She turned, stepped over to Jim and lay down next to him, her head on his shoulder and her hand resting on his chest.

"You see, Reverend Donovan," the giant said, his rich baritone seeming to be coming at Jim from all sides as if it was being amplified by some sort of sophisticated surround-sound stereo system, "all I want is for you to have a nice time this evening. This is Lanie." The giant's smile was mocking him now.

Jim's eyes widened in disbelief. "Wh . . . what? But I'm . . ."

"Yes. I know. You're married. And in your religion this . . . what do you call it? Ah, yes, adultery . . . this adultery is considered wrong. A *sin*, I think you Christians call it."

"Yes. Yes, that's right," Jim said. The young girl was softly fingering his chest. To his dismay he felt a twinge of excitement. Guilt and fear worked to suppress it. "And I love my wife," he continued. "So I beg you, leave us alone, don't do this, to Renee, to me."

"I'm so sorry, Reverend. But I must insist."

"But why? Why? For what possible purpose?"

"In due time, Reverend. In due time." The giant tapped his leg with the flat side of the spear point. "If you want to save your wife from what you fear, you will please Lanie. Now."

From behind him, Jim could hear Renee sobbing through the clapping and the chanting. He knew he had no choice. He turned his head and looked at the young girl lying at his side. She had a very attractive face with thick, inviting lips. The whites of her eyes shone against the backdrop of the darkness of the night with a fiery come-hither look. She kissed him. He didn't kiss back.

She leaned her head back slightly. Her excited eyes fixed on his. "Make Lanie happy," she said.

She put her lips on his again, then thrust her tongue into his mouth. Until this moment his fear and his desire to resist had kept him from getting sexually excited. But now, the sensation of her lush lips on his and her warm, wet tongue rolling all through his mouth sent waves of sensation through him and down into his suddenly erect penis. Despite his every wish and his every effort to resist, his lips and tongue began to dance furiously with hers.

As their tongues furiously groped each other, Lanie's left hand slowly moved down Jim's torso from his chest to the edge of his shorts. She slowly, deliberately withdrew her tongue from his mouth and got up on her knees. Her eyes, which now seemed almost mystical, peered into his. He felt the tips of her fingers slide under the elastic waistband of his shorts and, before he knew it, they were off. Without ever taking her eyes off his, she laid down beside him with her head again on his shoulder.

In the rising sexual heat, Jim had momentarily forgotten that he and Lanie were not alone. He looked up at the giant who was still standing over them. The giant showed a big, toothy smile watching their every move with obvious pleasure.

Lanie had waited long enough. She pulled Jim onto her and began to run her fingers up and down his back and his buttocks as she writhed suggestively below him.

From the position she had placed him in, Jim could see Renee again, and the naked men dancing around her. Without warning, the clapping and the chanting stopped. The sentries stopped dancing. They positioned themselves one on either side of Renee and stared straight ahead, in the direction of Jim and his captors. The three masked men turned and also faced the love scene now unfolding on the edge of the clearing.

It was suddenly very quiet. The only sound was the crackling of the flames. Jim could actually see Renee's face. It showed her confusion, and continued fear. But she kept quiet. She probably figured, Jim thought, that whatever had put a stop to the impending assault on her, she should just count her blessings for the respite, however brief it might be.

Lanie's body began to writhe more and more. She began to fondle his genitals and within seconds she placed him inside her.

All he wanted to do now was get this over with and get Renee out of there. He began to thrust hard and fast hoping to make it happen quicker. Lanie began to moan. In the dead still of the night the moans were almost deafening. Jim knew that the sounds must easily be carrying far enough for everyone within hundreds of yards to hear, including Renee. He lifted his head to see if he could see her reaction. What he saw instead, no more than six inches from his head, was the raised head and venomous fangs of a deadly cobra. He tried to leap up but Lanie, showing tremendous strength for such a small girl, held him down by his buttocks.

The giant's voice descended from above him. "The snake is frightening, is it not?"

"What is it? Some kind of trick to scare me some more?" Jim said nervously.

"Oh, I assure you Reverend Donovan, the snake is no trick. It is in fact, very real and very poisonous. It is an African cobra. If you are worried about it biting you, don't. You see, it prefers to shoot its venom. It particularly likes to target the eyes."

Jim could imagine the sadistic smile on the giant's face as he said this.

Lanie had slowed down her movements, as if to allow Jim and the giant to have their conversation. But she kept her hands firmly on his buttocks and his penis fully within her. With the cobra poised to strike six inches from his face, he wasn't inclined to move anyway.

"Can . . . can you control it?" Jim fearfully asked as the snake's eyes glared intently on his face.

"No," the giant said grimly. "I am acquainted with it. But I'm afraid it has a mind, and a will, of its own."

Jim and the snake continued their stare down.

"Then move it, just kill it," Jim pleaded. "Or let me go."

"Oh, Reverend Donovan. I would suggest that in your present position it is not wise to let the serpent hear you speak of killing it," the giant said with a chuckle.

He talks about it almost as if it's human.

"Then what do I do?" Jim asked.

"Exactly what you were brought here to do and what you're doing."

"But . . . but this is dangerous. I . . . Lanie could die."

"Isn't that how you like it, Reverend?"

"What do you mean?"

"Risky. Dangerous."

"I don't know what you're talking about."

"Really?" the giant responded sarcastically. "Here you are, making love with a beautiful young girl not more than fifty feet from your wife. And there is a deadly poisonous snake poised to strike at you."

"And I'm scared to death," Jim said through clenched teeth. He noticed for the first time that his whole body had broken out in a cold sweat.

"Yes, you are," said the giant. "And what happens to most men when they are truly frightened? Sexually, that is?"

The giant didn't wait for an answer.

"They lose their erection. Some become impotent for quite awhile afterwards."

Lanie began to thrust her hips faster again. Jim kept his eyes on the cobra, fearing that the additional motion would propel it into action.

"The excitement, the passion within you has grown. And, *Reverend* Donovan, you *haven't* lost your erection. In fact, it's even better now, isn't it?" *How does he know that?* Jim wondered. "The danger, Reverend, the danger is the ultimate aphrodisiac for you."

The giant was right. The passion of his lovemaking with Lanie was growing, not diminishing. Without realizing it, and in spite of the danger, he too had started thrusting harder and faster.

"You try to be so good," the giant continued, as Lanie and Jim continued. "But there is something within you, Reverend. Something you try to suppress, to hide from the world, and yourself."

How does he know these things? It didn't matter right now. All that mattered was the silky body beneath him. Lanie's head thrashed back and forth. Her groans turned to screams. The orgasmic pressure within him grew so strong he could no longer suppress the urge to cry out.

"YES! YES!" he shouted, so loudly that he knew Renee couldn't help but hear. But for the moment, he just couldn't, just didn't, care. As for the snake, *if this is how I've got to go,* he thought, *let it be!*

Finally, it happened. The release was as prolific as any he had ever experienced. His body was drained. His head flopped to the ground next to Lanie's. They were both exhausted and spent.

A couple of minutes passed, neither one of them moving beyond the heaving of their chests as their lungs sought replenishment. Then, into his mind jumped the snake. He slowly raised and turned his head. It was gone.

He lifted his head to look in the direction of Renee. He didn't know what to expect. He saw her head hanging down. Her body was limp. All of the natives in the clearing were kneeling in a prostrated position, with their heads and arms on the ground. He jumped off Lanie and looked up at the giant, who hadn't moved from the position he had taken when he first put the spear to Jim's head. Jim began to rise, but the point of the spear only allowed him to get up as far as a sitting position.

"What's happened to Renee?" he demanded.

"Perhaps all of the excitement wore her out," the giant answered mockingly. "Don't worry," he said. "She's only sleeping."

"Did she . . ."

" . . . hear or see anything? Who knows? You will have to ask *her.*"

Lanie sat up next to Jim. She took her hand, placed it on his cheek and gently turned his face to look at her. She kissed him gently.

"You remember always," she said. "Me good. Me, Lanie."

A sense of foreboding recognition washed over him. She smiled, kissed him again and then got up and scurried into the darkness.

Jim was shaken. He felt around and found his shorts. He looked up at the giant, wondering whether he could get up yet. As if reading his thoughts, the giant stepped back two paces and waved his spear as if to tell him to stand up. As he stood up, his legs felt as if he had just run a marathon. He slowly put his shorts on and looked up at the foreboding figure of the man who had, in essence, just directed his rape.

"You told me I would find out who you are in due time," Jim said slowly.

"And so you will."

"Now!" Jim insisted, feeling he had nothing to lose.

The giant smiled his big smile.

"For now it is enough to know that you have met me before—and you will meet me again."

"Where? When?"

"That is not important now. When it is, it will become clear to you."

"If it's not important now," Jim asked, "what did you want with my wife, and with me?"

"I want nothing with your lovely wife. She was only a means of getting to you."

"And what do you want with me?"

"Isn't that obvious?"

"No. It isn't."

"Why, your seed, Reverend Donovan. I wanted your seed."

"My seed? Why?"

"For insurance."

"Insurance? I don't understand . . ."

"Good Reverend, I strongly suggest that you waste no more time in retrieving your wife."

Jim turned and looked into the clearing. The natives were back on their feet dancing in place. He looked at Renee. The nude sentries both stood before her appearing to be taking a renewed interest in the naked white woman tied to the post.

Jim yelled. "STOP THEM!"

"No, Reverend. You came here to rescue your wife. Now go do it."

"How? What can I do?"

"It only takes one phrase to make them all scatter."

Jim pleaded with the enigmatic giant. "What? What phrase?"

"You are a man of God, Reverend. Ask your God."

Jim looked into the clearing again. The sentries were beginning to paw at Renee. She was awake and terrified. He closed his eyes and prayed—as hard as he ever had. The only words that came into his mind were *"In the name of the Lord, Jesus Christ, depart!"* He didn't know how that would chase the heathens away, but it was all he had.

He ran out into the clearing. He noticed that neither his shoulder nor ankle hurt any longer. He looked down and saw the swelling that had been around his ankle was gone. He didn't know how or why, but he couldn't think about that now. At least he would be able to run to Renee at full speed.

He turned his attention back to the fire. No one had appeared to notice him yet. He took a deep breath and broke into a sprint. As he reached the ring of fire he opened his mouth to shout his demand. But what came out wasn't his call to Jesus.

"Romanda iska manatu!" he yelled.

What on earth was that? he wondered in amazement.

He looked at Renee. She was looking at him with a look of both joyous relief and continued fear—fear that now extended to concern about both their fates. He turned and crouched into a defensive posture. He knew that as hopeless as it seemed, he was going to have to try to fend off over a dozen men. What he saw astonished him. Instead of men coming at him with spears, he saw all of the men and women running off in every direction. He turned his attention back to the fire expecting an attack from the sentries. They too were gone. Only Renee remained with him in the clearing.

She cried out. "JIM! JIM!"

The fire had grown larger since he first saw it. Its flames now reached higher than his head. It seemed to be getting closer to Renee. He had nothing to cover his head or skin and there was no water around to douse himself with. His only choice was to run through it. He estimated the depth of the fire to be about eight to ten feet, which wasn't too bad if he ran through it fast enough. He'd worry about how to get out with Renee once he freed her from the post.

Taking another deep breath, he put his head down and ran in. He could feel the searing heat of the flames on every part of his body. He churned his legs as fast as he could. The heat grew stronger. On every inch of his body he felt excruciating pain. He had heard that burning to death is the most painful way to go. Now he knew it was true.

He tried to open his eyes, but the heat was far too intense. *I only have to go ten feet,* he thought. *How can it be taking so long?*

Not only did he feel the heat and flames now. He could *hear* them, too. It wasn't the crackling sound of a campfire. It was more the roar of a forest fire. He began to panic. Perhaps he got turned around and was running around in a circle—in the center of the ring of fire. Whatever the problem, he knew he had to solve it fast. He may not survive the fire, but he had to at least save Renee.

Faster he ran and harder he pushed. Finally, he had no choice but to throw himself on the ground to kill the flames that had attached to his body and were melting away his skin. He rolled over and over and over. On the third roll he realized that he had cleared the fire.

He pulled himself up slowly and looked at his skin. It was red, but no more red than if he had sat in the sun too long. *How can that be?* he wondered, forgetting for the moment the damsel in distress he had come to rescue.

"Jim! Jim! Oh, thank God!"

He turned to the sound of Renee's voice. She stood strapped to the post, her spread-eagled legs tied to two stakes in the ground. Tears of joy ran down her face.

"Jim! Oh, Jim!" she cried over and over.

Jim rushed over to her. He had no knife so he began pulling at the ropes on her feet. They came untied much easier than he expected. Then he removed the ropes binding her hands. Renee fell into his arms. She sobbed uncontrollably.

"Jim. Oh, Jim." Her arms wrapped around his torso and gripped him firmly. Her head buried itself under his chin. "It was horrible. Oh, God. Thank God you found me."

He held her for several minutes as all of her fears and emotions poured out in her sobs and tears. When she finally calmed down, she looked at him quizzically.

"Thank God you came when you did. What did they want with me, Jim? Why did they do this?"

She put her head on his chest. She didn't seem to know that he had been just beyond the clearing most of the time—didn't seem to have heard him and Lanie. *Thank God,* he said to himself. *Thank God.*

After holding her silently for a few seconds, he answered her the only way he could. "I don't know, sweetheart. But let's get out of here."

What he expected to be the tattered remains of her nightgown were at the foot of the post, pretty much where it had been torn off of her. Even in its torn condition, he figured, it could at least provide some cover for her.

"Don't move," he told her.

He stepped the couple of steps to the nightgown and picked it up. *It can't be,* he thought. *It's all in one piece. It's not torn at all. How . . . how can that be? I saw* them *rip it off her.* He turned it over and around looking for the tears that he knew *had* to be there.

"Are you going to keep admiring my nightgown, or are you going to let me put it on?" Renee said with impatient sarcasm.

"Oh . . . I'm . . . I'm sorry," Jim stuttered. "Here. Here honey."

She took the nightgown from his outstretched hand and put it on. He walked over to her when she was done and put his arm around her.

She looked pleadingly up into his eyes. "Let's go home. Please."

Sure, he thought. *All I have to do now is figure out how to get us back through the fire.*

When he turned his eyes from Renee's, he realized to his surprise that the fire was gone, entirely. The ground was undisturbed and fresh. There was no sign that a fire had ever existed in this part of the clearing. The only light was that cast by the full moon above them.

"The fire," he said to no one in particular.

"What fire?" Renee said dreamily.

He looked at her as if she was some part of a massive practical joke.

"What's wrong, Jim. Why are you looking at me like that?"

His mind was spinning. Nothing made sense. He could no longer know what was real, and what wasn't. *I need to sleep,* he thought. *Tomorrow. It will be clearer tomorrow.*

He smiled what he hoped would be a comforting smile. "Nothing," he answered her. "Never mind."

Jim took Renee's hand. They walked slowly to the end of the clearing and into the tall grass. He didn't know how or why, but he knew that he was headed in the right direction to reach the mission home.

After three or four minutes of walking Renee stopped.

"Are you okay?" Jim asked. "Do you need to rest awhile?"

She shook her head.

"Jim," she said, tears welling up in her eyes. "I don't want to stay in Africa anymore."

He wiped the tears from her eyes with his thumbs.

"I know, honey. It's time to go home."

As they continued walking, Jim was gripped with guilt and fear—guilt at what he had done with Lanie, and the feeling that somehow everything that had happened was his fault—and fear of who the giant was, his power, and his promise that Jim would meet him again.

Then a strange thought entered his mind. *Where are you when I really need you, Father McTighe?*

The next morning Jim advised Les that he and his family would be leaving within two weeks. And later that day Renee received a telegram telling her that her father had suddenly passed away from a heart attack at the age of 57.

Chapter 29

J IM KNEW THAT IT WOULD take a long time for Renee to get over the death of her father. Reverend Smalley had always been her rock, the stable force in her life. The bond had become particularly tight after the violent death of her sister. Having learned of his death the morning after the vicious assault on her compounded her trauma a hundred-fold.

His father-in-law's death traumatized Jim as well, if for different reasons. There was, to be sure, the fact that he now had replace Bob Smalley as Renee's rock, a task few men negotiate with great success in the shadow of a woman's idolization of a strong father. But it was the events of that night in Africa and what they learned afterward that were most disturbing to him. When the details of Reverend Smalley's death were revealed to him he realized that the death had occurred at the very time he and Renee were going through their ordeal. A coincidence? He wondered. Or, in the person of the giant, had he come up against an evil that transcended the small African village where he had encountered it?

And what about his seed? Had he actually fathered a child that night? Perhaps a child designed to be evil? But if so, why him? Why Jim Donovan? And what did the giant mean when he said he needed insurance? Insurance for what?

What was paranoia and what was real? He didn't know. And did it really matter? Woody Allen's pithy saying played over and over in his head. "You're not paranoid if they really *are* out to get you." What he *did* know for certain was that he had been confronted by a powerful force, an evil force, and that he would face it again some day.

Initially, Jim coped with the unanswered questions and the fear by focusing his attention and energies on comforting Renee. After all, she was the one who had been kidnapped, probably drugged, and assaulted in the most shameful way. And it was she who had lost her father at the same time.

When they returned to the states they moved in with Mrs. Smalley. This was not only a big boost for Renee, and for Jim's mother-in-law who had not seen her grandchildren until then. It was good for him too. The comfort of her modest home and a couple of months free from the need to minister to the needs of those beyond his own family were like a magic elixir. It was the time he needed to clear his head and decide his future.

Just a small parish in a small town was all he wanted. Despite the frightening ending to their stay in Africa, his ministry there made him realize that his place wasn't in large cities serving well-off matrons and gentlemen and hobnobbing with the rich and powerful. It was in a small community, where he would know everyone's name, their children's names, their favorite movie stars and pies, their most vexing problems and deepest fears; where he could serve *all* of his parishioners' spiritual and counseling needs personally, one on one. Perhaps by bringing people closer to God in such an intimate way he could find the answers to the contradictions within his own character, calm the turmoil within his own soul, complete the relationship with his Lord that would ward off the evil that existed all around him, all around everyone, and bring him peace.

He called Dr. Westin. He asked him once again for his help—to find the right small parish in the right small town to serve. As always, Dr. Westin came through. He led Jim to Paradise—Paradise, South Carolina—a town that, if it didn't exist, Jim would have had to find a way to invent.

Chapter 30

MY WHOLE LIFE, FLASHING BEFORE *my eyes. That seals it. Quit hoping. No good. Death, please come soon.*

Perched on the cursed widow's walk, Jim's eyes stared up into the roiling storm swirling above him. Below him, the lady on the porch, confused and dazed, was experiencing pain, torment and fear like she had never known. Jim could actually feel her pain piled onto his own. Why did she have to suffer on his account, he wondered. If only he could help her. If only he could make it stop before it killed her too.

"Please, stop," he pleaded through motionless lips. "Take me. Take me now. I don't need to see any more. I know what I've done. It's my life. I know the story. If it's the end, then for God's sake let it end."

Laughter. Then the voice.

"The end? You think this is the end, Jim Donovan? Fool. The end of your story is just beginning."

Laughter.

This ends the first part of the Widow's Walk tale.

Every person is called to account for his or her actions.

The only questions are when and how--and sometimes ...where.

The story continues in Part 2 ~

Widow's Walk: The Reckoning